F. Marshall Ward

Waves on the Ocean of Life

A Dalriadian tale

F. Marshall Ward

Waves on the Ocean of Life
A Dalriadian tale

ISBN/EAN: 9783337036799

Printed in Europe, USA, Canada, Australia, Japan

Cover: Foto ©Andreas Hilbeck / pixelio.de

More available books at **www.hansebooks.com**

WAVES

ON THE

OCEAN OF LIFE:

A DALRIADIAN TALE.

BY

MRS WARD.

" Poor wand'rers of a stormy day,
From wave to wave we're driven ;
And fancy's flash, and reason's ray,
Serve but to light the troubled way.
The smiles of joy, the tears of woe,
Deceitful shine, deceitful flow ;
There's nothing true but heaven."

LONDON:
SIMPKIN, MARSHALL, & CO.
DUBLIN : MOFFAT & CO.
1869.

Ballantyne and Company, Printers, Edinburgh.

Dedicated,

By permission,

to

The Right Honourable the Earl of Antrim,

Glenarm Castle,

County Antrim, Ireland.

PREFATORY ADDRESS.

———◆———

LEST the description of the scenes during the latter part of the eighteenth century which have been introduced to elucidate the tale should lead the reader to suppose that the writer has any sympathy with the present Fenian movement, or that she agrees with the sentiments of its advocates, she quotes the words of an author on the same subject, as they completely coincide with her own views. "While Scotland preserves the memory of those who fell in the Rebellion of 1745, while their lives and actions are recorded by loyal Scotchmen, and read by loyal Englishmen, there can be no reason why the reminiscences of the Irish Rebellion of 1798, and of those who were unfortunately engaged in it, should not be faithfully recorded, without prejudice to the loyalty of the

writer or the reader of their history. We have out-
lived the wrongs which made rebels of these men.
In our times their descendants are possessed of rights
for the enjoyment of which they have reason to be
good and loyal subjects. It is not only their duty,
but their interest to be so."

Religious controversy is so frequently introduced
that life in Ulster would not be faithfully portrayed
were it omitted. Sectarianism and want of toleration towards different persuasions has been, and is,
the cause of much unhappiness in families, and has
engendered bitter feelings among the community.
It is fervently to be desired that members of Christian
churches who hope to meet in heaven would on earth
exercise mutual forbearance towards each other, and
unite in works of love and charity to their fellow-
travellers on their march to their home of peace, joy,
and love, instead of quarrelling on the way about
minor doctrinal points and church government. When
narrow-minded illiberal feelings, and the idea that
salvation is only within the limits of one particular
section of the Church, becomes prevalent, it proves
that religion is at a low standard. Dr Hamilton, in
his " Dew of Hermon," compares this state to "the
sands of the sea at ebb-tide, where there are many
little pools ; each has its little fish, to which the foot-

depth is all the ocean. He has no dealings with his neighbour shrimp; but when the rising ocean begins to lip over the margin of his lurking-place, one pool joins another, their various tenants meet, and by and by they have the ocean's boundless range to roam in.

" Happy church, farthest down the strand, nearest the rising ocean's bed, whose sectarianism shall first be swept away in this inundation of love and joy, whose communion shall first break into that purest and holiest, and yet most comprehensive of all communions, ' the communion of the Holy Ghost.' Would to God that church was ours ! "

WAVES ON THE OCEAN OF LIFE.

INTRODUCTORY CHAPTER.

WHEN "the Most High and Mighty Prince James, by the grace of God King of Great Britain, France, and Ireland, Defender of the Faith," &c., succeeded "that bright occidental star Queen Elizabeth, of most happy memory," he found that Ireland was a troublesome appendage to his other dominions. James was only the third monarch of Great Britain who bore the title of "King of Ireland," as previous to Henry VIII.'s reign the English sovereigns were merely styled Lords of Ireland. The ancient Irish dynasty of O'Nial were the last to submit to the title of king being taken from them; and as they occupied such a prominent position, were so intimately connected with Ulster, and involved in the destinies of other parts of Ireland, it is necessary we should here give a brief epitome of their history, and that of the province where the scenes of the tale in this volume are chiefly laid.

The family of O'Neill (as they are now called) are of Gothic origin, and trace their descent from a very

A

remote period.   According to tradition, Nial and
Magnus, sons of Belus, king of the Orkneys, left their
native islands in search of other possessions ; previous
to leaving home it was arranged between them that
he who touched the soil first should be king of that
country.   When they approached Ireland the vessel
of the younger was nearest the land.   Nial perceiving
that his brother was about to step out, seized an axe,
chopped off his hand, and flung it ashore.   " O'Nial,"
exclaimed Magnus ; " Hy Nial ! " (king or chief,) was
shouted by all the party, who unanimously acknowledged his supremacy.   This incident is said to have
given the name to the family and dynasty, and caused
the bloody hand, with the motto " Lamh dearg Eirin,"
(the red hand of Ulster,) to be the crest of the
O'Neills ; it also forms part of the armorial bearings of the province.   Some archæologists account
for it in another way, saying it is the opinion of
ancient historians that when the believing Jews (in
accordance with the Saviour's command) fled from
the doomed city of Jerusalem, previous to its destruction by Titus, many of them found refuge in Spain,
and from hence came to Ireland.   This belief is
strengthened when we know that Milesians (meaning military or hereditary soldiers) is a name de-
signating the ancient Irish.   It is evident from the
Scriptures, that the tribe of Benjamin were hereditary
men of war ; the name Benjamin signifying " son
of the right hand," a bloody or red right hand being
their banner or standard.

Do not we Irish, in many respects, resemble the

people of the " weary breast and wandering feet?"
It is also a current belief that when the final storm
of God's wrath is poured forth on the earth, Ireland
will escape, because when other countries oppressed,
persecuted, and acted cruelly towards the Jews, she
never did.

We are certain from time immemorial the O'Nial's
bore the title of " Kings of Ulster," and claimed to
be heirs of the whole dominion of Ireland, declaring
that previous to the coming of St Patrick, in the
fourth century, one hundred and thirty of the
Hy Nial race had swayed the Hibernian sceptre ;
but their supremacy was, however, often disputed
by the kings of the other provinces. In the eleventh
century, Brian, born king of Munster, in consequence
of having repulsed the invasion of the Danes, was
acknowledged supreme sovereign of Ireland by all
the chiefs and kings, with the exception of the
O'Nials, who made every resistance in their power,
but finally they were obliged to submit.

Malachy, King of Leinster, also distinguished himself in repelling the Danes. He has been immortalised by our poet Moore, as " wearing the collar of
gold which he took from the proud invader." Quietly
he took the place of a subordinate prince, and accompanied Brian on his progresses throughout the provinces to restore order, justice, equity, and religion
throughout the country ; and he succeeded in esta-
blishing a reign of peace, concord, and prosperity.
The people were inspired with such a spirit of honour, virtue, and religion by the example of Brian,

and by his excellent administration, that tradition and romance have vied with each other in recording the glories of this period of Irish history.   The reply of the beautiful maiden, adorned with gold and jewels, who rambled alone over the whole island, with no means of defence but a white wand, tipped with gold, is an illustration of the morals of the population then :—

> " Sir knight, I feel not the least alarm,
>   No son of Erin will offer me harm,
>   For though they love women and golden store,
>   Sir knight, they love honour and virtue more."

After the death of Brian the chiefs again quarrelled for supremacy ; his family acquired the ascendancy over the Hy Nial race, but they did not submit, and as their seat was Ulster, the two ends of the island were kept in a constant warfare during many generations, and continued so till towards the end of the twelfth century.

At this period a poor boy named Nicholas Breakspear was dependent for his daily food on the charity of the monks of St Albans, in Hertfordshire.   His father being only a servitor of the monastery, was too poor to pay for his attendance at the schools, and in consequence of the boy's deficiency in education, his wish of becoming a monk was denied at this Abbey.   He then passed over to France; his diligence, talents, and handsome person so recommended him to the monks of St Rufus, near Avignon, that he was admitted into their fraternity, and on the death of their abbot, was chosen to succeed him. Afterwards, when the monks were dissatisfied with him, and appealed to Pope Eugenius III. for redress, the abbot was examined by him, acquitted, taken into his service, and made a cardinal. Finally, in 1154 he became Pope, and assumed the title of Adrian IV., being the only Englishman who ever filled the Papal chair. When the news of his promotion came to the knowledge of Henry II. of England, he sent the abbot of St Albans, and three bishops to Rome, to congratulate him on his election ; the pontiff received them graciously, granted the Abbey many privileges, and also issued in favour of Henry the celebrated bull, or " letter of license to conquer Ireland."

At this epoch Ireland was divided into five principalities—viz., Leinster, Meath, Munster, Ulster, and Connaught, each governed by a king. He who took a lead in the wars was called monarch of all the kingdom ; Roderick O'Connor, king of Connaught, had then attained this dignity.

Dermod MacMurrough, king of Leinster, was a weak, licentious tyrant ; he carried off forcibly the daughter of the king of Meath ; her father being exasperated by this conduct, invaded Dermod's dominions, and, strengthened by the alliance of the king of Connaught, expelled MacMurrough from his kingdom of Leinster. Dermod had recourse to Henry II., king of England, (who was at that time in Guienne,) and offered to hold his possessions under the English crown, if the king rendered him assistance to recover them. Henry accepted the offer ; but being engaged with more important concerns, he only gave Dermod letters patent, empowering his subjects to aid the Irish prince. After some difficulty, Dermod formed a treaty with Richard de Clare, (surnamed Strongbow,) Earl of Pembroke, who agreed to reinstate him in his dominions, on condition of his being allowed his daughter Eva in marriage, and declared heir to all his territory.

Being assured of assistance, Dermod returned privately to Ireland, and concealed himself till the arrival of Robert FitzStephen, who landed with one hundred and thirty knights, sixty esquires, and three hundred archers; they were soon reinforced by another small body of men, who besieged and reduced the town of Wexford. When Dermod was reinstated in his hereditary dominions, he soon began to conceive hopes of making himself master of Ireland; aided by his allies, he took the city of Dublin from the Danes. Strongbow, having been prohibited by Henry, had not yet come over; but his avarice and ambition having been excited by the representations of Dermod, he applied and received permission from the king, and shortly after landed in Ireland, accompanied by two hundred horse and one hundred archers. The whole number of English forces did not amount to a thousand, but being disciplined, the greater part of the country was obliged to surrender. Ireland being thus partly subjugated, Henry became willing to share in person those honours and benefits which Strongbow and his adherents had secured, and also to take possession of the country which (as has been related) had been made over to him by Pope Adrian.

He left England with a fleet of two hundred and forty vessels, having on board five hundred knights and four thousand men-at-arms, and arrived in Waterford harbour on St Luke's day 1172, to take possession of the country as its rightful sovereign. He was joyfully received by the English, and by the natives of the country who were in alliance with them. The four provinces acknowledged his supremacy, but the province of Ulster refused to yield him obedience, and the O'Nials, in their fastnesses in Ulster, bade defiance to the English monarch. The chiefs who submitted to Henry thought they would be permitted to retain their lands and position, subject only to taxes, which as vassals would be imposed on them; but before leaving, Henry appointed Hugh De Lacy justiciary, or chief governor of Ireland, and consigned him about 800,000 acres of the best land. To John De Courcy he made over Ulster, although it never had acknowledged allegiance to the king. On the death of Henry II., Richard I. (who troubled himself little about Ireland) left his brother John in possession of the government. It had been called in former reigns "The Land of Ireland;" that part which had been subjugated was now named "The English Pale." The appointment of De Lacy to be governor so mortified De Courcy, (who considered he had a claim to the office,) that he asserted his right to Ulster, and determined to conquer it. For this purpose he set out with a chosen band of three hundred archers and twenty-two knights. Few enterprises recorded in history exhibit a more daring spirit, or a more triumphant issue. De Courcy's prodigious strength of body accorded with the unbending character of his mind; he had the policy to turn to account the prophecies of Columbkille regarding the conqueror of Ulster, who was to be a fair man, mounted on a white horse. His complexion answered the prophecy, and a horse of the right colour was easily procured. He continued to overrun Ulster, and plunder the country, fighting many battles with the inhabitants, who were famous for their warlike character. In the greater number of these engagements he was successful. The daring independence of De Courcy gave offence to King John, and De Lacy was ordered to seize him, and send him prisoner to England. De Lacy was then created Earl of Ulster, and at same time received a grant of that province. The O'Nials still remained unconquered, and retained possession, notwithstanding the many attempts to dispossess them in this and the following reigns. On some occasions they acknowledged fealty to the British monarchs, but more frequently they were found in open rebellion during the period which intervened till Henry VIII.'s reign.

As has already been stated, the O'Nial race of kings terminated with their subjugation by that king, who pardoned Con O'Nial on condition of his taking the oath of allegiance, and covenanting to adopt the English language and habits; for this submission, he was created Earl of Tyr-owen. In Elizabeth's reign, his son Shane was a constant source of annoyance and trouble to the English government, from his frequent rebellious inroads on the English Pale, but finally he was assassinated by the leader of the Scots in Ulster. Elizabeth confiscated his lands, took the title from his son, and bestowed it on his nephew, Hugh O'Neill or O'Neal ; but in a few years he too fomented fresh disturbances, incited the chieftains to revolt, united them, and placing himself at their head, set the government openly at defiance. An army was again despatched from England, and after many losses and disasters, the Earl of Essex arrived with further reinforcements ; but finding his army reduced by sickness and desertion, concluded a treaty of peace with O'Neill, and returned to England. Before long O'Neill broke the truce, and with his confederates overran the whole country, being aided by two thousand Spaniards ; but under the able administration of Sir Henry Mountjoy, they were defeated and obliged to leave Ireland. O'Neill fled to the Continent ; his possessions, with those of the chiefs who were implicated in this rebellion, became confiscated to the British crown.

The constant state of turmoil in which Ulster had so long been kept caused much of the land to be uncultivated ; and the wars having depopulated it, the greater part of the province was a barren wilderness.

King James I., shortly after his accession, turned his attention to colonise this province of his dominions ; he had it divided into portions, part he gave as Church lands, part he bestowed on his followers, and some he let out, under certain conditions and restrictions. These " undertakers," as they were called, were composed of English, Scotch, and a few of the native Irish. This mixture of nations has caused Ulster to be so different from the rest of the island, that the most casual observer will notice it in

the appearance, manners, customs, and habits of the
people.

Among the first settlers were many ministers who
had fled to escape from persecution in Great Britain ;
they were either accompanied or followed by members of their persuasion who were influenced to emigrate from religious motives.

The habits of these colonists were generally
prudent, and their demeanour grave.   These characteristics have descended to the generations who have
succeeded their Covenanter and Puritan ancestors,
cautiousness being apparent, and a love of religious
controversy and discussion of politics prevalent.
These peculiarities have stamped themselves on the
deportment and features of the inhabitants, who generally have a solemn impassive manner, and a shrewd
look, often accompanied by a dogmatic or a com-
bative expression.   Piety and gravity are strikingly
manifested on Sunday, (or the Sabbath, as it is generally designated in Ulster.)   Seriousness of character
is also shown by the prevailing indifference to public
amusements ; unfortunately it often proves a barrier
to progress in literature, music, and the fine arts.

One county especially has peculiar claims on England, being the property of London, the name showing its origin and dependence on that city.   Not
being able to induce as many families to accept of his
terms so as to populate the country, James requested
the Lord Mayor of London to influence the corporation to become colonists.   A court of common council was convened, and it was arranged that a deputa-
tion should proceed to Ireland to look into the matter,

and report accordingly. After their return it was agreed that the speculation should be entered into, and that a company should be formed in the city of London to determine and direct all matters connected with it. Alderman Cockayne was appointed governor, (from whose name it is said the soubriquet of Cockney had its origin.) The portion of Ulster which was assigned to them by the crown consisted of the County of Coleraine, with the towns of Coleraine and Derry, and the extensive lands attached, excepting sixty acres out of every thousand for Church lands, and certain portions to be made over to three 'native Irish gentlemen. On the part of the citizens, it was stipulated that they should expend £20,000 on the plantation. In order to meet the expenses of the colony, a tax was levied on the tradesmen of the city of London, which was considered by many as a great grievance ; and as it was compulsory, several poor men were sent to prison in default of payment. When three years had elapsed, the king was informed the plantation of Ulster was not in a prosperous state ; he then summoned the governor and assistants to attend a Privy Council at Whitehall to discuss the affairs of the colony.

Forty thousand pounds having been expended on the plantation, it was arranged that the land should be divided into twelve portions, which were to be appropriated by lot to each of the chief companies of the City, and so many of the smaller companies joined, as made their total contributions a twelfth of the entire sum. The chief companies were the mercers, grocers, drapers, fishmongers, goldsmiths, skinners, merchant tailors, haberdashers, salters, ironmongers, vintners, and cloth-workers; these were to act as trustees for the smaller companies which were incorporated with them. The allotment was managed by lottery in the following manner: the twelve proportions of land were entered on twelve sheets of paper, numbered from one to twelve, the lots with the figures on them being emptied into a hat; the lots with the companies' names and sums disbursed by them put into another; the sword-bearer of the City stood between the two hats; with his right hand he drew the figures, and with his left the name of the company to which the number belonged; he delivered them to the governor, who handed them over to the warders of each guild.

This company was incorporated by letters-patent from the king, and was styled "The Society of the Governor and Assistants of London of the New Plantation of Ulster, within the realm of Ireland." (It is now called "The Honourable the Irish Society.") By royal charter the territory was made over to the City, and the name changed from "county Colrane" to county Londonderry. Directions were issued to the companies, requiring each to send a certain number of artisans to Ulster, who were prohibited from taking Irish apprentices—boys from Christ's Hospital and other London institutions being sent over for that purpose. The companies were also ordered to have the churches repaired, and to supply the ministers with a Bible, prayer-book, and communion cup.

The trades recommended to be sent were weavers of common cloth, fustians, &c., felt-makers, and trim-

mers of hats, and hat-band makers, locksmiths, far-
riers, &c., also coast fishermen. " Paternes to make
the townes by" were drawn out, and were almost
all similar in plan, having a centre square (called a
diamond) from which the streets diverged. Frame
houses were made in Spitalfields, London, and sent
over ; when erected in Ireland, the interstices between
the wood were filled with wicker-work and clay ; the
ground floor having a pent-way projecting into the
street. Some of these houses remain to this day,
but the fronts have been modernised, so that they are
not discernible. The London tradespeople were
roused into indignation by further taxes being levied
on them, which they warmly opposed ; the coopers
and bakers broke into rebellion, and declared a determined hostility against " the wretched colony forced
on them by the king." Peace was made with the mal-
contents by the corporation agreeing to accept their
proportion, and to sustain hereafter all calamities
which might arise from its possession. The sum they
had paid in taxes did not amount to £400 ; the property they then resigned is now worth £1000 per
annum. The prices of provisions in Ulster at this
time were, a cow or bullock, 15s. ; a sheep, 1s. 4d. to
2s. ; a hog, 2s.; barley, 11d., and oats 4d. per bushel ;
and large salmon from 4d. to 8d. each.

A survey of the plantation, made 1622, is still preserved among the archives in his Grace the Archbishop of Canterbury's palace at Lambeth. As a
means of raising money to maintain the English
power in Ulster, James, at the suggestion of Sir
Robert Cotton, (the celebrated antiquary,) instituted

the order of English baronets, an hereditary dignity next in rank to the peerage. The number was at that time limited to two hundred gentlemen of good birth, possessed of a clear estate of £1000 per annum, (their number has since been enlarged at the pleasure of the crown ;) the conditions on which the title was bestowed being the payment into the exchequer, in three instalments, of money sufficient to support thirty soldiers for three years at 8d. per day. The coat of arms borne by English baronets shows plainly the origin of the institution, as it corresponds with the armorial bearings of Ulster.

Not only are the English indebted to Ulster for this addition to their nobility, but by the instrumentality of one who dwelt there centuries before, a right to claim the more exalted title of Christian was bestowed on them. It is well authenticated that St Patrick was taken prisoner by "Nial of the nine hostages," who sent him as a slave to a subordinate prince, who resided in the district called Dalriada. While young Succat was a captive occupied herding swine at the foot of Slemish mountain, his mind was enlightened to embrace the truths of religion, which had been inculcated on him by his pious mother. After being released, he was impelled by holy zeal to return and announce to the Irish the gospel of peace, which they gladly embraced. Columbkille, Aidan, Finian, and other holy men who succeeded St Patrick, became energetic missionaries. By their efforts Great Britain was evangelised, and Christianity spread rapidly over the land.

Ruins on Devenish Island, Lough Erne.

CHAPTER I.

NEVER did Lough Erne and the landscape around appear more beautiful than on a lovely spring evening in 17—. In the morning lowering clouds had cast their dark shadows on the placid waters, so that a gloom overspread both earth and sky, but all this had now vanished; copious showers had refreshed the parched ground, the face of nature was renewed, and everything looked bright, and seemed to rejoice in the glorious sunshine. The deep blue of the firmament, varied by a few thin vapour-like clouds, was reflected in the calm waters of the lake; while the numerous islets, ivied ruins, and tall round tower on Devenish island repeated themselves in the silver mirror beneath. Swallows flitted gracefully over its surface, and thrushes, blackbirds, and other feathered songsters warbled most sweetly amid its wooded banks. The fresh tints of the foliage glistening with rain-drops, the bursting buds of the trees, and the beauty and fragrance of the hawthorn blossoms, all combined to form a most exquisite scene.

Early in the afternoon, the roads leading from the then small but rising town of Enniskillen (in the west of Ulster) were crowded by persons returning from the half-yearly fair, and by herds of cattle which had been purchased and were being driven towards their new homes. But now the roads were clear of all obstructions, save a few old cronies, who had remained behind in the town to descant on the affairs of Church and State. Some of these were jogging home leisurely in the direction leading towards the county Tyrone, when they were passed by a young lady mounted on a spirited steed. Her cheeks glowed with health and happiness as she rode along at a brisk pace, evidently proving that she was accustomed to equestrian exercise. Her horse also stepped out as if familiar with the way. At a turn of the road the fair horsewoman came unexpectedly into the midst of a drove of cattle, which rushed before and around her horse, causing him to become restive; and although she maintained a firm seat, and reined him in with a practised hand, still her efforts were thwarted by the half-frantic motions of the cattle, who, notwithstanding the exertions of the drovers, continued to press around the infuriated animal. Every moment the lady's position was becoming more perilous, when a young man, who accompanied the drove, mounted on a powerful horse, dashed in among the wild cattle, and with the butt-end of his strong whip dealt heavy blows on the beasts that surrounded her; then seizing her horse by the bridle he led the lady out of danger.

After galloping some distance along the road till fairly out of danger, the lady addressed her deliverer, and, in a few stammering words, thanked him for his timely aid.

To this the young man replied, that "he felt he deserved blame instead of thanks, as the cattle which had caused her so much alarm belonged to him." He then expressed surprise at her venturing out on horseback alone.

"Oh," said she, "I often ride unaccompanied, but have never done so before on a fair day. My father, who came with me in the morning, left me at a friend's house in town. After the market he was obliged to return home on urgent business, and the rain coming on detained me until now."

"Permit me, then," said the youth, "although a stranger, to escort you to your journey's end." This the lady declined, saying, "As the way I am about to take is a by-path, which branches off the public thoroughfare, and free from cattle, I shall be quite safe; therefore I thankfully and gratefully bid you good-bye." Scarcely had she uttered the last syllable

B

when, reining her steed to the left, she darted off at a
brisk rate up the narrow road she had just described,
and was presently hidden from his view by an inter-
vening clump of trees. The departure of the lady
was so sudden, her companion was quite taken by surprise. For a moment he was spell-bound, and felt
bewildered. His first impulse was to follow her, but
being little accustomed to female society, and naturally of a retiring nature, he was deterred from doing
so, and in a mechanical manner pursued his journey.
Very frequently afterwards did his mind revert to the
events of that day; and as both parties will hereafter
make their appearance in these pages our readers
must learn more about them.

Although Irish by birth, they were of Scotch
descent; their ancestors had left the land of their
nativity under peculiar circumstances.

We have narrated in the introductory chapter some
of the plans which King James took to induce persons to emigrate to his favourite colony in Ulster.
Notwithstanding the persistency of his efforts to
populate the country, there still remained vast tracts
of waste lands. As a greater inducement to emigration from England and Scotland, he offered sixty
acres of land, at the yearly rent of six and eightpence,
to any who would go thither, erect houses, cultivate
the land, and maintain Protestant principles. The
unsettled state of the country, and the exaggerated
accounts of the savage character of "the wild Irish,"
deterred many from purchasing land during the early
part of James's reign. After a time the king's pro-

ject of peopling Ulster with English and Scotch
settlers was partially accomplished, though not by
the means he anticipated. Having attempted to co-
erce the people to adopt the liturgy and practices of
the Established Church of England, he found that
the Scotch, who had obliged him, when only king of
Scotland, to submit to be sermonised, would not now
allow themselves to be dictated to, nor would they or
the English use the forms prescribed for their worship. As these restrictions were not extended to
Ireland, many persons emigrated there to enjoy the
liberty of worshipping God according to the dictates
of conscience, without their lives being endangered.
Towards the middle of the seventeenth century, more
compulsory measures were taken against the Non-
conformists in England and Scotland. This caused
many to emigrate to Ulster, which was then in a more
settled social condition, and exempt from the storms
of persecution which swept over the sister kingdom.

Amongst those who left Scotland from religious
scruples was James Hunter, (grandfather to the fair
horsewoman who was mentioned at the commence-
ment of our tale ;) he was accompanied by his wife
and daughter Maggie. They were industrious, thrifty,
and frugal ; they belonged to the sect termed Covenanters. Hunter purchased a tract of country situated
near Enniskillen, erected a house, and settled down
to cultivate the land, living in the way that emigrants
to a new colony are compelled to rough it, tilling, en-
closing, and redeeming the waste around acre by
acre. Soon after the Hunters' arrival an incident

occurred which preserved Mrs Hunter's name from oblivion, or from only having the obituary of many of the patriarchs and centenarians in the Scriptures, merely the record of name, age, and death. Ireland was then densely wooded, but every year the trees were being thinned, as they were freely used for fuel, making fences, and in the erection of houses and cattle sheds. Wolves infested these woods, and a tradition has been handed down from father to son in the Hunter family, that Mrs Hunter slew one of these animals; in corroboration of which, a wolf-skin was preserved as a trophy for several generations, and often pointed out as "the skin of the wolf my great-grandmother killed."

It was then told how one day, when going to the "kail garden" with a large knife (or gully, as it was then called) in her hand, to cut vegetables for dinner, perceiving a wolf coming towards her, she stretched out the hand in which she held the knife, just as the animal sprung at her; it entered his throat, and he fell prostrate. She then ran off screaming in the direction of the fields where her husband and his labourers were at work; they soon appeared, and hastening towards the spot, found the animal with the knife still sticking in his throat, so disabled by Mrs Hunter's homethrust that he was easily despatched.

When the Hunters came to Ireland, they found the tract of land adjoining theirs occupied by a young fellow-countryman from Scotland, whose name was Macpherson. He and Hunter were glad to accommodate each other with the loan of farm implements, and various other articles.

Macpherson being unmarried, young females scarce, Maggie, a good-looking, loveable lass, and the young folk often together, it was but natural they should become attached to each other. Mr and Mrs Hunter approved of their union, and it was settled that the young people should be married, and all live together ; so that the two properties, as well as the two families, were henceforth to be united.

Their land was fertile, carefully and judiciously cultivated ; their cattle of good breeds, and well attended to. Farm produce rose in price, so that Hunter and Macpherson were soon in a most prosperous condition.

In the course of nature the old couple died in a ripe old age, having lived to see several grandsons and grand-daughters, who by their infantile prattle and endearing ways cheered and enlivened their declining years. We have been told by the poet, and often realised the fact from observation, that "the course of true love never yet did run smooth ;" but we find there are few rules without exceptions : in this case true love did run smoothly, and lasted during a long, happy, and peaceful life.

CHAPTER II.

THE extent and fertility of the pasture lands of the county Fermanagh induced the landowners to keep large herds of black cattle.

The long-horned cattle which, from a very remote period, had existed in Ireland, were slow feeders, inferior milkers, and took a long time to arrive at maturity. The landed proprietors became aware of this, and imported cattle from Scotland. Galloway had long been noted for the superior qualities of the polled or hornless cattle. A writer of the sixteenth century describes this region as " having mony fair kye and oxen, of quhilk the flesh is right delicious and tender." These animals throve well when put on Irish soil, the quantity of their milk was increased by feeding on the fioren or butter grass, which was indigenous to the country. Under these favourable circumstances, the farmers of Fermanagh, who had herds of cattle to dispose of, found a good market for them at the town of Enniskillen—the periodical fairs being frequented by farmers and graziers from the surrounding districts and neighbouring counties, to be supplied with an improved stock.

Mr Macpherson paid particular attention to the breeds and management of his cattle, and had large numbers to dispose of ; his beasts commanded a ready sale, were greatly extolled, and much sought after.

James Rutherford, a young farmer from Tyrone, having been sent by his father to the spring fair to buy cattle, had purchased a drove from Macpherson.

Riding out of Enniskillen, on his way homeward, his attention was attracted to a young lady on horse-back, surrounded by a drove of wild cattle, the particulars of which we have already described.

Young Rutherford's purchases pleased his father greatly, so that when the next fair came round, he was again commissioned to buy more cattle. This he readily undertook to do, especially as he had often thought of the young lady whom he had rescued, and whose appearance had impressed him so favourably as to make him desirous of becoming better acquainted with her, wished that he knew what was her name, where she lived, and hoped that he might see her again, &c. &c.

On his way to Enniskillen, she returned more vividly to his memory, he recalled her every word and look, and when he came near the spot where they had parted, he gazed anxiously about, but she was not in sight, nor did he get a glimpse of any lady at all resembling her at the fair that day.

Business, however, must be attended to ; he sought out Mr Macpherson in the fair ; told him how well his former purchases had been liked by his father, said he had been sent to buy more cattle, described the

uses for which they were intended, the kind of pasture
they were to be put on, &c., requesting Mr Macpherson
to assist him with his judgment in making the selec-
tion.   This was complied with, the drove collected,
and given in charge to the men who were to take
them home.

" How long does it take the cattle to reach your
place ?" asked Mr Macpherson, when business was
concluded, and they were seated together in the inn,
over a glass of wine.

" That depends on the state of the roads, and the
weather," replied Rutherford.   " Sometimes it takes
three, and at other times four days."

" But you do not accompany them ?" said Mr
Macpherson.

" Oh, no, I only take two days to reach home."

" Then you need not be in any hurry leaving ; my
house is on your way, a few miles distant from this ;
will you accompany me there and remain over night ?
You will then be fresh for your journey next day."

To this proposal the young man acceded, and
shortly afterwards they rode out of Enniskillen, in
the direction by which Rutherford had reached the
town in the morning.

As the pair proceeded along the road, Rutherford's
eyes wandered to the spot where he had first seen the
lady who had since that time occupied so much of his
thoughts, and when, leaving the highroad, they entered
the same byway she had taken, the young man's
mind was so occupied thinking about her, that for
some time he was quite abstracted in his manner, and

replied incoherently and at random to Mr Macpherson's various questions and observations.

After riding several miles into the country, a large substantially-built house came in view, picturesquely situated on a rising ground, overlooking Lough Erne, with its islet for every day in the year.

" This,"said Macpherson, entering a straight avenue which led towards the end of the house, " is where I live."

" How beautifully situated it is," responded Rutherford.

Just then they came to the end of the avenue, opposite to which was a large gate.

" The way to the stables," said Mr Macpherson, pointing with his whip in that direction. At this moment the hall door opened, and a young lady appeared ; a single glance convinced Rutherford that she was the person who had occupied so much of his thoughts during the day. She seemed to recognise him also, as her face and neck were suffused with blushes.

" Here I am, Meg, and a friend with me—tell your mother we are hungry as troopers ; and see, girl, that supper be quickly ready."

It was fortunate that dismounting, unstrapping the valise, and taking off his spatterdashes, required Rutherford's attention, thereby affording him time to regain composure before entering the house.

The youthful stranger was then shown by Mr Macpherson to the bedroom he was to occupy. James Rutherford had never till then thought of his personal appearance, nor had his toilet ever occupied longer than was absolutely necessary for cleanliness and comfort; but this evening he spent more time than ever he had before done opposite the looking-glass, and made extra attempts at adornment, tying and untying his cravat several times, until the knot was made to please, brushing his hair first one way, then another, trying to make himself look to the best advantage.

Miss Macpherson had hastened to her mother to tell of her father's arrival, and that he had brought the young man home with him who had rescued her when in danger, returning from Enniskillen on last fair day.

When James came into the parlour he was heartily greeted by Mrs Macpherson, who said, " We owe you a debt of gratitude for preserving our child from being killed, and I am glad to have it in my power to thank you."

" But why," interposed Mr Macpherson, turning to his guest, " why did you not tell me you were the preserver of my daughter?"

" How could I," stammered James; " I did not know the lady's name."

" Well, Meg Macpherson is her name; come here, girl, and shake hands with Mr Rutherford."

A very awkward salutation was gone through by both, the lady blushing, and James attempting to say something complimentary, but in a most confused and hesitating manner.

During supper Mrs Macpherson elicited from him

that his father was an immigrant from Scotland, his mother was dead, he had a brother and sister, that the family were Covenanters, and Peden was the name of the clergyman under whose ministry they sat.

" Pray," said the hostess, " is not Mr Peden a descendant of that man of God, Alexander Peden, who suffered for maintaining the truth, and upholding the faith during the times of persecution ?"

" Yes," replied James.

" Then it is the same Mr Peden we know," said she, turning to her husband ; " he assisted our minister on the special day of humiliation last year."

These and other topics which James could join in Mrs Macpherson introduced, so that his shyness gradually wore off, and he found himself entering quite freely into conversation with his host and hostess ; but with the young lady he could not find any subject of discourse.

Next morning James was invited to remain another day, Mr Macpherson wishing to show him over the farm ; he was reluctantly obliged to refuse, as his father would be uneasy at his absence ; but he promised at some future period to do himself the pleasure of remaining longer.

When next fair day came round, it rejoiced James to go again to Enniskillen.

Mr Macpherson was glad to see his young friend, and reminded him of his promised visit to Lakeview, "where," said he, " you are expected ; Mrs Macpherson will have the friend's bed-room ready for you."

James was but too glad to have the invitation renewed, and accordingly rode home with Mr Macpherson, but this time Miss Macpherson did not appear at the hall door, nor was she in the parlour when James arrived. When she did come she was quite constrained and flurried. James's shake-hands was also given in a nervous, tremulous manner. A little boy and two girls then entered, and were introduced as "the children."

All were soon seated at a plentifully spread table, cheerful conversation enlivened the meal, causing it to pass pleasantly, and be enjoyed by the whole party.

The farm was gone over next day, and Mr Macpherson found his young friend shrewd, sensible, and well versed in the rotation of crops, management of stock, and farming operations generally.

When Mrs Macpherson was bidding him good-bye, she said, "Perhaps when you next visit us my sons will be at home; as our minister, who is now educating them, is talking of going to see his friends in Scotland, and the boys are to have their vacation then."

James from this concluded that he had permission to renew his visit without waiting till fair day came round.

Again and again did James return to Lakeview, and although reserved and reticent, gained favour with Mr and Mrs Macpherson; Meg also welcomed him, if not with words, in a manner that proved she was glad to see him.

After some time James came to Lakeview accompanied by his father, whose object was to ask Mr and

Mrs Macpherson's consent for their daughter Maggie
to be married to his son, and to state his prospects,
&c. He frankly told them his farm was not large
enough to divide, but if whatever sum of money Mr
Macpherson would give his daughter was expended
in the purchase of land, he would stock and crop it,
furnish the house, and supply the young couple with
the means of going on until after the first harvest.

As Mr Peden had given a favourable account of
the Rutherford family, the union was approved of by
the parents. Mr Macpherson acceded to the plan of
purchasing a farm, and as shortly afterwards "a deed"
(freehold property) was to be sold in the county
Tyrone, some miles distant from Lough Neagh, and
near the rising town of Slievedhu, Mr Macpherson
bought it on advantageous terms.

Meg and James were married, and removed to their
new home, which was called Thornbrae.

They lived happily and comfortably together, with
hopeful prospects for the future; but who can calculate what is in store for us,—" man proposeth, but God
disposeth." Before twelve months had elapsed poor
Mrs Rutherford's health became very delicate; however, it was hoped that after her confinement she
would get stronger.

Mrs Macpherson sent a trusty Highland woman to
her daughter, who had lived with herself many years;
she had great experience in the management of children and tending invalids, so that Mrs Rutherford
had every care and attention.

After the birth of "wee Maggie," Mrs Rutherford

improved so much in health, it was confidently expected she would soon be quite well again ; but these
hopes were doomed to be blighted.   She who so
lately had been blooming with health, surrounded
with every comfort, radiant with hope, and with the
prospect of living many years, was taken away before
her ear was greeted, and her heart rejoiced, by hearing
that sweetest of all sounds, "Mamma," lisped by her
infant's lips.

> " And thus how oft do life and death
>   Twine hand in hand together ;
> And the funeral shroud and bridal wreath
>   How small a space may sever !"

Within two years James Rutherford had been a
bachelor, a husband, a father, and was now a widower.

CHAPTER III.

HIGHLAND KATE, who had superintended and assisted in the household duties during Mrs Rutherford's life, was now sole manager of the establishment at Thornbrae, so that all went on much as formerly. She had also the entire charge of the child, who did not experience any change by her mother's death, and, as she knew no other, called her nurse "Mammy Kate."

Rutherford felt his wife's death keenly, as he had been devotedly attached to her; but, among his sect, to betray any feelings of emotion, or express sorrow in words, was considered sinful. He rarely spoke of his bereavement, and seldom paid the slightest attention to the child. His nearest approach to any demonstration of affection was gazing for a few minutes on the sleeping babe, and ejaculating, "Poor motherless bairn! may the Lord cause His face to shine on thee, and be very gracious unto thee."

Three years passed over; the child was healthy and happy. Sometimes her childish prattle and artless ways elicited a caress from her undemonstrative father.

One Sunday Kate was drenched with rain coming from meeting, caught fever, and became dangerously ill. Mr Peden, the minister, came and took the child, for safety, to his residence, about four miles off. His wife, never having had any family, was at a loss what to do with her, particularly as the poor child continued weeping and begging to be taken home to her "Mammy Kate."

Mrs Peden, who was a bustling housewife, felt relieved when the minister's sister, a maiden of mature years, who resided in the house, offered to try what she could do with "the puir bit lassie." Her woman's instinct suggested that the only way to relieve the grief of the child was to turn her affections on other objects; so, taking her to the farmyard, she showed her a brood of young chickens, then gave her some corn in her pinafore to throw to them, telling her if she was a good obedient girl she would be allowed to feed the chickens, but if she cried she would not.

To this Maggie abruptly said, "Won't I be taken home to Mammy Kate then?"

"Well, child, that cannot be now."

Poor Maggie's lip trembled; her eyes filled with tears; she was just about to burst into a fresh paroxysm of grief, when the hen and chickens clucked past her; then, rushing abruptly forward, she buried her agitated face in Miss Peden's apron for some minutes, and, looking up, exclaimed, "Will you be another mammy, then?"

The lady, though unaccustomed to sentimentality,

was touched by this appeal,. and, stooping down, demurely kissed her forehead; but Maggie insisted on "a mouth kiss, like what she got from Mammy Kate."

Days wore on. Kate's fever came to a crisis. The case was pronounced hopeless; she could not live many days longer. When her death took place, Rutherford rode over to inform the minister. Maggie saw her father coming, and ran to meet him with the usual question, "Where's Mammy Kate?"

She was gravely told, "You will never see her again in this world, child; she's gone to heaven."

"Oh, then take me to heaven, to my Mammy Kate; oh, do take me!"

Rutherford was shocked at such a manifestation of the power of the old Adam in his daughter, and attempted to reason with her; but she was so young, her feelings strong, and too much excited to be controlled immediately. She was carried away to her room by Miss Peden, who laid the sobbing child on the bed, and commenced singing the 23d Psalm. This was the last task Maggie had committed to memory. It now turned her thoughts off her grief. Her sobs became less frequent, and ere the last verse was sung, she had dropped over into the happy sleep of childhood.

Miss Peden left the room, and after some time returned to look at her charge. There she lay, with smiles wreathing the mouth which had been so lately twitching with sobs. Doubtless in her dreams she was feeding the chicks, chasing butterflies, or en-

C

gaged in some infantile pursuit which afforded enjoyment.

Weeks passed over, and Maggie had forgotten her grief and bereavement. She was a great favourite with the whole household. Even the minister, though "cast in humanity's sternest mould," relaxed from his gravity on seeing the gambols, or hearing the joyous sounds of "wee Maggie's" voice; and rough old Robin the ploughman lifted her with such gentleness before him on the horse he was riding home from the field. It seemed as if each member of the family felt a favour had been bestowed when they were permitted to do anything for "the bairn."

Whenever her father spoke of the child's return he was put off by being told "she is better cared for here than she would be at home." For some weeks James passively submitted to his child's absence, being convinced of the truth of the remark that she could not, under existing circumstances, be attended to at Thornbrae in the same manner as she was at the manse. Kate's death was a great trial and loss, as she had not only filled the place of mother and nurse to Maggie, but had also carefully managed and attended to all the household duties at the cottage. As home was so cheerless, James, as might be expected, was a frequent visitor at the manse, where he was sure of a hearty welcome from the minister and his wife. His grief was lessened by the caresses and prattle of his child, and his troubles and cares soothed by the quiet sympathy of Miss Peden, and the solicitude and tender

care which she bestowed on his daughter. He began
to realise that it is not good that man should be alone.
It is not therefore to be wondered at that Miss Peden
now took possession of his thoughts, as being a suitable companion for himself, and a helpmeet in his
daily pursuits. If she would become his wife, his
child still could have almost maternal care, and he
would again have Maggie at home with him. Pondering on all these matters, he came to the conclusion
that "it was a providence which took the bairn to
the minister's, and a special providence that put it
into Miss Peden's heart to take to the bairn, and the
bairn to love her in return."

Accordingly he rode over one afternoon to ask the
minister if he thought his sister would marry him,
and if he approved of the union. The minister,
worthy man, had foreseen such a *dénouement*, and
cordially gave his assent, agreeing with Rutherford
in pronouncing that "altogether it was plainly a
special providence."

Miss Peden was duly informed by her brother of
the state of affairs ; and as she never had an offer
before, and never might again, all was arranged for
the marriage, which took place shortly afterwards in
a manner becoming the ages and situation of the
parties.

Rutherford took his bride home on horseback,
seated on a pillion behind him ; the minister's wife
and Maggie followed in a cart.

After the lapse of a year Mrs Rutherford presented
her husband with a son, whose birth had nearly a

second time made James a widower, but this time both mother and child were spared.

"Wee Maggie" looked upon the doctor with affectionate regard for bringing such a treasure, which she considered as her own exclusive property. Poor child! her woman's nature could not be suppressed; she must have an object for her affections to centre in, and brother became her chief care; she never wearied looking at him, and sitting beside his cradle became her especial duty, rocking and hushing him to sleep by singing Sternhold's version of the twenty-third Psalm, then in use :—

1. "My Shipheard is the liwing Lord, nothing therefore I need;
   in pastures faire, with waters calme, He sets me for to feed.
2. He did conwert and glad my soule, and brought my mind to frame,
   to walke in pathes of righteousnesse, for His most holy name.

3. "Yea though I walke in vale of death, yet will I feare none ill,
   thy rod, thy staffe dothe comfort me, and Thou art with me still.
4. And in the presence of my foes, my table Thou shalt spread;
   Thou shalt (O Lord) fill full my cup, and ekè annoint my head.

5. "Through all my life Thy fawour is so frankly showed to me,
   that in Thy house for ewermore my dwelling-place shall be."

The little nurse then took her knitting and sat guarding his slumbers, roused by his slightest movements; and when during his infantile ailments he cried, Maggie wept too, and would willingly have endured the pain rather than see him suffer.

James looked on the child as a gift sent by the Lord, and determined to devote him from his birth to His service, intending to bring him up to be a minister of the Covenanter persuasion.

In accordance with James's plans for his son's future prospects, he resolved to name him for his maternal relative, Alexander Peden, who is mentioned in the " Scottish Book of Martyrs" as " Peden the Prophet."

"But a man cannot tell what shall be, and what shall be after him who can tell?"

When the minister was informed of his brother-in-law's intention he was greatly gratified; shook James warmly by the hand, prayed that the babe might be " a babe of grace," and that he might follow in the footsteps of his sainted ancestors, Peden and Rutherford; requesting that he might be permitted to give his assistance in furthering the good work by educating the boy till he was ready to be sent to Glasgow College.

Years rolled over; all went on prosperously at Thornbrae; crops were abundant, cattle and sheep increased exceedingly; all the in-door duties were thriftily managed; and Rutherford's house became a scene of bustling activity.

As the household was arranged according to the general style of the period, and as it belongs to the things which have passed away, we shall describe it in the following chapter.

Some readers may not feel interested in this chapter, and as it is not connected with the narrative, it can be skipped.

CHAPTER IV.

THORNBRAE FARM contained one hundred and fifty-seven acres, arable and pasture land, besides the privilege of cutting turf (peat) in unlimited quantities out of a bog a few miles distant, and the range of a hill-side for grazing cattle. The house was a stone-built, whitewashed, thatched cottage, and behind it were stable, cowhouses, pig-styes, &c. Narrow windows, one pane wide and four high, were on either side of the strong front-door. These were recessed inside, and in each stood a red earthenware flower-pot, one of which contained a horse-shoe geranium, the other a gooseberry geranium. These were the only flowers about the place, with the exception of sweetbriar and honeysuckle, which had been planted outside the door by Maggie's mother.

The interior of the house was divided by a wall at either end, the centre being the kitchen, and the ends the apartments, over which were lofts (approached by a ladder) for sleeping-places, for " the boys " on one side of the house, and for the lasses on the other.

The outside door opened into the kitchen, which was, however, partially hidden from view by a slight wall about six feet high and eight long. This made a hall or passage to " The Room" *par excellence,* which was only used on Sunday afternoons, or when the minister, his wife, or any other great personages came to Thornbrae. The floor of this apartment was of spotlessly clean wood uncovered, carpets at that time being too expensive a luxury. In centre of the room stood an oval table of dark wood and strong massive proportions ; another larger table, with falling leaves, was behind the door ; on it, placed upright against the whitewashed wall, the tea-tray, and in front the big Bible covered with calf-skin, with the hair on, and at either side a pair of tall brass candlesticks. Two arm-chairs, and several other chairs of hard-wood corresponding with the tables, the seats of chairs being also of solid wood, were little adapted from their luxurious ease to encourage laziness, and the upright unornamented straight backs indicated that they had been designed, made, and were to be used by a plain matter-of-fact set of men. Over each window was a valence of blue and white linen checquer, and on either side a curtain of the same homespun material.

Opposite the door was the fireplace : it was filled with a bunch of hawthorn or sycamore in summer ; and in winter, when the room was occupied, the grate contained a peat fire.

On the mantel-shelf was arranged the family library, consisting of the following volumes bound in

strong dark leather : " The Confession of Faith,"
" Fox's Book of Martyrs," " Baxter's Saint's Everlasting Rest," " Willison's Afflicted Man's Companion," " The Pilgrim's Progress," " Fleming on the
Papacy," " Keith on the Prophecies," " Venn's Whole
Duty of Man," " Boston's Crook in the Lot," " Bun-
yan's Come and Welcome," &c. &c. Above these
hung the former Mrs Rutherford's sampler. The
ponderous size of frame, and the quantity of hard
wood employed in it would in the present day be
valuable for mechanical purposes. Poor Maggie
often looked at and admired this marvel of female
achievement in art. Samplers of late have been hidden out of sight by old ladies, as in addition to the
date when worked, the age of worker was also stated,
but as the fingers are now powerless, and the tongue
is also silent of the worker of the sampler which hung
in " The Room " at Thornbrae, we can describe it
without giving offence.

Unbleached canvas was the ground-work ; length,
twenty-two inches ; breadth, eighteen. Round this
was wrought in cross stitch, with green silk, the pattern we term Grecian, but then called " Walls of
Troy ;" and at each corner, birds which, from colour
of plumage, shape, and attitudes, must have belonged to some species now extinct. Certainly, if
such ornithological specimens could be procured alive
now, the Regent's Park Zoological Society would
gladly give a large sum for them, as they would be
sure to attract crowds when once they had been seen
poising themselves upright, and standing on their

tails in the attitude of a dog begging. Then came the alphabet in Roman letters worked in red, then Italics in blue ; various patterns and colours of lines dividing each row of letters ; next followed large capital letters formed of eylet holes, (each alternate letter a different colour.) This was the stitch used in marking blankets, towels, bed and table linen ; then followed the texts of scripture, " Favour is deceitful, and beauty is vain ; but a woman that feareth the Lord, she shall be praised." " Give her of the fruit of her hands, and let her own works praise her in the gates."—Prov. xxxi. chap. 30th and 31st verses. " Wrought by the hands of Margaret Macpherson, April 23rd, 1735, aged nine years and eight months." But the "*chef d' œuvre*" of art was reserved for the last. The bow-pot of flowers in centre was pronounced most beautiful, and the bunch of cherries on one side, and strawberries on the other, so natural, it would be useless for us to do otherwise than agree with the testimony of so many admirers.

Between the fireplace and windows facing the door " solemnly ticked the brass-dialled clock," in its blackoak case. On opposite side of fireplace was the chief ornament of the room, the beaufet ; this was a mahogany corner cupboard, with panes of glass in the doors ; it contained the china tea-service, arranged so as to show each article to the best advantage ; also a pair of crystal decanters, and a dozen wine-glasses mounted on high stalks, which showed a white spiral pattern in centre of stem ; the sugar-bowl to match decanters was placed in a prominent position, so as to display the silver sugar-tongs and dozen tea-spoons, on which were engraved $_{J\overline{R}}^{M}$, it being the fashion of the day to have the initials of husband and wife combined together.

A door opened out of the room to a sleeping apartment; this was the stranger's or friend's chamber. The walls were whitewashed; the curtains of bed, and drapery of window, were blue and white chequer. The bedstead was of equally substantial proportions with the other furniture; it was called a tester-bed. In these days of French and Albert beds such a piece of furniture would be a rare curiosity; the four posts were large, and strong enough to form pillars to support the gallery of a church; on them rested a square canopy, round which was a projecting cornice of highly-polished dark wood, and under this was a valance, with curtains of checquer. The feather-bed, of the best white-goose feathers, was part of the "plenishin" brought by Meg Macpherson to Thornbrae; the tick of strong linen had been spun by herself; also the sheets, towels, and curtains. The patchwork quilt had been her handiwork; it was made of hexagon scraps of coloured print, alternating with white linen. This patchwork was called the "Causeway Pattern." A table, a couple of chairs, and white bedroom ware completed the furniture. Alongside the bed was a width of carpet, made of strips of different coloured cloth sewed together, and woven with coarse thread, the cloth forming the warp, the thread the woof. A bedroom corresponding in size with the stranger's bedroom opened off the kitchen ; it does not require particular description.

The other end of the house was similarly divided, the large apartment being the " gudeman's and gudewife's " bedroom ; there was a tester-bed in it, also a large oak chest, to hold the blankets, &c., and a strong oak-press, containing the " go-to-meeting " clothes, and underneath it large drawers to hold the " napery." *   Opening off this apartment was the store-room, containing webs of linen, chequer, ticking, spangles (bunches) of linen yarn and wool, the saddle, bridle, pillion, &c., &c.

The other small apartment on this side, leading out of kitchen, was used as pantry, and held barrels of salt provisions, oat, barley, and wheaten meal, groats, and seeds ; also cheese, bannocks of bread, crocks of butter, and a wooden pail containing butter-milk, on which floated a small wooden bowl or basin, called a " caap ;" this beverage was *pro bono publico*, and was often resorted to by both male and female servants when they felt inclined to slake their thirst.†

The kitchen must now be described.   It was large, being forty feet long and thirty wide ; the floor, formed of clay and lime, so incorporated, smoothed, and

---

* Bed and table linen.

† The milk that remains after the butter has been taken off the churn is called " butter-milk ;" this in Ireland is delicious when fresh, not at all like what is called by that name in England.   In Ireland, milk as well as cream is churned ; in England, only the cream is used, so that what remains, after taking off the butter, is thin whey, only fit to be used by pigs, and not a favourite drink with them either.

kneaded down as to form a hard, even surface, like the asphaltic pavement of the present day.

The chimney, built on the " butt " end of house, (in distinction to the " room " end, it being " ben the house;") towards roof this chimney was about four feet broad, two wide, and gradually enlarged its proportions till, at the distance of five feet from the floor, its breadth was nearly seven feet, and it projected fully four feet out on the floor; this projecting part was designated the " brace." Inside this ample chimney were hung up hams, sides of bacon, tongues, "hung beef," and black puddings; outside was suspended an old blunderbuss, used for shooting birds for scarecrows ; also scythes, bill-hooks, reaping-hooks, &c., and any other articles requiring to be kept dry. On the ground, in centre of chimney, was a large, round, hard stone, (such as those used in mills for grinding grain ;) it formed the hearth, and on each side, and in front, it was paved with oval flint stones ; it should have been mentioned that on either side of hearth were stone seats, called " the chimley corner." Built in across the chimney was a strong bar of iron, about four feet above the hearth; this was " the crane," and on it were iron chains or " links," to fasten the " crooks " in—namely, iron hooks of various lengths, to hang the pots, kettle, pan, or girdle on over the fire, when required for cooking.

It may be asked how roasting, or any other kind of cookery, could be done at this fireplace ; but let me assure my readers that, notwithstanding the many kinds of roasters, hasteners, bottle-jacks, ovens, close

ranges, kitcheners, and American stoves in present
use, I have never yet tasted a goose so well cooked
by any of them, or which had such a delicious flavour,
as one cooked in a farm-house at a similar fireplace.
Many, many years have passed over, but the savoury
remembrance of that goose still causes me to "smack
my lips."

The goose having previously been stuffed with
mashed potatoes and onions, was put into a large pot,
with a little water about it, and allowed to stew slowly
over the fire ; after some time the gravy was taken
out, the pot placed on hearth, some butter put in
along with goose ; turf embers were then placed under
the three-legged pot, also on top of iron lid ; in this
way it was nicely browned, and tasted tender and
juicy.

All kinds of meat and fowls were cooked in this
manner ; also apple and other pies. Peat was the only
fuel used, the lighted embers being placed on hearth ;
pieces of trees, dug out of the bogs and well dried, were
added; this is bog-wood, (not bog-oak, but fir, white and
reedy ;) turf, shaped like long bricks, were piled round
this, and over it were suspended the potato-pot, the
stirabout-pot, the broth-pot, or the yarn-pot, as occasion required.

In centre of partition opposite fireplace was the
"dresser," of ample proportions, made of white deal,
clean, and well "scoured ;" it was well "plenished"
with pewter plates and dishes on upper shelves ; then
followed delf "bowls,"* trenchers,† "caaps," (before

* Basins.   † Wooden platters.

described,) "noggins," and "piggins." These were
vessels made of staves of wood, fastened together
with bands of "sally," (willow,) round a circular piece
of wood. One of the staves was a few inches longer
than the others, and narrowed in, for the fingers to
catch by, forming a handle; the noggin was the
smaller vessel; piggins were used for milking into.
On hooks in front of shelves were suspended jugs,
porringers, mugs, &c. Two drawers in dresser contained knives, forks, and horn and iron spoons; under
it were pots of various sizes. These were all three-
legged, and had "ears" (loops) on either side to hook
the pot-hooks into; the frying-pan and griddle* were
also to be found there. The bakeboard, rolling-
pin, potato-bruiser, beetle, † pot-stick, ‡ and a large
wooden ladle for lifting broth hung upon wall beside
the callender and sowen-sieve; the use of latter shall
again be described.

The ceiling of the kitchen was lofty, as it was not
covered over between the partitions, but left open
the height of the roof. On a level with the floors of
servants' apartments were strong beams across the
kitchen. On one of these was fixed the "glaiks,"
(used for churning with;) this was a transverse piece
of wood, to which a handle was attached to form a

---

* A circular plate of iron to suspend over the fire. On it the oat-
cakes were firmed, previous to being placed to "har'en" opposite the
fire, supported in an upright position by a turf.

† A round wooden mallet, used to beat clothes with, as a substitute
for mangling, also for pounding (mashing) potatoes.

‡ Used for stirring the meal in porridge, (in Scotland it is called a
spurtle.)

lever; the churn-staff was fastened to the "glaiks,"
and was moved up and down by the motion of the
handle working it like a pump. The churn used in
this way was in shape like the present toy churns.
Along the window, in a line with the door, was a
settle-bed ; this was made of white deal wood, formed
like a sofa; the closed up seat contained a bed,
blankets, and quilt, and, when folded down, formed
a bedstead, for use on extra occasions ; beside this,
when not in use, stood the mistress' spinning-wheel,
and on the wall hung the reel for winding the yarn ;
and, at the time we write of, the strong wood cradle
stood between the settle-bed and fire. On the opposite side of the kitchen were two windows; under
both were tables, and between them the back-door,
beside which was a pair of water-cans, (water-pails
or stoups,) for carrying water from the well or burn
(rivulet.)

Deal stools, and chairs with seats formed of straw
ropes crossed, and the lasses' spinning-wheels, completed the furniture of kitchen.

Close to the back-door, outside, was the milk-house,
and near to this the "byre" (cow-house) and pig-styes.

Having now described the house, its furniture and
belongings, we shall reserve the management of the
household for another chapter.

CHAPTER V

ALL went on in the usual routine at Thornbrae for years. The children were healthy, and had got over their infantile ailments.

As Maggie grew older, she was able to assist in all the household work. Her "mammy" taught her to read, knit, and sew; the minister set her writing copies; from him also she gained a knowledge of geography, and learned the simple rules of arithmetic. During this time, Alexander was acquiring the elementary branches of education. When he was older, he rode over to his uncle's every morning to be instructed by him, and as the boy had a good capacity and capital memory, he made rapid progress in his studies.

Matters went on in this manner for years, only varied by going to "the meeting" on Sabbaths and fast-days, and occasional tea-parties amongst the neighbours.

"Quiltings" were the occasion of many a party being assembled. They were almost the only places where the boys and girls had an opportunity of seeing each other, except at "the meeting." When a patchwork quilt had been sewed together ready to be lined, a number of girls were invited to come to put it into the frame and quilt it. When finished, they baked " fadge," (potato cake) and " slim cake,"—namely, puff paste cut into squares with a knife, or made round by being cut out with an inverted tea-cup. These cakes were cooked on the " griddle," some eaten hot and buttered, others used cold.

The minister, his wife, and the fathers, mothers, and brothers of the girls came to spend the evening. When all were assembled in " the room," the males generally ranged on one side, the females on the other. Tea was then " masked," (infused.) After a long " grace," said by the minister, tea was poured out by " the mistress," and handed round by the young men in a sheepish, awkward manner ; but this did not seem to be observed by the fair young girls, who, in return for a cup of tea, bestowed many a sweet smile and bright glance on their respective favourites. Then laughter and jest gradually overcame the silence which previously had reigned, and fun and merriment prevailed.

During the repast the men talked little, the minister generally taking the lead in conversation, inquiring of each matron about the welfare of her children, &c. ; and informing the company in general the latest news of the war, the state of the Church in Scotland, reforms about to be introduced into the kirk-session, enlarging and explaining the nature of the abuses about to be rectified, deploring the influence that Popery and Prelacy were gaining over the length and breadth of the land, &c. &c. Occasionally the

D

matrons, during a pause in the conversation, praise the
tea, descant on the merits of black or green tea, discuss whether they are better separate or mixed, each
telling who they thought sold the best tea in Slievedhu.

After returning thanks the tea-things were removed;
the table, which had been most plentifully supplied
with bannocks, cakes, and cheese, was lessened considerably of its load; what remained was left on the
table, and glasses, whisky, sugar, and hot water immediately placed on it. The elder portion of the
males drew their chairs round the table, and commenced to make their tumblers of punch, of which,
however, they partook in moderation. They talked
of the weather, discussed the proper rotation of crops,
the best methods of scutching flax, the failure of the
hay crop, the prices of grain compared with former
years; mingled with news of the war, the probable
effect it would have on the price of pigs, &c. &c. &c.

Meantime their better-halves gathered into a corner,
and between the sips of their whisky-punch, (which
had been made and handed to them by their lords
and masters, with the remark, " Hot, sweet, and
strong, the kind of punch ladies like; hope it may
please,") they commenced to " shannagh" (gossip)
about who was going to be married; the price yarn
brought at the last fair; whether it was likely to rise
or fall in price; how many " cutts" (skeins) they
could spin to a " spangle," (bunch ;) the best remedies for chin-cough ; what they did when Johnny had
measles, and baby the chicken-pox ; calculated how
many spangles of yarn it took to buy Mrs Brown's

poplin dress, or Miss Adams's Dunstable bonnet, trimmed with "bloom"-coloured ribbons, (of course neither of these ladies were present;) what herbs were the best to put in rennet; the surest method of keeping moths out of clothes; who was going to have an addition to her family, *et cetera*.

Immediately after tea the young folks had retired to the kitchen, and began to play round games, such as "Hunt the slipper," "Blind-man's buff," "Twirl the trencher," "Whistle the key." The two latter were great favourites, as they entailed forfeits, to release which kissing was principally the penalty. Dancing would have been considered highly immoral; but releasing pledges, which were forfeited by the "long kiss in the corner," or being sentenced to

> "Wink at the wittiest,
> Bow to the prettiest,
> And kiss the girl you love best;"

or condemned to stand in the corner and repeat the poetical and highly sentimental distich, appealing to the sympathies of the fair sex—

> "Here I stand as stiff as a stake,
> Begging a kiss for charity's sake."

All these, of course, were innocent compared to dancing. A penalty often imposed was "the monk and the nun," which was a prime favourite. The monk or nun, whose pledge was to be redeemed, went outside of closed door and knocked. The question was then asked, Who are you? Reply, A monk. What do you want? A nun, was the answer. Name her. Then the girl who was called went to be kissed outside the door ; she called a monk, and he in return a nun, till the whole party had been gone over.

These amusements were varied with the puzzling demand before a forfeit was redeemed ; namely, " bite an inch off the poker," or repeat six times without making a mistake,

" Peter Piper picked a peck of pickled peppers.
    Did Peter Piper pick a peck of pickled peppers ?
    If Peter Piper picked a peck of pickled peppers,
    Where is now the peck of pickled peppers that Peter Piper picked ?"

Or sit on the floor on the " beetle," (the round mallet already described,) with legs crossed, and right arm tied across breast, then take three sips of water out of a " noggin," brimful of water, without spilling a drop, (the latter was only a gentleman's forfeit,) and from the difficulty in performing this feat, and the mishaps it led to, elicited peals of laughter.

About nine o'clock the young people came into " the room," a jug of whisky-punch was made, and a wine-glass of it handed by a young man to each damsel, accompanied by " slim-cake," or " bannocks " and cheese ; sometimes the punch was refused, and the gallant request was made, " Just taste it then to sweeten it for me." The minister then gave out a psalm, all voices joining in singing it to the air of " Martyrdom," " Dundee," " Montrose," or the " Old Hundred ; " the slow-measured, long-drawn, doleful strains, contrasting strongly with the mirthful sounds which had previously resounded from the kitchen, made it seem like martyrdom indeed. A chapter was then read, followed by a long extemporary prayer

by the minister, and the party broke up ; the females
who lived at a distance going home in the usual way,
riding double—viz., mounted on a pillion behind their
father, husband, or brother, the rest walking.

As might be expected, " courting " made up a
large share of the enjoyment of the evening, and
most of the love-making commenced at " quiltings "
terminated in weddings.

At one of these festive meetings Maggie Rutherford
(now grown into maidenhood) met a young man
named Wilson, who, after a few other interviews, sent
his father to propose to Rutherford for his daughter ;
and as Wilson had been pronounced by the minister
to be " a well-to-do, God-fearing boy," the fathers
entered into preliminary arrangements, settled the
" tocher " (marriage portion) to be paid with the
lass ; the number of acres of land, the cattle, sheep,
carts, ploughs, &c., to be given by the other father.

The marriage shortly afterwards took place, and
Maggie removed to her new home about twelve miles
distant, taking with her the sampler and all the other
articles previously described which had belonged to
her mother.

CHAPTER VI.

WE shall now redeem our promise of giving an account of the domestic arrangements at Thornbrae; they may prove interesting, as almost everything was managed differently from what it is in the present day in the north of Ireland farm-houses. The habits of both farmer and labourer are changed, their social position and relation to each other, as master and servant, altered; they seem quite like a different race of them. Servants, both male and female, were engaged by the half-year, at one of the statute fairs; they were fed and lodged in the house, wages for boys being from £2 to £2, 10s.; girls, 20s. to 25s., with the proviso that the girls were to spin so many spangles of yarn in the week.

Farm labourers were paid 10d. to 1s. per day, " cost anent," (this term means that the men were to provide their own food;) women got 4d. to 6½d. for weeding, but in "har'st" (harvest) 8d. to 10d.

A description of how one day was spent will suffice for each, with little variation. At five in the summer mornings, or later as the days shortened, Mr Rutherford took the ladder from the lasses' bedroom door,

and placed it at "the boys',"* calling on them to
"get up;" the last down carried the ladder back to
the girls' door. Bannocks, cheese, and milk were
then given to "the boys."

By this time the girls had dressed in their coloured
bed-gowns and black petticoats; their toilet did not
occupy long, as they had neither stays, crinolines,
shoes, nor stockings to put on. They came to the
kitchen, kindled the fire, brought in "a go" of water
from the well, in the water stoups, and put it into a
large pot which was hung over the fire, set forward
the churn, fastened the churn-staff to the "glaiks,"
and when the water was sufficiently warm to add to
the milk, commenced to churn; the girls working the
"glaiks" by turns. Meantime, stirabout (oatmeal
porridge) or potatoes were boiling, and the mistress
had laid the cloth on the table for breakfast, placing
on it butter, bannocks, and cheese.

When the butter was ready to be taken off the
churn, the lid was rinsed down with water, also the
churn-staff, to remove any particles of butter sticking
to them. The mistress having previously well washed
and "scalded" her hands, and rubbed them with salt,
lifted the butter with her right hand into a large
wooden bowl, which she held in her left; a "gather-
ing brush" was then given to collect the remaining
butter; all was then well clapped to take the milk out,
and salt added; a blunt knife passed through it, to
catch any stray hairs which might have fallen off the

---

* In the same way as negroes are designated in the United States, an
Irish boy may be of any age from childhood to sixty, if unmarried.

cows while milking, and escaped through the strainer. The butter being well washed, the milk and water pressed out of it, then put into crocks or wooden butts, except what was required for immediate use, which was made up in " miskins" (namely, rolls containing about a pound each) made in a triangular shape, and a few " prints" (pats) made to " mense the table," when the doctor, minister, or any town friends called. Previous to removing the churn, a " brash" was given to make " pedlar's cream ;" this was frothy milk, containing a few particles of butter ; it was skimmed off with a "caap," and was considered an especial " bon bouche."

Meantime the lasses milked the " kye." Stirabout being then dished into large " caaps," was placed on the table to cool ; one of the girls went either to back or front door, or either gable, in whichever direction the labourers were at work, and shouted, " H-o-o-y, H-o-o-y, come in." Presently the horses were heard entering the yard. Mr Rutherford then came in, washed his hands, and after a lengthy blessing was invoked, his wife and he partook of the stirabout and milk, or potatoes, finishing with bannock, butter, and cheese ; he then went out to send in the boys, and see if the cattle had been properly foddered.

After the servants had got their breakfast over, (of the same fare,) the big family Bible was brought out of " the room," and placed before "the master," who read a few verses of the Scottish version of a psalm, he then " raised the tune," (commenced singing,) joined by all the household, every two lines being repeated previous to being sung; a chapter was then read, followed by an extempore prayer. " Morning exercise" concluded, the men went to their out of doors employments; while the lasses "redd" (tidied) up the house, the mistress attended to the baby, arranged what was to be for dinner, and then sat down to her spinning-wheel :—

> " With hand ever stirring,
> And heart ever light,
> The spinning-wheel burring
> From morning to night."

" H-o-o-y, h-o-o-y," resounded at two o'clock, announcing dinner, which was served in much the same manner as breakfast had been; it consisted of potatoes, and broth made of salt beef, bacon, or " hung beef," thickened with barley or groats; occasionally it was varied by having leeks, cabbage, or marigolds, instead of barley or groats, to which was added a quantity of oaten meal.

When dinner was over, and the house again "redd up," the "stirabout" or "sowens," were prepared for supper. The latter was made of the outer covering or husks which came off oats, in making groats; they were put in water to " steep," (soak ;) the mealy particles that had adhered to the " seeds" sank to the bottom, the seeds were then lifted out by the hand into the " sowen sieve ;"* what strained through being of a thickish consistency, was allowed to remain some

---

* This was a square wooden frame, about eighteen inches long, and twelve wide, the bottom of which was made of perforated tin, forming a strainer.

days to ferment; when boiled, it formed a kind of
acid jelly; this was a favourite dish, and partaken of
either hot or cold, with the addition of sweet milk.
Beastins was the rarest treat of all; this was the
second milk taken from a cow after calving; it was
put into a pot over a fire, the heat caused it to thicken
like rennet milk, only being stronger in taste, and a
deep yellow, as if coloured with saffron. The girls
then sat down to their wheels. Spinning linen yarn
was a productive source of revenue to the farmer's
wife, and every servant had her appointed task to perform weekly; many girls prided themselves on the
number of " spangles " they could spin in a month.

The declining shadows indicated the time for coming in from the fields, without having to be summoned
by " H-o-o-y, h-o-o-y," as before.

Supper over, horses and cattle attended, cows
milked, and all tidied up, spinning was resumed,
some of the boys winding on the reel what the girls
had already on their pirns, (reels attached to the
wheel,) or chopped fir for firewood, repaired the cart
harness, mended sacks, &c. In winter all this was
done by light produced by pieces of bogwood, thrown
from time to time into the fire, causing a most cheerful light to gleam over all the kitchen.

Evening devotions over, which were conducted in
the same manner as in the morning, the boys went to
bed, the girls raked the fire; this was done by lifting
the peat embers aside with the tongs, then with a turf
making an opening in the ashes, the embers were
placed on them, covering them over with ashes so as

to preserve them for kindling the fire next morning.
Of course there were occasional jobs, such as the
May and November cleanings, when every article was
taken out of each room, brushed, dusted, washed,
rubbed, scrubbed, and subjected to every possible
form of purification. Then there were the washing
days, the bleaching, drying, and ironing days, and the
extra big washings, when blankets, quilts, curtains,
&c., were done.

While the out of door work and domestic duties
were progressing, love scenes occasionally occurred
between the servant lads and lasses. Jamie M'Gwiggan (who had been many years living with the
family) was so blindly in love with Nelly Donnelly,
that he forgot his shamefacedness, and was caught
on several occasions kissing her. When reproved
by the mistress, he declared he " thought Nelly
had bewitched him, as he couldn't get her out
of his head day nor night." " God forgive me, she
goes atween me an' my prayers." " Och mistress,
dear, don't be angry wi' me, maybe you were in the
same way yoursel' afore you were married, an' troth
I'm all through-other just now."

This so amused Mrs Rutherford, she said, " Well,
Jamie, do you really love Nelly ? "

" Och, love's not the word at all, mistress, dear ;
sure I love her very shadow on the wall, and I'm
nearly wrong in my head about her, or I wouldn't be
making the freedom I'm doin' wi' ye, mem, dear ; so
don't scowld me, and get the master not to be angry
wi' me."

"But," interrupted Mrs Rutherford, "how could you support a wife, Jamie?"

"Och bravely, if ye lets us be married, sure, we'll be your servants all the while, and if ye gives us the wee cabin down bye, and lave to set a rig or two o' praties, me an' Nelly can pay the rent out of our work, and we'll be as happy as the king on the throne, and far happier, and we'll pray for you and the master, not forgetting Master Alick; and shure we'd go on our bended knees to sarve ye-es, or rise at the hour of midnight to do yer biddin'."

Mrs Rutherford pleaded Jamie's suit so well with "the master," that he acceded to Jamie's wishes, and Nelly and he were married, and went to live in the cabin, their places being filled up by another "boy" and "lass."

CHAPTER VII.

SHORTLY after Maggie Rutherford's marriage, her father was informed by the minister (his brother-in-law) that Alexander "was fit for College."

Preparations were then commenced to get ready his outfit for going to Glasgow. They were on a sufficiently ample scale to supply a traveller in these days with more than would be necessary to take with him on a voyage to Australia, with a prospect of not getting a further supply for many years. A journey had to be taken to the neighbouring market town of Slievedhu for the express purpose of buying cloth, leather, and other necessaries for the occasion.

A tailor was brought to the house to make up several suits of clothes, also a shoemaker to manufacture as many shoes and leggings for use during the winter as might have sufficed for three or four years' wear in an active occupation.

When the making and bleaching of shirts and towels, the knitting of socks and comforters, and the baking of "bannocks" was completed, the crock of butter, the cheese, bacon, and hung beef were packed in a capacious wooden chest made expressly for the purpose.

All was then pronounced ready for departure. Alexander and his father rode off to Londonderry, the port of embarkation for Glasgow, followed by Jamie M'Gwiggan bringing the chests in a cart, who was also to bring back the horse Alexander had ridden.

Alexander had never been so far from home before, and Londonderry being associated in his mind with historical recollections, was regarded by him with the greatest possible interest.

Being obliged to remain some days awaiting the sailing of the vessel, he had frequent opportunities of walking about and gaining information concerning this ancient fortified city.

Here we may realise (said he to his father one day when standing on the wall looking towards the sea) the situation of the besieged in the autumn of 1688, when they assembled on this spot to witness the progress of the ships up the river, containing the supplies, not only of men, arms, and ammunition, but of food to relieve them from perishing by hunger. With what high-strung feelings, and with what breathless suspense must they have beheld the ships approach the boom placed across the river! and when the " Mountjoy " snapped the barrier, how must they have been relieved! and when Browning's vessel was fired on by the enemy and went aground, oh what a revulsion of feeling they must have experienced, and what anguish must have wrung their hearts! and what must have been the agony endured by Mrs Browning on witnessing her husband's perilous situation! We may imagine how that heroic and venerable man, Governor Walker, spoke soothing words to the mourner, reminding her that they had been sustained so long by the mighty hand of God, and for her faith not to droop now ; that His arm was still mighty to save, and that the prayer of faith would be answered, and a way of deliverance opened up for all who trusted implicitly in His power. Methinks while he speaks a cheer is raised ; " Thank God, we are saved ! the vessels are free !" is uttered by quivering, pallid lips, while many are suffused in tears, and others are so weak, they can only lift their feeble hands, and look up to heaven, murmuring thanks to God for their deliverance ; the soldier-clergyman was ——. But here the enthusiasm of the youth was checked by his father saying in a stern voice, " Enough about the man of Prelacy ; he was only the instrument raised up, and he never would have been able to sustain the place, had it not been for that godly minister John Mackenzie, who urged on the apprentice boys, and the lad Robert Morrison, who was the first to close the gates of the city against the traitor Lundy. Were they not of the true faith ? I tell thee, boy, had it not been for Mackenzie's assistance, notwithstanding that Walker is so lauded for it by the prelatical party, Derry would not have held out against James and his Popish adherents."

Alexander was obliged to keep silence, but nevertheless retained his own opinion.

Rutherford saw his son on board the vessel, and with many a solemn caution against getting among bad companions, begged him to remember the high position he was to occupy, reminding him he was descended from those men of God, the sainted Peden and Rutherford. And with a husky voice the fond father implored the Almighty to protect his son from danger during his perilous voyage on the deep; he then bade him farewell.

Rutherford was surprised and overpowered with the enthusiasm which his son had manifested while talking of the defence and deliverance of Derry, pondering deeply over it on his way home, foreboding evils which he feared Alexander's impulsive nature would lead him into, and praying fervently that he might be kept from being led away from the faith of his fathers.

On the fourth day after leaving Londonderry Alexander arrived in Glasgow, and here for the first time his self-importance was prostrated; at home he was known to almost every one he met, had all his wants supplied, and he considered himself a personage of some importance. But now, among the many faces with which he was surrounded, he knew none; every one seemed intent on his own affairs, and he felt solitary and depressed; but he must rely on self; and engaging a "hurley" (cart) to convey his luggage, he started off to deliver his letter of introduction from the minister, his uncle, to Mrs M'Farlan, who "lodged students."

After a hearty breakfast, his spirits returned; he wrote to his mother announcing his safe arrival, then walked out to look about the city, and we shall allow him to go along the "Trongate," through the "Salt-

market," the "Candleriggs," the "Cowcaddens," &c.,
without detailing his peregrinations and reflections ;
but when he saw the Cathedral, he could not refrain
from exclaiming, " Truly it proved an independent,
liberal spirit influenced the trades-folk who interfered
to prevent such a noble pile being pulled down by a
set of bigoted fanatics ; what sacrilege would it have
been to have destroyed such an edifice !"

When Alexander underwent an examination preparatory to commencing his College course, his self-
esteem was mortified by finding that, although
pronounced by his uncle to be "very forward in all
his studies," he was in many respects deficient ; but
he determined to apply himself closely, and attend
regularly the lectures and classes, so that at the close
of the session the professors declared he "had made
the most of his time, and had progressed rapidly in
his studies." During his stay in Scotland, Alexander
had associated with persons of various religious denominations, and had gone to different places of
worship. He began to think that there were more
people right than merely those of his own sect ; and
thought that although there were differences of
opinion on minor points, if they agreed on the funda-
mental doctrines of religion, it showed bigotry and
narrow-mindedness to quarrel about trifling doctrinal
points, or church government, or outward forms and
ceremonies. He also considered that it was a proof
of the want of a spirit of Christian charity to dwell so
much on the persecutions which in years gone by had
been inflicted by the party who were in power against

E

the other; and felt that, instead of cherishing such remembrances, it would be well to encourage a spirit of love and unity amongst the members of all Christian churches, and to bear in mind that there had been faults on both sides, and blame attached to all parties. He also saw that, had a little more toleration and forbearance been practised, such angry and vindictive passions would not have been called forth, nor so many lives sacrificed.

With these enlarged views, he left Scotland to return home.

CHAPTER VIII.

AT this period, going up or down the Clyde was quite a journey of magnitude, owing to the circuitous route of the river. Its navigation occupied, according to the state of wind and tide, never less than a day; frequently two or three days were required to accomplish it. Being considered highly dangerous to sail "after. dark," vessels were brought to anchor during the night.

The picturesque scenery of this noble river, with its fertile and wooded banks, its rocks, towers, ruins, and mountains, fraught with so many recollections to the historian, can now be seen daily at a very trifling expense, and in a few hours, by going on board one of the numerous steamboats which leave the Broomielaw every hour. True, the Greenock lad, Watt, had at this time, by experimenting with his grandmother's tea-kettle, found out the power of steam, which afterwards was developed in the invention of the steam-engine, but it had not been applied to navigation, as Bell, whose first vessel propelled by steam in this country, had not yet commenced to run "The Comet" on the Clyde between Glasgow and Greenock. It was not till the summer of 1812 his first trips were made, the journey occupying a day to Greenock, and the same period for return.

When Alexander came to Glasgow it was in the beginning of winter. The weather was inclement, and the scenery on the river bleak and unattractive. He was also suffering from the effects of sea and home sickness, so that even if the landscape had "spread o'er each scene its brightest of crystal and fairest of green," it would have had no charms for him.

But now the summer had set in. The weather was fine, the landscape verdant, and his own health and spirits good; so that the voyage was contemplated by him with pleasure.

The localities he passed brought before his fervid imagination, and called forth from his well-stored memory, scenes of bygone days.

The first place pointed out to him was suggestive of many ideas. This was the site of the ancient Bonavern, where it is said St Patrick was born, in the latter end of the fourth century. It is now an insignificant village called Kilpatrick. Here, thought Alexander, young Succat received from his pious mother, Conchessa, the first lessons of love to God and his fellow-creatures, which in after years caused him to devote himself to the service of his Creator. How wonderful to think, when he had been sent to be educated at Tours by his uncle Martin, who was archbishop there, that he should be seized by pirates, carried off, and sold as a slave to one of the Irish chieftains, who employed him to herd swine in the

fields at the foot of Sleimish Mountain ; but his energetic mind, upheld by his heavenly Father, did not
sink under this degrading occupation, but, like all
truly great minds, rose above adverse circumstances,
so that young Patrick in his loneliness had time for
reflection and prayer, his constant supplication being
a reiteration of what had been his mother's early
lessons, that God would increase love in his heart
more towards Him. Being rescued and again made
captive, at last the lad was restored to his parents ;
but even the love and endearments of his mother
could not prevent him from wishing to return to the
country where he had, though a captive, felt so happy
in communion with his God. Even in his dreams his
mind was occupied with this idea, and he fancied he
heard voices issuing from the dark woods of Dalriada
inviting him to come back again to Erin. Being now
near manhood, Patrick determined to go and proclaim
to the Irish the glad tidings of the gospel in their own
language, which he had acquired during his captivity.
And now the holy youth has accomplished his heart's
desire. He collects the people together in the fields
by beat of drum, to tell them in simple language the
story of grace and the doctrines of the Christian religion, preaching and teaching. He caused many to
become converts. St Patrick explained the doctrine
of the Trinity in Unity by showing to his pagan
auditors the trefoil called shamrock, which is known
as the emblem of my native Erin.

Here we come to Dumbarton Rock and Castle.
Poor unfortunate Mary Queen of Scots! what a host of

recollections this place calls up ! Here she was sent off
by her mother secretly to France ; here again she returned, a lovely young widow, and was enthusiastically
received by the stern barons, who in after years
turned against her, insulted her, and made her miserable, and at last imprisoned her in Lochleven Castle ;
but being chivalrously assisted to escape by young
George Douglas, she unfortunately fled to England
for protection from the power of her turbulent barons,
where she was detained as prisoner for eighteen
years, and finally beheaded, with the sanction of the
Virgin Queen, whose cognomen of Good Queen Bess
I never can subscribe to.   Certainly the times were
troublous, and the people in a barbarous state ; but
preserve us from again having a repetition of those
acts which entitled this queen to be called good !
But while my imagination is accompanying Mary
Queen of Scots through her trials, and villifying the
virgin monarch, we come in sight of Bruce's Castle. I
wonder, was it after or before his *sixth* defeat that
this monarch lived here, and did he ever permit a
housemaid to destroy a spider's web in this castle,
after the lesson of perseverance given to him in the
cottage where he was hid from his enemies, by the
spider uniting its broken thread the seventh time,
after having made six futile attempts, exactly the
number of battles Robert Bruce had been defeated
in ?   But here we are at the mouth of the river;
islands in sight, the Argyle mountains in the distance,
lowering clouds overhanging them ; "a stormy night
may be expected," the captain says.   The water is

also getting very rough ; even now the demon sea-
sickness has seized on me. I must retire, and thus end
all my romancing. True to the prognostications, the
passage to Londonderry was boisterous ; but as the
wind was most favourable, the vessel arrived at her
destination in an unusually short time, having only
been thirty-four and a half hours coming from Glasgow. Shortly after reaching Derry, Alexander heard
the bells of the cathedral ring for evening service, and
determined to go there. Had his father come for him,
he would as soon have permitted his son to go into a
theatre, gambling-house, or ball-room, as to have gone
into the "apostate building ;" but Alexander went,
and was greatly struck with the manner of the worship ;* he thought that the mode of the congregation
responding to and joining in the prayers which they
knew, was better than one man praying for the whole,
in language in which the congregation did not join
by responses, or follow him with their thoughts all the
time he was speaking. This being the first time he
had heard an organ, it astonished and overpowered
him ; nothing could exceed the rapture with which
he listened to its strains. "Surely," thought he, "if
music is mentioned in the Scriptures as being one of
the enjoyments of heaven, it cannot be wrong to use
it in the house of God in His service on earth, and
when our Maker has put it into the mind of man to
invent, and enabled his hands to construct, an instru-

---

* The service was then plain, not choral or intoned, and continued
to be so till 1860, this being the last cathedral in the three kingdoms
which adopted the regular cathedral service.

ment which produces such sweet sounds, and calls
forth such rapturous devotional and elevating feelings,
it must be right to employ it to assist us to offer praise
to our Maker, Redeemer, and Sanctifier, the great
Jehovah.

Jamie M'Gwiggan was sent with a horse and cart
to take Alexander's luggage home, and a saddle-
horse for him to ride on.

" Well, Jamie, how are you ?" said Alexander.

" All the better for seeing yer honour agen, Master
Alick ; but, och, but yer whitely by what ye were
when ye went away."

Alexander smiled and said, " I 'll get rosy enough
to please you when I am home a little. But how are
my father and mother, and all at Thornbrae ?"

" Bravely, bravely ! They 'll all be so glad to see
you, Master Alick ; and the mistress has been getting
the world and all done for yer home-coming; an'
she 's got the 'room' and strangers' chamber whitewashed yellow, an' a carpet to cover the whole places;
and dimity curtains, as white as the driven snow;
an' it's all so gran' now."

" Well, Jamie, tell me about Nelly and the young-
ster—how are they ?"

" Och, Master Alick, shure they 're hearty and well,
and Nelly 's only too rich now, wi' both a pig an' a
wean."

" Indeed," said Alexander, (smiling at the account
of Nelly's riches,) " how has she got to be so rich as to
get a pig ?"

" Well, Master Alick, I 'll just tell ye. Ye see Nelly

had always a spurit, an' she said she had always been
fore-hook on the har'st rig, an' she just said : Jamie,
says she, I'll not be bate this time neither; so she kept
her word, and when the 'churn' was won, the mistress
gives Nelly a whang aff a cheese ; and Nelly, says she,
take that home, you'll require to have something to
give the women when they're wi' ye about the New
Year ; an', says she, the master bid me tell ye that
Jamie's to take you home a little pig, an' we hope
it'll thrive wi' ye. God bless both the master an'
mistress ; shure enough I got the purtiest slip of a pig
ever I clapped my two eyes on, and isn't it a darlin'!
But ye'll see both it an' wee Betty when we get to
Thornbraĕ."

"Fore-hook," and "winning the churn," must now be
explained. "Fore-hook" was the person who reaped
on the first ridge, and led the rest of the band ; it
was considered a post of honour, as the position was
given to whoever was thought to be the best and
quickest reaper. There was also a rivalry to be "fore-
hook," as whoever retained it for several years was
entitled to a present. "Winning the churn" was
cutting the last handful of grain left standing after all
the rest had been reaped. It was plaited, to make it
stand upright on the ridge, and called "the hare."
The reapers then threw their reaping-hooks at it,
and the person whose hook cut it through was said
to have "won the churn."

The girls, in turn, hung it over the house door, and
the first male who entered was to be their future husband, or else one bearing the same Christian name.

CHAPTER IX.

ALEXANDER was gladly welcomed home by his
father and mother. His uncle, aunt, and all
his friends vied with each other in showing him they
were glad to see him back again; indeed all the
people in and about Thornbrae regarded him with
respect and reverence; their intercourse with him,
however, was often constrained, being intermingled
with feelings of awe, in entering into conversation
with "the minister that was to be, who had just returned from getting so much ' larnin'' at the college."
All this flattered his self-esteem, and made him again
feel he was an important personage, which was increased by seeing the many alterations and improvements which had been made for his reception in and
about the house.

His mother agreed with Jamie in thinking he did
not look as strong as before he went away, but her
anxiety was relieved when her brother said it was
to be expected after studying so closely during the
winter; but a few weeks' relaxation, the country air,
and nourishing substantial food would soon restore
him to his former robust health.

The first Sunday services he attended at the meet-

ing after his return seemed very tiresome, and he
could not help being wearied with the long-winded,
roundabout prayer, the prosy sermon, with its seven
heads, and, hydra-like, each head dividing itself into
innumerable branches, divisions, digressions, and rami-
fications, followed by an application, then a summary
of what had previously been enlarged on, lastly, reflections, and finally the conclusion practically considered; this discourse having been preceded by the
first forty verses of the 119th psalm, read, expounded,
and commented on, and as this lasted longer than
an hour, Alexander thought it was more than sufficient for any memory to retain, and ample subject for
reflections without the addition of the sermon. During the singing of the psalms the version seemed so
unpoetical, and the strains so harsh, they put to flight
all his devotional feelings, causing him by the contrast to recall vividly the service in Derry cathedral,
and the glorious, never-to-be-forgotten organ accom-
paniment to Tate and Brady's version of the Psalms.

On returning home from the meeting they retired
to " the room," and, previous to partaking of a frugal
meal, consisting of eggs, cheese, bannocks, and milk,
a long discursive grace was said by Mr Rutherford.

During the repast there was very little conversation,
but near its conclusion Alexander said to his father,
" I wish my uncle would give over using Sternhold
and Hopkin's version of the Psalms, they are so unpoetical, and the tunes to them so discordant; no
wonder they were called in derision ' Geneva jigs.'
Rowse's version is bad enough, but they are not so

rough as what you use here; they are now almost universally used in Scotland, and the tunes adapted to them are scarcely so doleful and uncouth." Rutherford was dumbfounered, and looked horror-stricken at his son; at last he energetically exclaimed, " Alter the Psalms of David, and put new tunes to them—not content with the tunes the sweet singer of Israel played on his harp, and sung to the psalms of his own composition! O Scotland! land of saints and martyrs, art thou indeed become such a backsliding generation? Where will thy profanity end? After a time, no doubt, they'll be for introducing 'the kist fu' o' whistles, the squealing abominations,' which were destroyed by the men of God, who with a strong arm silenced this vile remnant of Popery."*

Alexander was about to launch forth in a panegyric on the organ, and a defence of its use, but Mrs Rutherford looked pleadingly at her son, and motioned him to keep silence.

It was now the time for the girls and boys to come to be catechised. She summoned them to "the room," and this put an end to the subject for the present.

During the week the minister and Alexander had a long discussion on the same topic, neither being convinced or swayed by the other's reasoning, the minister maintaining that innovations were dangerous,

* Rutherford's speech seems to have been prophetic, as an organ has lately been introduced into several churches in Scotland; and it is now a matter of debate among the Scotch whether the use of them will be permitted generally in their Presbyterian churches. Hymns are also now used in some of the Scotch churches.

and that "the use of the old Scottish version of the Psalms had been purchased so dearly by their fore-fathers, it would be wrong to use any other."

Alexander insisted "that as progression was the order of nature, we should keep pace with the times; and as arts and sciences advanced, bring them forward to raise the mind, and elevate all its powers for the worship of the Creator."

"Alexander," said the minister, "you have partaken of the tree of knowledge of good and evil, may you be preserved from the effects of partaking of the forbidden fruit, and may grace be given you to discern between good and evil before it is too late; but I fear you are temporising in your present course."

On the following Sunday Alexander walked across the fields to meeting; his father followed by the road, mounted on horseback, his mother seated behind on a pillion. At this period there were stables adjoining the country meeting-houses for the accommodation of the horses of the worshippers during the service, and in the enclosed green space which surrounded the meeting-houses there were one or two sets of stone steps for the facility of riders dismounting. (In Scotland this was called the "louping-on stane;" in Ireland, the "getting-on stone."

The day being sultry, the meeting-house close, the sermon long and prosy, and the minister's voice monotonous, Alexander became drowsy. In vain he tried to keep up his attention, opened and shut his Bible, turned over the leaves, shifted his position, fixed his eyes on his uncle the preacher; at last drowsiness so overcame him that he fell into a doze, his Bible dropped out of his hand, which caused him to wake up with a start, and he saw his father gazing on him, with displeasure strongly depicted in his stern countenance.

After service Alexander hastened home, in time to assist his mother to dismount off the pillion; while doing so, she pressed his hand, and motioned him to follow her into the house.   When out of her husband's hearing, she said, "O Alick, what have you done this day! what can you say for yourself?"

" Mother, indeed, indeed, I tried all I could to keep awake, and keep up my attention, but the service is so long, it is utterly impossible for any one's thoughts to be concentrated for such a lengthened time on one subject; besides, my uncle's voice is so monotonous, and having often before heard all he brought forward, and the house was so overpoweringly warm, I felt the truth of Matthew Henry's saying, ' When weariness commences, devotion ends;' and as for what I said about the Psalms it was truth.   Look," said he, pointing to the sky, " you see that lark singing as it rises in the air, you hear how its notes mingle with the song of your favourite thrush which is singing on the tree at the foot of the garden, are they not both praising the God who gave them being? and do not their notes blend together in unison?   If I, like the lark, wish to soar aloft, and my father, like the thrush, chooses to sit and sing on the tree, provided only our hearts accompany our melody, and our praises ascend to God, surely it will make no difference to our heavenly Father, who has endowed us with various feelings and capacities for praising Him."

"O Alick, Alick, my son, your reasoning might convince me, but your father is so rooted and grounded in his own faith and opinions that he could not be influenced by any of your arguments, so pray try and avoid provoking him to anger."

Rutherford now entered and proceeded to " the room," followed by his wife and son ; the frugal repast was partaken of in silence. At the conclusion of the meal, Rutherford said, in a stern voice, "Alexander, are you not ashamed of your conduct in the house of God this day ? "

" Well, father, I really tried to keep up my attention," and was about to excuse himself as he had before done to his mother ; but a deprecating look from her changed his intention, and wishing to ingratiate himself with his father, said, "I am truly sorry I was so overcome, but hope next Sunday I'll behave better."

" Who dares in my house to name the Sabbath in the profane manner of heathens and idolaters ; this is another newfangled device of the present generation to call the Lord's day after the creature, instead of the name the Creator himself bestowed on it."

" But, father," interrupted Alexander, "we live in different times from those in which the law was given, even the very day has been changed from the seventh to the first day of the week. Our language was unknown when the commandments were instituted, and surely it cannot signify our calling it Sunday any more than our calling the other days that God made, Monday, and so forth."

Rutherford, who was by this time fairly exasperated, exclaimed loudly, " I say, boy, in my presence never again dare to desecrate the name of the Sabbath, by calling it in your idolatrous fashion by that profane name."

Poor Mrs Rutherford looked imploringly at her son, who rose and left the room.

The catechising commenced, and Alexander's absence seemed unnoticed by his father.

Scarcely a day passed that there was not some difference of opinion between father and son ; the latter had imbibed more of a liberal spirit by intercourse with his fellow-students of various creeds, and endeavoured to prove to his father that narrow-minded sectarian views did not glorify God, and were not calculated to advance the cause of religion ; but instead of being convinced, Rutherford daily grew more dogmatical, and got more confirmed in his belief that all sects and denominations, except the one of which he was a member, were erroneous in their doctrines, church government, and practices.

Alexander was equally firm in maintaining his antagonistic opinions, so that discussions only tended to make each more determined and dogged in adhering to his own peculiar views.

Mrs Rutherford was to be pitied ; she had a hard task to mediate between her husband and son. Alexander was devotedly attached to his mother, and to avoid giving her pain, endeavoured to restrain his tongue from giving utterance to the sentiments which called forth his father's anger. To her husband she still held out the hope that their son would come round after a time to acknowledge the rectitude of his father, and to coincide with his wishes; and as she had implicit faith in her brother's power of refuting Alexander's arguments, she begged her husband to desist from controversy with him till the minister had fully ascertained his sentiments, argued with him, and proved to him the unreasonableness of some of the ideas he entertained.

Week after week passed over, and the father and son rarely met, except at meals, and at the morning and evening devotions; they seldom spoke to each other; it seemed as if each feared to provoke a discussion.

Mr Peden tried in vain to check Alexander's "new-fangled notions," as he called them, and came to his sister's conclusion, that it would be "better to leave him to himself for a little, as arguing and opposition might have a contrary effect to that which they all so much desired."

Alexander's time began to hang heavily on his hands, and hearing that Lord Southend required a tutor for his son, he applied, and got the situation.

The Hall was only two miles off, and Alexander walked there each morning, returning late in the evening to Thornbrae, so that he scarcely ever saw his father, except on Sundays, and these had become to him so wearisome that he determined one day to attend the parish church. Accordingly, after breakfast he left home, as his mother thought, to walk

F

across the fields to meeting, but on her arrival she found he was not there.

During the services she could not refrain from feeling great anxiety about him; but on her return home, was rejoiced to be lifted off her pillion as usual by her son.

Her joy, however, was damped when she heard where he had been; she knew her husband would never forgive him for this.

As on previous occasions, the meal was partaken of in silence; but from Rutherford's lowering brows and stern expression, both mother and son saw that the thunder-cloud was about to burst, and felt that matters were coming to a crisis; so they were not surprised when they heard Rutherford say, in a trembling, choking voice, "Alexander, have you forgotten what is said in the Scriptures concerning those who forsake the assembling of themselves together on the Sabbath-day, and the judgments which are denounced against those who keep their foot from going to the house of God?"

"Oh no, father, I have not forgotten all the Scripture proofs which you taught me out of the Longer and Shorter Catechisms on these subjects."

Darting a keen glance at his son, he replied, "Therefore greater will be thy condemnation when thou knewest the law and kept it not."

"But, father, I was at the house of God to-day."

"Where did you sit then? I saw you not."

Alexander could scarcely refrain from smiling, and replied, "I was at the parish church."

"At where ?" gasped his father. "Call you the prelatical building the house of God ?"

"Indeed, father, I heard a most excellent sermon on the text, 'God is love ;' it was delivered in less than half an hour ; I could almost repeat it verbatim, showing forth how great was the love God had manifested to sinners by sending His Son to save us ; the love we should in return feel towards Him for our 'creation, preservation, and redemption, for the means of grace and for the hope of glory ;' and proving that if our hearts were filled with love towards God, it would flow forth towards our fellow-creatures in patience, forbearance, and acts of love and mercy."

Alexander was stopped in his enthusiastic speech by the sight of his mother's pale, agitated countenance. His father seemed overpowered with astonishment, placed his elbows on the table, and covered his eyes with his hands, shook with agitation, moved his head backwards and forwards, and at length groaned heavily, "Ichabod, Ichabod, the glory is departed, my idol has been laid low," then relapsed into silence.

Alexander rose and left the apartment, almost regretting that he had been led on to say so much, and felt sorry to have grieved his mother; but "what is past who can recall, or done undo ?" He could not unsay his words now, and, besides, he felt he had not done anything wrong.

When the servants came into "the room" Rutherford roused himself up, but went through the catechising and devotions as if in a dream; his voice faltered so in the singing and prayer that Mrs Rutherford feared he would break down entirely; but the exercises were got over as usual, and the servants retired to rest.

Previous to going to bed Rutherford vowed solemnly on his knees, that if Alexander again entered the Church of England, (the doctrines and church government of which was so obnoxious to him and his sect, and the disowning and disagreeing with which had been the cause of so many of his ancestors losing their lives,) that he would disown him as a son, and hold no further intercourse with him.

When Alexander was informed by his mother next morning of his father's resolve, he said, in the most decisive manner, " Then I'll leave this at once. I have a right to liberty of conscience as well as my father, and I am determined never to be a Covenanter preacher." Remonstrances were useless; Alexander left his mother bathed in tears, and without bidding farewell to his father, left Thornbrae, never again to enter it during his father's life.

When told of his departure, Rutherford muttered, " My son is dead, mention him not again to me," and maintained ever afterwards a morose silence regarding him.

CHAPTER X.

ALEXANDER attended as usual his pupil at the
Hall during the day, and in the evening walked
into the town of Slievedhu, which was a short distance
off, where he procured lodgings, and took possession
of them at once.

On the morning of the following market day, he
was visited early by Jamie M'Gwiggan, who, having
many commissions to execute in Slievedhu, Mrs
Rutherford had given him Alexander's chests, containing his books and clothes, and, carefully stowed
away in the foot of one of his stockings, the savings
of many years, thirty-five spade guineas. When
Jamie delivered the chests, and handed the keys to
Alexander, he looked round the room furtively; then
in a husky voice stammered forth, "Och, Master
Alick, sure you'll soon come back to Thornbrae,
the poor mistress is so donsy like,* an' as if her
heart was broke with your lavin'; an' the master
niver spakes unless you spake to him, an' jist goes
about wi' his head down an' his han's ahint his back,
doited like. Och, hoch! the light's gone out o' the

* Weak, or delicate-looking.

place intirely; an' Miss Maggie away, too. Won't you come back, avick? Och, Master Alick, yer grown a cliver* young gentleman now, but didn't I give ye mony a ride afore me, goin' out to the fields, on Sally, the ould mare, when ye weren't the height of a turf, and Nelly, the crathur, cried, an', says she, mony's the drap o' crame an' strippin's † she gave ye unknownst; an' she niver forgot, when ye were wee, to bake ye a bannock wi' a hole in it to string roun' yer neck; an' she slipped bits o' butter into the pedlar's crame for ye. An' to think o' ye lavin' us all now;" and poor Jamie fairly broke down, and burst into tears.

Although suffering great mental agony from the step he had taken, and the account given him of the affliction of his father and mother, Alexander could not help feeling amused at Jamie's reminiscences, and replied cheerfully, "All will turn out well yet, Jamie. I'm going to Dublin with Lord Southend's family, and when I come back I'll bring Nelly half a pound of tea."

"Och, Master Alick, won't she be the proud woman! an' she'll jist say, Didn't I tell ye, Jamie, that 'God niver sends mouths but he sends mate;' an' won't she be as gran' as ony lady to hae tay when she lies-in; an' if it's a boy, plase God, won't she be proud to git lave to call it for ye."

---

* In the common parlance of the north of Ireland, "cliver," (clever,) when applied to the appearance of a person, means tall and portly.

† The last milk taken from the cow, and richer than the first milked.

"But, Jamie, didn't my mother give you a letter or message for me?"

"Och, I disremimbired it althegither; the trouble fairly put it out o' my head. Well, ye see, the misthriss, God bliss her, jist came to the stable, an', Jamie, ses she, ye'll take Mister Alick his chists when ye go to Slievedhu, says she, an' ye'll give him this key, ses she, an' he'll likely give ye a letter, ses she; an' when ye comes back, ye can jist give it to myself, ses she. Now, a nod's jist as good as a wink to a blin' horse, an' I jist tuk it up that the master wasn't to see it. Och, that ye niver had gone to the college! It's all owin' to the larnin'. If ye'd stayed at yer hot, full* home, an' contentid yerself, an' not minded the master's dour way for all his time o't, ye might hae been as happy as the day's long."

"Well, Jamie, I'll have a letter ready for my mother. You can call here when you are leaving town. Meantime, here is a thirteen † to drink my health."

"Och, an' won't I do that wi' all my heart. Master Alick, may ye live long an' die happy."

Jamie went off, and, long after he was out of sight, was heard invoking blessings on "the young master's head."

Alexander had not time to indulge in grief, as his duties required his immediate appearance at the Hall. He wrote the following few lines to his mother:—

---

* Hot and full means comfortable and plentiful.

† A silver coin, value thirteen-pence.

"Mother, dearest, words cannot express how it grieves me to be the cause of so much sorrow to you and my father, but I really cannot bring my mind to entertain such narrow, sectarian, illiberal views as he does on religion and church government.

"I shall not return to Glasgow College again, but as the family at the Hall are going to Dublin next week, and Lady Southend has requested me to accompany them as tutor, I shall go on with my studies there, and enter myself as student at Trinity College. Thanks for your generous gift. I can now pay the college fees. I will write to you from time to time, and trust you 'll ever find me your loving son,

"ALEXANDER."

Next evening Alexander had a visit from his uncle, who had been sent by his mother, to try to dissuade him from fulfilling his promise of studying with the view of becoming a clergyman of the Established Church. When the first greetings were over, Mr Peden introduced the topic at once which had caused him to come to his nephew, by saying, "Alexander, I have just come to have some serious conversation with you. Is it possible that you, a descendant of men whose blood was shed in handing down a pure faith to you; is it possible that you, who bear the name of two of the saints who gave themselves up to persecution because they would not subscribe to the prelatical Church; I say, can it be possible that you are about to turn against the religion of your fathers, and join the party who oppressed and destroyed them, and, had they not been upheld by the mighty hand of God, would have exterminated them ? "

" Uncle, it seems to me that, among the sect of which you and my father are worthy members, toleration of any other than your own belief is the greatest of all sins ; and you are not willing to accede to others the liberty of conscience to worship God as they consider right, though you claim that liberty for yourselves ; and as for the persecutions the Covenanters endured from the Episcopalians, you and I have often discussed this, and you must acknowledge that when the Covenanters and Puritans had the ascendancy, they persecuted the Episcopalians, and put them to death. But all this is past and gone ; why should it be recalled now, unless as a warning to deter us from disunion, and a motive to induce Christians to practise more charity and toleration towards all denominations ? This illiberality and bigotry have confirmed me more and more in my determination to join the Church of England ; besides, I am like poor Charles II., who was compelled on a fast-day to listen to six sermons preached without intermission. The strictness and doleful manner in which the Sabbath observances were kept in my father's had almost, like the poor monarch, given me an aversion to religion altogether; so that it is well I did not, like him, neglect religious services and observances, and become utterly profane."

" Well," said Mr Peden testily, " surely, nephew, you would not wish to have sports and games introduced, such as were sanctioned and approved of by that godless man to be played on the Sabbath ? But, as you have made up your mind to act after the rules of that apostate Church, you may as well approve of "The Book of Sports" as any of their other words and mummeries. Oh! to think of a descendant of Alexander Peden wearing that 'rag of Popery,' a surplice, keeping saints' days, and reading prayers for the man Charles, who was drunken with the blood of the saints."

"And no wonder, uncle, that the Church of England venerates the memory of King Charles I., and looks upon his execution as having been martyrdom in the cause of upholding their faith, and time-serving by making promises which he did not intend to fulfil. He always declared the Episcopalian to be the Apostolic Church. The Duke of Hamilton and some other of his Scotch friends conjured him on their knees, and with tears implored him to accept the proposals of Parliament to allow Presbyterianism and the 'Westminster Confession of Faith' to supersede Episcopacy and the 'Book of Common Prayer,' and thereby save his life ; the queen also wrote pressingly on the subject ; but all he would grant to their most urgent entreaties was, that Episcopacy and Presbyterianism should be established side by side ; but this the Parliament would not allow. He was beheaded ; and they would not even permit the funeral service of the Church he loved so dearly, and sacrificed his life for, to be read over his headless body previous to its being consigned to the tomb."

"Enough, enough! I'll not listen to such profanation any longer. I fear, Alexander, you are 'in the gall of bitterness and in the bonds of iniquity.' May the God of your fathers forgive you, and pluck you as a brand from the burning. Farewell !"

When Mr Peden returned to Thornbrae, and told his sister the result of his interview with Alexander, she saw it was useless to hope to change him in his determination. Of course Mr Rutherford was also told ; but it seemed as if the former shock had so overpowered him, that he was incapable of feeling now. He never recovered parting from his son, and from the disappointment of the expectations he had indulged in from his birth ; his hopes had all been frustrated, and he felt the blow keenly, the more so as he brooded over it in sullen silence ; he seemed to lose interest in anything, and moped about the farm.

Mrs Rutherford had to look after everything, but this kept her from sinking under the trial also.

For three years all was managed as usual at Thornbrae ; the only variety being an occasional letter from Alexander to his mother, one of which, showing the state of his mind, and the course he was pursuing, is given in the following chapter.

CHAPTER XI.

"MERRION SQUARE, DUBLIN, *Feb.* 7, 17—.

MY DEAR MOTHER,—I have now got my degree of A.B. at college, and hope soon to get a curacy, be ordained and admitted into the ministry of the 'Episcopal' Church. In the meantime, I have remunerative occupation as tutor here.

"What you say about abuses and errors is, I acknowledge, quite true ; but, mother dearest, can any church on earth be perfect ? Was there not even among the twelve disciples of our Lord a Judas ? But a reformation and improvement will soon be effected. At present a most singular and energetic man is going about preaching, who is likely to rouse the Church of England from its deadness and formality. I have heard Wesley preach ; he is a member of the Established Church, and does not aim at schism or separation from it. He is short in stature, and thin ; enthusiastic without being fanatical; has great fluency of speech, and makes use of simple but persuasive language. He has gained a great number of followers, and as he is very methodical in his rules and habits, his adherents have been called Methodists.

"You may judge of the sensation he has made, and

the popularity he has acquired, when he can collect thousands to hear him preach every morning at five o'clock. Should the weather prove favourable, he is obliged to preach in the open air, as a building cannot be found sufficiently large to accommodate the numbers who flock to hear him.

"Mr Wesley is liberal in his sentiments towards all denominations of Christians, as will be seen from the following dream which he narrated.

"'Methought,' said Wesley, 'I had died, and found myself in another world beside two open gates. One was wide, and looked gloomy within; the other was narrow, and inside shone a bright light, surpassing the brilliancy of the sun in its meridian splendour.

"'I had no difficulty in deciding that the broad gate was the entrance to hell. Both entrances were guarded by angels. Well, thought I, though I don't wish to enter the broad gate, I'll ask the gatekeeper some questions; so approaching the stern, gloomy angel, I said, Have you many people inside? Yes, a great many, was the reply. Have you any Episcopalians here? Yes. Have you any Roman Catholics? Yes. Any Quakers? Yes. Any Presbyterians? Yes. Any Methodists? Yes. Well, I suppose you have some of all sects inside? Yes, said the angel, laughing sarcastically; there are a great number here who were professors of religion on earth.

"'I turned sorrowfully away, and approaching the narrow gate addressed the guardian angel, asking if there were many persons in heaven? Sweetly smiling, he replied, Oh yes; from every nation, tongue, and people on the earth. I suppose you have a number of Methodists? Not any, replied the angel. You have Episcopalians, then? No. Quakers? No. Presbyterians? No. Covenanters? No. Jews? No. Mohammedans? No. Well, said I, getting quite alarmed, who have you, then? The angel looked pitifully at me ; then smiling benignantly, said, We have neither sect nor denomination in heaven. They were followers of the Lamb, and have washed away all their sins in His blood. Then opening the gate I heard sung by thousands of voices, Worthy is the Lamb that was slain. Blessing, and honour, and glory, and power, be unto Him that sitteth on the throne, and unto the Lamb, for ever ; for He hath loved us, and washed us from our sins in His own blood, and hath made us kings and priests unto God and His Father ; to Him be glory and dominion for ever and ever. Amen.

" ' I then awoke, and am more fully persuaded than I had hitherto been, that being a member of any particular church will not get us to heaven. The main question is, Am I in Christ, or out of Christ?' Never shall I forget the expression of Wesley's face, beaming with devotion, love, and Christian charity, while he pronounced the benediction. ' The peace of God,' which he had so earnestly implored, seemed indeed to have rested on the attentive audience, as the dense crowd separated, evidently deeply impressed.

" Dearest mother, I have written you a long letter, and although it may not give you satisfaction, that I have acted and feel so differently from what my father and you wished, I have done only as my conscience dictated. But however much I may have changed in other respects, believe me I have not intentionally given you and my father pain ; and I still remain ever your affectionate son,

"ALEXANDER P. RUTHERFORD."

During the time Alexander was pursuing his studies in Dublin, his father was gradually getting weaker and wasting away ; latterly he was only able to come from his bed-room to the kitchen. As Jamie had said, "He seldom spoke unless spoken to," and then replied in a moody abstracted manner.

For hours he would sit in his chair, leaning on the top of his staff, muttering to himself. Occasionally he was heard to mention his daughter Maggie's name, then shake his head, and say, "It must be made all right to her yet."

At length he was so weak he could not leave his bed, and the doctor told Mrs Rutherford if her husband had any arrangements to make about his affairs, it would be well to do so soon. The minister was then sent for. On his arrival he came to his brother-in-law's bedside, and, grasping the dying man's hand, said, "Brother, the decree has gone forth, Set thy house in order, for thou must die. Are you afraid of the dark valley and the shadow of death ?"

To which he answered with a firm but feeble voice, "The Lord's will be done. Yea, though I walk through the valley and shadow of death, I will fear no evil : for Thou art with me ; Thy rod and Thy staff they comfort me. I have fought a good fight, I have finished my course, I have kept the faith. O death, where is thy sting? O grave, where is thy victory? Death is swallowed up in victory."

"My brother, is there anything you would wish to settle of your worldly affairs?"

"Oh yes," replied the dying man, eagerly; "send for Lawyer M'Cormick immediately." So saying, he sank back in his bed seemingly relieved, after having come to this determination. Jamie was despatched to Slievedhu to bring the lawyer. During his absence the sick man lay quiet, occasionally murmuring in an almost inaudible voice, "Maggie will now be righted—Maggie will now be righted," frequently glancing towards the door. The lawyer was not at home when the messenger arrived, but hastened to Thornbrae a few hours after he had been sent for. By that time Mr Rutherford had become unconscious, and could not be roused to understand anything; he fell into a heavy slumber, from which he never awoke.

> "When from flesh the spirit free
> Hastens homeward to return,
> Mortals cry, A man is dead;
> Angels sing, A child is born."

Thus passed away James Rutherford, the sincere but rather stern, unbending Christian. He was a worthy descendant of the Scottish Covenanters, who sealed their testimony with their blood, and whose sufferings, heroism, and magnanimity cannot be surpassed in the annals of ancient or modern history. The liberties and precious privileges which they secured to all coming generations cannot be too highly appreciated, and must ever be remembered with feelings of heartfelt gratitude by their posterity. Imbued with the same soul-stirring devotion, staunch principles, and rectitude of purpose, Rutherford would have suffered martyrdom rather than submit to what was contrary to his religious belief.

The facts narrated of his individual case are not, however, to be taken as representing the feelings of the whole body to which he belonged, as among them were, and are to be, found many large-hearted, liberal men. May his treatment of his son act as a beacon to warn persons of all parties and persuasions against immoderate sectarian and narrow-minded views ! Happy would it be for Christendom if all denominations would hold out the right hand of fellowship to those who love the Lord Jesus Christ, irrespective of creeds or church government.

His son Alexander succeeded to the property ; Maggie had got her dowry when she was married, and never asked or was offered anything more. Thornbrae, it will be remembered, came to Rutherford by Maggie's mother, and it was thought that her father intended bequeathing it to her, and this was what preyed on his mind, and what he was so anxious to get the lawyer to arrange previous to his death. Alexander and his mother had possession, and kept all—

> " For why ? Because the good old rule
> Sufficeth them ; the simple plan,
> That they should take who have the power,
> And they should keep who can."

G

CHAPTER XII.

PREVIOUS to Mr Rutherford's death, Mrs Rutherford had invited a relative (a widow, without any family) to come and reside with them, and assist in the household duties, while her own time was occupied attending her husband.

As Alexander was obliged after his father's funeral to return to Dublin for some months, Mrs Cooper remained at Thornbrae, and so far ingratiated herself into Mrs Rutherford's favour, that she was solicited to live permanently with her as companion.

Lord and Lady Southend would have wished Alexander to have continued with them, as they liked him, not only as an occasional companion, but were highly satisfied with the progress their son had made under his tuition. They had also hoped he would have accompanied him on "the tour of Europe" previous to leaving. His mother, however, could not manage the farm without assistance, and it was arranged that he should return home when Lord Southend would find a tutor who could fill his place. Some months elapsed before a suitable person was met with; Alexander then took leave of his pupil and noble patrons with regret. Lord and Lady Southend expressed their sorrow at his departure, thanking him for the manner in which he had discharged his duties, not only at the Hall, but also in Dublin; assuring him of their continued good wishes, and that if at any future period it were in their power to serve him, they would gladly do so. Alexander left Dublin with great reluctance ; but as his mother had earnestly desired his return, he yielded to her entreaties, not wishing to add to the sorrow which he had already caused her. It was therefore with feelings far from pleasurable that he arrived at Slievedhu ; but his depression vanished when he saw honest, faithful Jamie's delighted countenance, and heard his hearty " Welcome home, yer honour ; shure I 'm proud to see ye back agen ! "

After hearing that his mother and all at Thornbrae were well, he relapsed into silence ; his thoughts were occupied with recollections of his father, and of the sacrifices he was now making to gratify his mother. His spirits became so depressed that he groaned aloud, forgetful that Jamie was riding alongside. He was soon recalled to a sense of his presence by the exclamation, " Och, Master Alick ! won't it be the blissid sight to the misthress to clap her two eyes an ye this evenin', an' ye 'll get a blissin' for comin' to yer mother, she 's fail'd so, iver since the day ye went to Dublin first ; but then she had to look after and attind the master, an' now that he 's gone, shure ye 're all the comfort she has."

Poor Jamie's sympathy was so sincere, genuine, and unsophisticated, that Alexander reproached himself for giving way to selfishness, and felt he was unkind in being so occupied with his own thoughts as to neglect asking for Jamie's wife and children. This he knew was an inquiry which would gratify this faithful domestic, and a topic on which he would become eloquent, as, if once started, Jamie would dilate on it all the way to Thornbrae, and he would merely have to say " Yes " occasionally, or assent by a nod. Then rousing himself, he said, " I hope, Jamie, that Nelly and the youngsters are quite well ? "

" Och ! and what wud ail them, yer honour ? Haven't they lots o' praties ? An' the misthress niver lets them want a sup o' butter-milk ; an' Biddy 's fit to take care o' the pig an' the wean ;* an' Betty, (ye min' wee Betty, yer honour ?) she 's grown quare an' big ; she goes out wi' her mother to weed, an' they 're makin' saxpence halfpenny a day atween them now, ivery day barrin' the wet yins ; but we 'll hae plenty o' fine weather (the Lord be praised) atween this an' winter, an' of coorse be able to do a power o' work, an' make lashins † o' money." Jamie continued in this strain until they reached home.

It was indeed a great consolation for Mrs Rutherford to have her son with her again ; she fondly hoped he would settle down, and be happy and comfortable on his property ; but Alexander was not happy or contented. He found the monotony of the country tiresome ; longed for society such as that to which of late he had been accustomed ; and having an active mind and fervid imagination, he often chafed at being in solitude. Almost everything in and about Thornbrae reminded him of his father, to whom, notwithstanding his stern, injudicious treatment, Alexander had been devotedly attached. Opposition had

* Infant.   † Plenty.

only strengthened his dislike to the sect of which his father was such a warm and worthy adherent, and driven him to extremes, defeating the long-cherished purpose of his parents with regard to his profession. Now, however, that the old man was gone, Alexander overlooked his failings, and only thought of him as the sincere Christian and devoted father, and blamed himself for embittering his last days and hastening his death. These and many other reproachful thoughts preyed on his mind, so that he often gave way to melancholy. When in his gloomy moods, as he sat absorbed in " the room," or reclined under a tree in the garden, Mrs Cooper would come and rouse him from brooding on his own thoughts, asking him to explain something to her, or read while she knit or sewed beside him. Her manner was so gentle and unobtrusive, her voice so low and musical, that her presence soothed his troubled spirit. Week after week he sought her society, finding that it was a relief to enter into conversation with one who, by looks and tones of voice, evinced sympathy for him. New graces both of body and mind were observed ; a desire felt to gain her confidence, and pity awakened for her desolate widowed state.

She also had her dull moods, being occasionally absorbed in silent sorrow. In return for her sympathy, Alexander endeavoured to rouse her into cheerfulness, and cause a smile to play over her statuesque features. By degrees she confided her griefs to him, and he then realised that " pity is akin to love ;" finally, he concluded that she was very dear to him, essential to his happiness, and that she would be a good companion for life, and make the best of wives.

Mrs Cooper also felt that Alexander had gained her confidence, and a place in her heart, by manifesting sympathy for her desolate condition, and she gladly accepted his proposal of becoming her husband and protector.

The union was approved of by Mrs Rutherford, to whose comfort (as well as her son's) Mrs Cooper had become essential. The trio being unanimous, it was arranged that the marriage should at once take place· So without any romance, Alexander and the widow walked to the parish church one morning and were united in "the bonds of holy matrimony." There were not many persons present but those who officiated, and the necessary witnesses to the ceremony, which, in the service of the Church of England, ends with the word " amazement." This event afterwards called forth many expressions and exclamations of great amazement from many who heard of it. As the scandal-mongers said, " To think of Alexander Rutherford, the ' turncoat Protestant,'* marrying the Widow Cooper, who," &c. &c. But what will not Mrs Grundy (or the world) say on the occasion of a marriage which, of all matters, is less their business than any other occurrence, and only of chief consequence to the two persons concerned.

* "Turncoat" means changing religion. In the Ulster dialect, to be a Protestant or go to church is also understood to signify an Episcopalian, or member of the Church of England and Ireland; to go to meeting—a Dissenter; to go to chapel—Roman Catholic.

CHAPTER XIII.

IT has often been remarked that most couples who
are married bear a resemblance to each other;
but Alexander and his wife were totally unlike in appearance: she tall, thin, and angular, he of middle
height, stout, and muscular; she with long visage,
small mouth, and thin compressed lips, sallow complexion, and light gray eyes, her husband's face round
and rubicund, his upper lip long and firm, his mouth
large, chin massive, and his eyes dark and penetrating,
surmounted by shaggy eyebrows, forehead rather low,
hair black, stiff, and thick, brushed to stand upright
on top of forehead; in the clerical fashion of the time,
every vestige of beard and whisker were shorn off,
which, if they had been allowed to grow according to
the present mode, would have formed magnificent
whiskers and a flowing beard, but, from the constant
use of the razor, left a black ground over the greater
part of his face, as if gunpowder had been rubbed into
every pore.

The colour of the lady's hair we have omitted to
mention, it being confined under a thin muslin cap,
with lace borders, closely fitting round the face; perhaps as gray predominated over the original brown,

little of it was to be seen.   However, it must not be
inferred from this that the bride was old ; true, she
was two years her husband's senior, but remember he
was not then twenty-six years old, so it could not
have been age which had silvered her locks ; but Mrs
Cooper had, 'twas said, " been abroad, and suffered a
great deal of affliction," but of what nature none of
the most assiduous scandal-mongers could ever ascertain, though " intent to hear and eager to repeat," nor
could the most prying of her friends surprise her to
confide her trials to them " in confidence ;" she maintained so strict a guard over her expressions, and was
so reticent, that all that could be gleaned was only in
a general way, " that she had had many trials," but as
they were not specified, Mrs Grundy could only shake
her head, look sage, and hint more by looks and nods
than words that something had occurred which could
not be revealed.   Nor was a cap assumed for the purpose of covering those silvering locks.   No such thing,
gentle reader, it was the custom of the period in
Ulster, (and continued to be so till within the last
twenty years,) that a girl when married wore a cap to
make her look matronly, as it was considered quite
indecorous in a married female, if only in her teens,
and having luxuriant curls, to be seen without one.   A
similar custom was observed in Scotland at an earlier
period.   Perhaps caps were worn as outward and
visible signs that married females were then in (or
should be in) a state of subjection to their lords and
masters.

Mrs Rutherford's dress was scrupulously neat and

clean, and was of that wishey-washey, colourless description, which is generally adopted by females of her age and appearance, who wish to look plain and genteel.

Mr Rutherford (as we shall henceforth call him) settled down to live at Thornbrae, his wife and mother managing the household as formerly. He began to enlarge the house, make a different approach to it, and several other improvements. The new building stretched across the south gable; he laid out the grounds opposite to it tastefully with shrubs and grass plots, had a trellised porch in front, and creeping plants trained over the windows. The old part of the cottage remained unaltered, with the exception of a glass door out of the stranger's chamber, which opened into a flower garden. " The room " was now used as dining, breakfast, and general sitting room. The furniture of the new apartments was adapted to the size of the rooms, and suited the requirements of the inmates; the carpets, hangings, and paper contrasted harmoniously; the pictures on the wall, though of little value, were well selected; books, scattered about, showed that taste and intelligence went hand in hand, giving all a look of refinement without pretension, and still retaining an air of comfort.

Mr Peden for a time came frequently to Thornbrae, hoping by persuasion and arguments to win his nephew over to the belief of the Covenanters; in vain did the minister argue with him, and exclaim against the hierarchy, the Book of Common Prayer, the Thirty-nine Articles, vestments, rites, and ceremonies, confirmation, the signing of the cross in baptism, kneeling at the communion, &c. &c.

Every conference only confirmed each party more firmly in his own views. Alexander's remarks were often couched in bitter, sarcastic language, to which the minister as tartly retorted. Unkind words and feelings were almost always the result of such arguments, and as neither party was willing to abstain from controversy, it was finally arranged that the minister should not visit Thornbrae, and that all intercourse between uncle and nephew had better cease.

Mrs Rutherford, sen., visited occasionally at her brother's, and attended the meeting as usual, but Alexander and his wife became regular attendants and communicants at the parish church.

Alexander, however, so far acceded to his mother's wishes as to promise that during her life he would not take orders in the Episcopal Church. This was an end to all his cherished hopes. Since the day he had heard service in the cathedral at Londonderry it had been his constant aim to become a minister of the Established Church of Ireland. He had studied for that purpose, and had every prospect of obtaining a living. The remembrance of Lord and Lady Southend's parting words now only deeply grieved him. The Lord Bishop of Derry was a connexion of the Southend family, and if he, through their influence and patronage, had got a charge in that diocese, he might well have expected speedy promotion, perhaps even on the decease of the Very Rev. the Dean of

Derry he might have been appointed to the vacancy. Truly it was a great sacrifice both of his feelings and prospects; still it was alleviated by the reflection that he made it for a mother who was nearly deprived of life at his birth, and whose whole existence since had been a constant ministration to his wants and wishes, and who latterly had suffered so much on his account. He also dreaded making her feel that he was embittering her last declining years with sorrow, as he had done those of his father.

Year after year passed over, adding to the inmates of Thornbrae child after child, till there were two sons and three daughters born to Mr Rutherford, who educated them himself, determining to allow the boys to choose their own professions in life. Whether this was a prudent course or not remains to be seen.

At the epoch we now take up, the eldest son was in the twenty-third year of his age, two sisters came next, then another brother, and the youngest, a girl 'in her fifteenth year. Hilary, the first born, (so called because born on the thirteenth of January, St Hilary's day;) his grandmother insisted he should be baptized by that name, to fulfil a vow, which she recalled to her son's remembrance as having been made by him while arguing with his uncle, who had brought forward, that "as he was called for his great ancestors Peden and Rutherford, he should walk in their footsteps, and feel proud of doing so, and of being named after them." To which argument Alexander testily and passionately answered, "Nonsense, uncle; I vow if ever I have a son, I'll call him for whatever saint or sinner is mentioned in the calendar on the day he is born, and see if he follow in their footsteps."

This son very closely resembled his father, not only in appearance, but seemed to be an exact counterpart of him in character, if placed in circumstances to call forth similar traits.

Margaret, the eldest girl, was of middle height, very erect in her carriage, oval face, aquiline nose, dark, intelligent-looking eyes, firmly compressed mouth, and brunette complexion ; in character energetic and decisive. Being educated with her brothers, and having a good capacity and memory for acquiring languages, she was almost as well versed as they were in classic lore. She was her father's universal factotum, keeping his accounts, arranging his books, &c.

Agnes, the second girl, was rather tall and slight, more resembling her mother than any other of the family, but unlike her in character, being sensitive and impulsive.

John, the other son, was like Hilary, only on a smaller scale ; his eyes were not so dark and penetrating, and his mouth showed that he wanted the decision and self-reliance possessed by his elder brother ; he was affectionate in his disposition, and greatly attached to his mother and sisters.

Lucy, the youngest, was the pet of the household ; her rounded form and white and red complexion, her light step and merry laugh, were often afterwards spoken of ; her hazel eyes beamed with love and happiness ; her light brown hair flowed in wavy ringlets over her shoulders. She seemed to be a creature made to love and be beloved by all. The poultry, dogs, cows, horses, and sheep knew her voice, and were caressed by her ; the little boys about the farm sought out birds' nests "to show Miss Lucy ;" and the old men and women gazed with loving looks after her, saying, " Och, but she's a winsome bit lassie ; bless her bonny face." At this time there was another inmate of Thornbrae, a lad of seventeen, an orphan, named Edward Talbot. His parents had both died in Jamaica, and he was sent by his paternal uncles, who were West India merchants in London, to be educated and brought up by Mr Rutherford with his family ; he promised to be a very handsome man ; his slight, well-made figure and finely-chiselled features age would improve ; bright dark eyes lit up his countenance, and black, curling locks clustered closely over his well-formed head.

He and Lucy were often together ; for though so different in appearance, their tastes corresponded ; he also petted all the animals ; the pony " Rodger " knew his voice, came at his call, ate out of his hand, and followed him like a dog ; he had also the good wishes of all the servants and labourers, who proved their regard for him in every way that lay in their power. If a bird's nest was found, or the slightest incident occurred likely to gratify him, it was sure to be communicated to him.

Edward's education had progressed favourably, and his removal to London was soon expected.

Hilary had years ago served an apprenticeship to an apothecary, and completed his college course of study for the medical profession. He had obtained his degree of M.D., was now located in the town of Slievedhu, and was known by the sobriquet of "the young doctor."

The girls were proficient in all the feminine accomplishments of the day, as well as good housewives, being *au fait* in pickling, preserving, baking, &c., relieving their mother of household duties by taking week about of housekeeping. Their grandmother was not long dead; till within a few weeks of her decease she enjoyed good health, and her energy never forsook her. So long as she had strength to move about, she attended to all as formerly.

John had attended Trinity College for the first term, and had just returned home. One day he, Edward, and the girls had gone to the banks of Lough Neagh to spend the afternoon. The evening dropped down, and the father and mother sat awaiting their return.

"Alexander," said Mrs Rutherford, addressing her husband, "I 've been thinking that John does not look so strong as before he went to college, and Lucy is delicate; would you advise our going to the seaside for a month? Margaret and two of her girls are, by Hilary's advice, going to Portrush, and we could be accommodated at Dunluce."

"Well, well, wife; it is likely you womenkind have arranged it all between you, so I suppose there is no use in my objecting; the matter is, can Jamie and the horses be spared just now?"

"Oh, yes, Alexander ; Jamie says he has done moulding the potatoes, and that all the other work is far forward."

"Just as I said," responded Mr R. "Settle all, then ask my advice ; so you have nothing to do now but pack up and start."

"But," said Mrs R., "if you don't wish us to go, of course we will not."

"Ho, ho ; so you think I can't do without you ; but Margaret and I can manage well enough."

"But, Alexander, won't you come for us, and bring Margaret too ?"

"We'll see, we'll see ; but here comes the party from the lake. I wonder if John has had a good fishing ; most likely not, when Lucy and Edward were with them. How that boy does grow ! why, they are wild with mirth. Lucy is mounted on Rodger; her hat is wreathed with eglantine. Hector has also a wreath round his neck, and is scampering on before them. Margaret and Agnes are carrying the fishing-basket, and John strides on, seemingly well satisfied with his afternoon's sport."

Here he was interrupted by Edward, (who had run on before the rest,) shouting, "Here we are, as hungry as troopers. Put on the frying-pan ; John has caught his basket full of pollans ;" then, darting back, he seized the pony by the bridle, led him opposite the open window where Mr and Mrs Rutherford were seated, and after assisting Lucy to dismount, bowed to them, waved his hand towards Lucy, and in mock heroic tones repeated—

" Field and flowery grove,
He spoil'd of all that 's sweet and fair,
Wherewith to grace his lady-love."

The young people were greatly pleased with the
project of going to the shore—all but Edward, one of
whose uncles was expected daily; but it was arranged
that after his uncle's visit he should follow them to
Dunluce.   Thornbrae is distant nearly forty miles
from the sea ; and as in those days there were neither
stage-coaches, vans, railways, nor any public conveyance, and as jaunting-cars and gigs were very expensive, (they had not come into general use,) there was
great planning how the journey could be accomplished.   All was bustle preparing for the departure,
and packing up whatever would be required during
the sojourn at Dunluce.   At last all was ready, and at
six o'clock on a bright July morning the party were *en
route.*   John, mounted on a strong horse ; and behind
him, on a pillion, Agnes, followed by Mrs Rutherford
and Lucy on a car, (a vehicle which is rarely seen
now, and that in out-of-the-way districts in Ireland ;)
it somewhat resembled a jaunting-car of the present
day, without the rails at each end or in centre, and on
each side a hanging board for the feet to rest on ; the
wheels had not spokes, but were solid blocks of wood,
hooped round with iron ; on this conveyance was laid
a feather-bed, covered with a patch-work quilt.
Seated on it were Mrs R. and Lucy, who loudly pro-
tested against being on the car, begging to get on the
pillion, which was promised her when they halted at

noon to feed the horses and rest during the heat of the day.

Our old friend Jamie M'Gwiggan was car-driver; and the cart which followed containing the provisions and luggage was attended to by his son Alick, whose exclamation on first seeing the sea was, "Lom-minny! Oh, Master John, but the say's quare an' big; it bates the Lough hollow; there must be lashins an' laivins o' pullans to be got in it!"

Having accompanied our travellers to Dunluce, we now leave them to get refreshment, and retire to their comfortable beds, to sleep away the fatigues of the journey, while we in another chapter renew our acquaintance with Mrs Wilson, formerly "wee Maggie Rutherford."

CHAPTER XIV.

IT will be remembered that, previous to her brother's going to Glasgow College, Maggie had been married to a farmer called Wilson, who resided about twelve miles from Thornbrae. They lived happily together for years, adding annually to their live stock, cattle, pigs, sheep, horses, and children. Being anxious to give their sons the advantage of a liberal education, they sold their farm, and removed to the neighbouring town of Ballynacraig; they purchased a farm in the vicinity, bought building ground in the town, and erected an hotel (or inn, as it was called) and posting-house. As stage-coaches had not yet been introduced, gentlemen were accustomed to travel on horseback, and the families of the gentry in their own carriages, which were supplied with post-horses and postillions at the different stopping places along the road; post-chaises were also kept in the various towns to convey persons to and from Dublin, or to any other part of the country. This was the way lawyers went in those days to attend their terms, and milliners and mantuamakers to obtain the latest fashions.

Of course not only was the journey a matter which

required deliberation beforehand, but it was also a matter of grave consideration of whom the party should be composed who were to share the expenses and dangers of the undertaking.

As the time occupied on the road was mainly regulated by the weather and length of the day—no travelling being performed after nightfall—it is not to be wondered that in a journey which occupied three days in summer, and four or more in winter, it should indeed be considered a momentous question what persons should be cooped up together in such narrow space ; and many a petty manœuvre was resorted to in order to gain agreeable companions. A journey to Dublin was then considered such an undertaking that, previous to leaving, friends came to say farewell, wills were made, and everything settled before such an important step was taken.

The " Royal Arms " soon became noted as a good resting-place, the house being kept clean, the beds comfortable, the provisions good, plentiful, and well-cooked, the horses in good condition, servants and postillions civil, charges moderate, and the host and hostess attentive.

The two sons, Francis and James, were liberally educated, made choice of the medical profession, and were pursuing their studies to prepare them for situations in the British navy.

The eldest daughter, Nannie, belonged to a class of girls to be found in all ages, moderately well-looking, fond of dress, frivolous in conversation, dawdling in her time.

The second girl was quite different in every respect, quick, intelligent, enterprising, and ardent ; her elder sister rather looked on her with contempt as not being fair, a blonde complexion being with her the *sine qua non* of female beauty.   There were also the other girls, who were, as their nurses declared, "too good to live long ;" but as in their short lives they did nothing "to point a moral or adorn a tale," we shall not describe them.

Francis was older than Mary ; James came between her and the sisters who died.   Mary, the second girl, did not pass through life so quietly ; her appearance shall now be described.   Short in stature, slight and erect in carriage, well-shaped head, and an abundance of straight raven-black hair.   From her finely-marked features, thin long nose, brunette complexion, and dark intelligent eyes, she might have been taken for a Jewess ; indeed, it was told of her that when the celebrated Mr Whalley (known by the soubriquet of Buck or Jerusalem Whalley) stopped at the "Royal Arms," *en route* from Dublin, just after his return from the Holy Land, he was so struck with her Jewish appearance that he remarked to his valet, "If we had seen this girl in the Jewish quarter of Jerusalem, we should not have taken her for any other than of Abrahamic descent."

Mrs Wilson's health became delicate, and on Mary devolved the entire management of the establishment ; besides assisting her father with accounts, she found time to read and improve her mind.   Having a great thirst for knowledge, whenever she met her cousins Hilary and John, she applied to them for information ; and having a most retentive memory, she acquired a fund of general knowledge, to which she took every opportunity of adding.

Her greatest pleasure was having her cousins, particularly John, to converse with her on books and scientific subjects. Hilary's mode of imparting information was terse and uninteresting, and he was annoyed if stopped, by being asked questions which arose in Mary's quick imagination.

John had a greater fluency of language, possessed a fund of anecdote, and a more lively imagination, was minute in description, and had no objection to being questioned ; he was pleased to have an attentive auditor, and to be applied to, particularly by cousin Mary, who was so gratified by his conversation ; it was therefore with most pleasurable feelings that both looked forward to many pleasant walks and talks while at the shore together.

Shortly after the Rutherfords arrived at Dunluce, John went across the fields, in the direction of Portrush, walked along the top of the White Rock cliffs, often stopping to admire the bold headlands formed of white limestone, perforated by the action of the winds and waves into caverns and arches, and here and there assuming the form of gigantic profiles, as if chiselled out of the rock ; these from time immemorial have been known by the names of the "Giant's Head," "Sheelah's Head," &c. He then descended to the sand-hills, which are covered with bent ; mosses also are to be found in great variety in boggy hollows among the sand-hills, and many other botanical specimens indigenous to the soil.

John noted all as he passed on, calculating on being questioned about them by cousin Mary. Procuring a large burdock leaf, he collected a quantity of wild strawberries, which in sheltered nooks among the hills grow in abundance, and are of a most delicate flavour, wrapped them up carefully to take to his aunt Wilson ; then descending on the strand, after a walk of two miles along the hard sands, where the tide was ebbing, reached Portrush, where his aunt and cousins had arrived the evening before.

The many tourists who at the present time have, through the agency of Bell, Watt, Stephenson, and Dargan, visited Portrush, on their way to and from the Giant's Causeway, and who now see a thriving watering-place, with every hotel* and lodging accommodation, baths, railway, steamboats, churches, chapels, &c., will smile at a description of the appearance of this village at the end of the eighteenth and beginning of the present century, and the accommodation it then afforded visitors.

At that period there were only about thirty stone-built cabins, thickly thatched with straw, and firmly secured across and along the roof with strong ropes made of twisted bogwood, (the same which has already been described as used for fuel and light.) These houses were tenanted by fishermen and pilots,

* Hotel accommodation in Portrush is universally acknowledged to be good, and is pronounced in Murray's Guide Book to be "the very best in Ireland."

who earned a scanty livelihood by fishing when the weather permitted, and steering timber and slate-laden vessels into the small basin or dock of Port-rush, or taking them over "the bar" (sandbank at the mouth of the river Bann) to the port of Coleraine.

At the entrance to the village the houses were in straggling rows, but near the dock assumed the form of a street; at the dock-head were a row of cabins; conspicuous among them was the only three-storied house of which the village could boast, being roofed with slates, and so superior in size to the dwellings around that the inhabitants looked on it as quite a splendid mansion, and called it " The Castle."

At this time it was tenanted by Dr Richardson, Rector of Clonfeacle, (of fiorin grass celebrity,) one of whose maxims was, " The man who made two blades of grass grow where only one had previously been, deserved well of his country." The marks of his attempts at cultivation may to this day be seen on the part known as " Ramore Head," the termination of the promontory on which Portrush is situated.

It may here be mentioned, *en passant*, that some years afterwards Portrush became unexpectedly the birthplace of a peer of the realm who now holds a prominent position in the House of Lords. In the autumn of 1805 the first Baron R——, being on a tour through the north of Ireland, accompanied by his lady, were returning from the Giant's Causeway, when the lady took prematurely ill in the post-chaise. The postillion, on being interrogated, told his lord-ship that " there was no place of entertainment for man or baste nearer nor Cowlrain," but when he heard the lady's moans, and saw the distress of the gentleman, said he was " certain sure they would be taken in at ' The Castle' at Portrush, as Dr Richardson is a quare an' good man."

" Then drive there at once," eagerly replied his lordship.

Dr Richardson was noted for his hospitality. His sympathies were now called forth ; and with all the urbanity of manner and warmth of heart which characterised this Christian gentleman and learned divine, he received the baron and his suffering lady.

Madame Richardson and a lady visitor exerted themselves in every way to add to the comfort of their unexpected guest, to allay her fears, and soothe her distress of both body and mind. The postchaise was dispatched instanter to Coleraine for Dr Thomson, who immediately came off in his gig, accompanied by his apprentice, to be in readiness, if required, to return for anything which they had forgotten in their hasty departure.

All went on well ; and after a few hours, the population of Portrush had a male child added to its number, greatly to the relief of the apprentice, who was benumbed with cold, and his patience nearly exhausted by driving about in the gig waiting for his master. Years rolled on ; the Doctor died, and the apprentice inherited his title, but did not practice. He acquired wealth and position by other means, and was unanimously chosen by his fellow-townsmen to represent Coleraine in Parliament, for which borough he was returned several times. On one occasion, when he wished to carry through "the House" some measure for the benefit of the town he represented and so dearly loved, he was opposed by Baron R——, but he was gained over by Dr B——, who, with that ready wit and dry humour which made him such a pleasant companion and welcome guest at the houses of the aristocracy and gentry, told Baron R—— the incident of his birth, hoping that even at "the eleventh hour" his lordship would remunerate him for the discomfort he experienced on the night his lordship first made his appearance in Ireland.

Baron R—— may not like to be considered an Irishman, particularly at the present time, when the name is too frequently coupled with outrages and disgraceful conduct, but it is to be hoped his lordship will not judge "the noble many by the rascal few."

We Irish are proverbial for wishing to be thought like St Patrick, "come of dacent people;" and claim as "natives of the sod" all who are good and great; therefore we recognise Baron R—— as a "true-born Irishman."

Lodging accommodation was of course of the plainest and most meagre description, so that it was necessary to bring beds, bedding, and other requisites. The lodging Mrs Wilson and daughters got was considered "quite fit for gentry and 'quality' to come to." This house still remains in the main street; its gable towards the dock has a small window in it, and two similar windows face the street. These were in

the room occupied by Mrs Wilson. This apartment
is about fourteen feet wide by sixteen long. Across
the end of it were two four-posted bedsteads, with
plaited straw palliasses; along the ceiling, in front
of bedsteads, was a drapery of white and blue
chequer. Curtains also hung down at the top of each
bedstead; the windows were draped with the same
material. The whitewashed walls were adorned not
only with a sampler, (similar to that already described,) but, as the house belonged to a sailor's wife, there
were numerous pictures of ships, and a really rather
good water-colour drawing of Vesuvius in eruption,
purchased by Donald Nevin in Naples, during a voyage to the Mediterranean with a cargo of salted Bann
salmon, from " The Cranagh" and " Cutts," near Coleraine. On the mantel-shelf was a case of stuffed
birds, shells, &c., collected during many a voyage.
Over one window hung a toy canoe, ornamented with
coloured porcupine's quills, and in the other an
ostrich's egg. The floor was covered with matting
made of the bent which grew on the adjacent sand-
hills; and between the front windows hung a looking-
glass, beneath which was a large wooden chest, painted
red. This did duty for both sideboard and wardrobe;
on it, against the wall, stood the tea-tray, depicted on
which was a landscape in glowing colours, surrounded
by a wreath of flowers of the most brilliant hues; in
front were arranged a pair of glass decanters, several
jugs, two large brass candlesticks, and a number of
painted wooden bowls, (such as we now see in grocers'
windows filled with tea or fruit;) these had been

brought by the aforesaid Donald Nevin on his return from a voyage up the Baltic.

In addition to the hardwood tables and chairs, there was also an eight-day clock, and a buffet which held the tea things and glasses. The door into this room was quite close to the street, and opened out of the kitchen.

John was heartily welcomed by his aunt and cousins. After inquiries had been made and answered concerning the journey of both families, " I must tell you," said John, "that I stole off without letting any one know where I was going; so pray, aunt, allow the girls (I know you are too fatigued) to return with me to obtain my pardon from my mother and sisters for playing truant. I 'll bring them back safely in the evening ; so, like a good kind aunt, don't refuse my request."

Mrs Wilson having given her permission, the party soon set out for Dunluce by the route we have already described. On leaving the house, as Mary opened her parasol, she heard Bell Nevin shout, " Come, come, mother; the quality here has got the same as Madame Richardson holds over her head." While the party proceeded along, the children ran after them, gazing at the unusual sight ; and many a hand and brow were uplifted in astonishment as they passed through the village. Mary, as usual, had many questions to ask about the various objects on their way to Dunluce. Short as had been the time she was in Portrush, she had ascertained from the oldest inhabitant, Randy MacCallister, that his grandfather had told him that there had been arable land where it was now sand-hills. "Yes," said John, "had it not been for this most useful plant, *Arundo arenaria*, sea mat-weed or bent, much more damage would have been done; but wherever it takes root, it binds the sand together, and prevents it drifting about. Queen Elizabeth prohibited its extirpation; and a recent Act of Parliament protects this plant throughout the places of its growth in this kingdom. Few if any in the vegetable world are more wonderfully constructed, and show so plainly the purpose for which it is designed. You observe that the stems are ridged, and the leaves pointed and thorn-like. The root of this species of grass is creeping, and often twenty feet in length; and being very tough and penetrating, and sending forth numerous fibres, it serves the important purpose of binding together the loose sand. The ridged stems readily resist sand-drifts, however sudden; and the pointed leaves allow the sand to fall between them, as through a sieve, from which the wind may not again chase it away. The sand is evidently adapted to the plant, and the plant to the sand. The leaves too are defended with a firm, hard cuticle, which effectually prevents the fine particles of salt that fly off the waves from penetrating into the pores. Without this admirable provision, the *Arundo* would soon perish; doubtless the surface of the leaf is endued with a filtering power, by means of which sufficient moisture is derived from the atmosphere to sustain its existence and growth."

With nimble footsteps and light hearts the trio

arrived at the White Rocks. "Surely," said Mary, "the poet must have been here when he composed the lines—

> ' In every object here I see
> Something, my heart, resembling thee ;
> Hard as the rocks that bound the strand,
> Dry and unfruitful as the sand ;
> Deep and deceitful as the ocean,
> And, like the tides, in constant motion.' "

"There are many places I daresay," replied John, "to which the words would be equally applicable, and a still greater number of persons whose hearts these objects symbolise ; but I prefer the following verse, leading me to look beyond myself from nature up to the God of nature and of grace :—

> ' In every object here I see,
> Something, O Lord, that leads to Thee ;
> Firm as a rock Thy promise stands,
> Thy mercies countless as the sands ;
> Thy love a sea immensely wide,
> Thy grace an overflowing tide.' "

After ascending to the rising ground—" Here," said John, " we 'll take a seat on this thyme-covered bank ; and while we enjoy the cool breeze, I 'll repeat to you lines written by a friend about this locality. It was composed on the occasion of a trip to the ' Skerries ' and ' White Rocks.'

> " Come let us ride
> On the bounding tide ;
>   Why idly mope on shore ?
> Find us a boat
> That can safely float
>   And glide the proud waves o'er.

" We'll spread our sail
  To the rising gale,
    And steer for 'Island Dhu ;'
  The merry song
  Will cheer us along
    As we sweep the waters through.

" On the ' Skerry Isles,'
  'Mid sunny smiles,
    We'll repose 'neath the rocky shade :
  And drink from the spring
  Where the waters ring
    Through the caves the sea hath made.

" The conies dark
  We'll chase, but hark !
    The sea-birds loudly scream ;
  Your rifles use,
  The wild sea-mews
    Will serve us well for game.

" Our course we'll veer,
  And off we'll steer
    To the rocks of snowy white ;
  From the limestone caves,
  Which the water laves,
    We'll view the wild dove's flight.

" Those arches spann'd
  By nature's hand—
    Fair temples of the deep ;
  Like fairy forms,
  That 'mid the storms
    Their lasting vigils keep.

" Through every cove
  We'll sail and rove,
    Amid the living spray ;
  Each nook explore
  Along the shore
    From morn till closing day."

Agnes and Lucy, who had suspected where their

brother had gone, were on the look-out, and ran off to welcome their cousins, first scolding John for going away, then thanking him for going, as it gave them the pleasure of seeing their cousins sooner than they expected.

Dunluce Castle.

CHAPTER XV.

AFTER partaking of curds and cream, for which Mrs Moore of Dunluce was celebrated, an inspection of the castle ruins was proposed. No padlocked iron gate, guarded by a guide, then opposed the progress of visitors ; all were free to wander about when and where they pleased.

"Now," said Mary, "John will begin at the beginning and describe all to us."

"Well, coz, I can tell you very little about it, as there is no authentic record of when Dunluce Castle was built ; but we know it was a stronghold in Queen Elizabeth's time, and that the Duchess of Buckingham lived some time here. But now, as Schiller writes of a similar ruin—

' The wanton winds are clambering there,
And desolation broods within ;
Through yawning breach and window rent,
Over the roofless tenement,
The clouds of heaven, careering high,
Lower as they pass, and wistfully
Look in.'

This large aperture is where the outer courtyard
gate was ; and those buildings inside served probably
as residences for the retainers, and for stables and
other offices. One of these apartments is said to have
been the hall of justice where offenders were tried,
and, if found guilty, hung on yonder hill, (pointing
to one on the right, which to this day retains the
name of the " Gallows Hill.") Look out of this opening, which was once a window. From this situation
the castle is well seen ; you will perceive it is situated
on an insulated rock, and is joined to the mainland
by a narrow bridge or arch of mason work, which is
the only way of access to the ruins."

" Indeed," said Agnes ; " is that the only way of
getting into the castle ? Why, it is only the top of
a wall, not more than eighteen inches broad."

" Well, Agnes, it is just what you say, the top of a
wall ; but it is wider than you imagine. I measured
it this morning, and find it is twenty-seven inches
wide, and twenty feet long. 'Tis said there was a
corresponding arch to lay a drawbridge on ; but I
cannot find any traces of where it has been. My
opinion is that there never was another ; but there
may have been some subterranean passage from the
cave which you see underneath to the interior of the

I

castle. You will perceive that many of the stones in the walls are of basaltic formation, and the mortar which binds them together is very strong and hard. Look at this chimney which has been blown down; it has fallen *en masse*, and retains its shape entire."

Here they were interrupted by the clapping of hands and a merry peal of laughter. It was caused by Lucy, who had crossed the bridge, and called exultingly, " I have got over the dangerous place; it's nothing at all to be afraid of. Shall I go over to assist you across ?"

To which John rather angrily replied : "I say, miss, if you don't be less adventurous, you'll rush into some dangerous situation, where there may be difficulty in rescuing you, or you may fall over the cliffs into the sea ; you must behave yourself quietly." At which reprimand Lucy looked very demure ; but after watching them come over the bridge, she darted off, seated herself in a round tower, and commenced singing " Here in cool grot."

Attracted by her voice, they followed to the spot where she was.

" Here," said John, " is Lucy in Mava Roe's room. You naughty girl, what would you have done if the fairy or banshee had come to you ?"

" A fairy !" said Lucy. " Oh, I'd like to see her, if she is a kind, good fairy, like Order in the fairy tale, who came to assist a poor untidy, thoughtless girl like me, or Cinderella's good fairy. But preserve me from seeing the banshee ; she's a doleful little old creature, always wailing and wringing her hands, and giving notice of approaching evil, as if sorrow were not soon enough when it came."

"But, John," said Mary and Agnes, "do tell us the legend?"

"This tower," he replied, "is said to be haunted by Mava Roe, a cleanly fairy, who always sweeps the floor, so that there never is any dust to be seen. Boreas, however, it is evident, is the sweeper, and a nor'-wester his besom. The banshee's wail may be accounted for by the whistling of the stormy breezes through the walls and loopholes. It is still, however, believed by some old retainers of the Antrim family that a supernatural noise is heard here previous to the death of any of its members. There is also a tradition that the story had its origin in lamentations being heard issuing from this chamber, where the daughter of the chieftain M'Quillan was confined by her father, to keep her from being carried off by her lover, M'Donnell of the Isles. He had been shipwrecked in the neighbourhood; and when hospitably received and entertained at Dunluce, won the affections of M'Quillan's daughter, whom he carried off; and then finally dispossessing her father, turned him out of the castle, and took possession of the adjoining lands.

"But, as I have already said, no authentic records have been preserved. The descendants of M'Donnell up to the present time are owners of the castle and lands about; and the eldest son of the Earl of Antrim derives the title of Viscount Dunluce from these roofless walls.

"This tower must have been erected at a very early period, from the rude style in which it is built. The arched roof, you will perceive, is formed of stones, and has evidently been made by raising a mound of earth, firmly pressed together, then laying wicker-work on the top, and paving it all over with blocks of stone, then pouring over it mortar in a semi-fluid state, so that it penetrated into the interstices between the stones, (this I believe was called 'grouting.') See, here are not only the marks of the rods employed in the wicker-work, but also some pieces of rods remaining. When the mortar was firmly hardened, and the masonry bound together, the mound of earth was removed, leaving the roof arched as it now is."

"Ho, ho!" said Lucy; "our John talks like a book. You would think he had been architect at the building of the castle; but can you tell us anything more about the fairy?"

"Granny Garland introduced a fairy into the legend she told me," said John.

"Pray tell it," was the general request.

"It is too long," replied he, "to enter into now."

"Oh, John," said Lucy, "tell us who is Granny Garland; is she the banshee?"

"Not that I know of, Lucy. Certainly she does not correspond with your description of that personage, as she is not little, and does not wear a red cloak; notwithstanding, she is a remarkable woman. If you wish, I shall tell you how I became acquainted with the old dame; but as it will occupy some time, let us leave this windy chamber."

The party then went to another spot in the ruins ; and when seated on the fallen walls, John proceeded to gratify the curiosity of his auditors as follows :—

" Having heard from some of the inmates of the farmhouse at Dunluce that 'Granny Garland,' who lived about two miles off in the 'toon o' Ballymagarry,' when in a good humour would tell incidents of bygone days, which had been communicated to her by her grandmother, who had in turn been told them by her great grandmother ; and as they had all been remarkably long-lived, some of her traditions went back to three or four centuries ago; I determined to visit the old dame, and endeavour to extract some information from her relative to Dunluce Castle and the neighbourhood.

" The Lords of Dunluce, you may remember, had a mansion at Ballymagarry, to which they removed in the beginning of the seventeenth century, leaving the sea-girt castle untenanted, to become a prey to the destroying effects of time, tempests, and rain.

" The ' Toon ' is situated at the top of a hill, and consists of a few mud-built, straw-roofed cabins on each side of the highroad. As I slowly ascended the steep acclivity I began to consider in what manner I should accost granny so as to gain her favour. I then thought of her having more than numbered the term of years now allotted to man, and that life was becoming to her a burden. Occupied with these thoughts, I would not have noticed a woman who was standing in a stream which ran in a deep channel along the roadside. The noise of my footsteps had caused her to raise herself out of a stooping posture to look who was coming, and thus she attracted my attention. There she stood, a woman rather above the middle height, strongly and muscularly formed; her features massive and weather-beaten; her keen bright gray eyes and firm long upper lip showed that she was neither wanting in shrewdness nor intelligence. Her linen cap, with a narrow frill round it, was dazzlingly white; her grizzled hair was turned up over a pad on her forehead, and the cap confined round her head with a parti-coloured cotton bandage, which I believe you call a binder.

"The dark blue and white stamped linen bedgown, (loose jacket, with sleeves to the elbow,) though patched, was clean, as well as the blue drugget petticoat, which was turned up and fastened round her waist, forming a tunic, which only reached to her knees, permitting her to stoop without 'drabbling her tails,' as the phrase goes. At her feet, in the water, resting against her strong limbs, was a bushel basket full of potatoes, which she had been washing when interrupted by my approach. Of course I did not stand gazing at her for so long as I have taken to describe her appearance, and the impressions I formed of her; nor was she fascinated by me, for in an abrupt, hasty manner and firm voice she echoed my 'good day,' which plainly meant, 'Go on your way, and don't bother me,' and, stooping, resumed her occupation without again lifting her head to look at me.

"For some minutes she shook the basket vigorously, then holding it up till the water had nearly all dripped away, she stepped out of the stream, carrying the basket, and walked with a firm step in her bare feet to the road in the direction of the houses. I followed her, saying, 'Will you be so good as to tell me where Granny Garland lives?'

"Turning round her head, but not slackening her pace, she said, 'It's Granny Garland ye're speering for? What may ye want we her?'

"'Well,' said I, (rather taken aback by her abrupt manner,) 'I want to have a little conversation with her about old times, and should feel obliged if you will tell me which of these houses she lives in.'

"'An' what would be the use o' ye goin' to her at this time o' the day, when she hasna time for cracking,' (chatting.)

"'But surely,' I replied, 'such an old woman is not able to work at anything which will occupy her so busily; at any rate I should like to see her, and give her some tea and tobacco which I've brought for her.'

"By this time we had reached the cabins, and, halting opposite an open door, she said, while a shrewd smile played over her countenance, 'Ye may come in, but I canna crack we ye till I put on the praties, for they'll all be in for their dinner, and pulling flax is a hungry job.'

"'Is it possible,' I exclaimed, 'that you are Granny Garland?'

"'An' why for shouldna I be? But, as I afore said, the dinner must be got ready; so, young man, if ye'll just step along the plantin', an' walk about the owld place below, in a wee time I'll be ready for ye.'

"As this was notice to quit, I was turning away

when, in rather a loud voice, she said, 'Ye may as well leave me the bit tobaccy ; a smoke whiles brings many an owld story o' granny's into my head.'

"Gladly I presented it and the tea to her, feeling assured that I had found favour in her sight. The belt of trees, 'the plantin',' is at the base of the hill, and is all that now remains of the oak woods of Ballymagarry. There was little left of the mansion which had been occupied by the Lords of Dunluce. A common farm-house had been erected out of the building materials of the castle ; all that remains of the original building is a tower, now used as a barn and granary ; the threshers and farm-labourers never thinking about the departed glories of the place, or the different use the edifice had been applied to in former days. ' *Tempus edax rerum,*' I exclaimed, and retraced my steps to granny's cabin, hoping that the pipe had caused her to be in a more sociable mood.

"I was not disappointed. On a stool, opposite a peat fire made on the hearth, she sat, gazing intently into the fire, her right elbow resting on her knee, and holding a cutty (short) pipe in her mouth, which she seemed greatly to enjoy. Having given a closing whiff, knocked the ashes out of the pipe, and deposited it carefully in a hole in the chimney-corner, she turned round to me, and drawing her commanding figure up to its full height, waved with her hand, saying, 'Now, young man, sit down on the settle, an' I'll keep my seat on the creepy.* I must watch the

---

* An oblong or triangular piece of wood, having strong wooden pegs fastened into it so as to form a stool.

praties,' looking and nodding at the pot suspended over the fire. 'I've a noggin of water here beside me to check them when they come to the boil; so I'll not have to stop the discourse. Ye'll aiblins be the young minister, his reverence's son, that's lodging in Mistress Moore's beyant, an' ye'll be wanting some screed about the owld castle I'se warrant.'

" I replied that she was correct about who I was, and that she had also rightly guessed my errand, and hoped that she would favour me with one of her grandmother's tales.

" The tobacco and the deference I showed her had a good effect. As a mark of the respect she felt for me she had put on a blue and white apron of ample size, to which she attracted my attention with evidently as much pride as a duchess would feel when displaying her hereditary diamonds, saying, ' This was my grandmother's ; the flax was sown by grandfather more than sixty years ago ; weeded and pulled by his wife ; steeped, dried, scutched, milled, beetled, and all that by grandfather ; spun and dyed by grandmother ; woven by grandfather ; and finally made into its present shape by grandmother ; and the aprons were so strong she could never wear them out; she meant to leave them to wee Molly, her great granddaughter.'

" During this preamble about the aprons I began to fear I should not hear any of the legends, but the old woman's garrulity was roused, and with a look at the fire, evidently meaning *tempus fugit*, said, ' Now for one of granny's owldfarrent histories of Dunluce.

Ye'll doubtless hae heard about the wars o' the
M'Quillans, and about M'Donnell marrying the
chief's daughter, and about the rock splitting, an'
that then they all came away bodalilty to Ballymagarry ; and ye've heard o' Mave Roe's chamber, and
that she comes to sweep it ; but all ye've heard
about the tower is just havers (nonsense).   I'll tell ye
the true way o' the story ; I had it word o' mouth frae
granny when she was bordering on a hundred ; and
she had it from her great-granny, word for word,
when she was near fourscore an' ten ; and she had it
from them who knew all the outs an' ins o' it ; and
as it's all about love and murder, ye'll like to hear
it.   I mustna forget to look at the praties though.'

"I had great difficulty in following the digressions
in the tale, but I was anxious to take advantage of
her communicativeness while she was in the vein, as
I felt assured that when the potatoes were cooked
she would not talk any more to me, and I feared that
the tale would not be concluded.   Granny's tongue,
however, could spin a yarn as fast as her grandam's
wheel could possibly have spun the thread for the
prized and valuable aprons ; and she came to the end
of the legend just as the goodman and all the troop
of labourers returned from the fields.   Having
thanked her heartily for the gratification she had
afforded me, I turned my steps towards my home
pro tem. at Dunluce.   Afterwards I wrote out the
tale told to me by Granny Garland.   I shall read it
to you in the evening.

"Let us now enter this large apartment opposite,

which was evidently used for the banqueting hall; and while seated among the ruins picture to ourselves a scene which doubtless often occurred here. We will suppose that the chieftain M'Donnell and his haughty wife, formerly Duchess of Buckingham, who resided here in 1639, have invited all the neighbouring chieftains, their families and retainers, to a grand banquet. The floor has been strewn with freshly cut rushes. A long table runs down the centre of the hall, on the upper end of which are wine flagons and cups of silver, pewter plates, and dishes containing barons of beef, saddles and legs of mutton, boars' heads, haunches of venison, and pasties, game, fish, poultry, &c. Along the lower end of the board, for the use of the less distinguished guests, are wooden platters and methers,* containing mead and a spirituous fermented liquor made out of rye and barley. There is also a plentiful supply of rye bread, and the coarser pieces of beef and mutton. The ladies and chieftains then enter and take their places at the table.

" The lower end is speedily filled by the other guests and retainers.

"The viands disappear rapidly, and are washed down with copious draughts of wine, mead, or 'usquebaugh.' The hall now resounds with the clatter of plates and tongues, and as the feast progresses, toasts and songs are introduced, and mirth and revelry prevail.

* A drinking vessel made out of a solid piece of wood, forming a circle at bottom, and square at top. It was hollowed out to contain from three pints to two quarts. Some methers had two handles, but the greater number had one on each side, four handles being more convenient for passing it round from one to another.

"MacBhaird, the chief minstrel belonging to the castle, now enters the hall.

> ' What tho' time's wintry touch hath somewhat marr'd
> His minstrel craft, and rudely here and there
> Jangled the tuneful chime ? yet not so jarr'd
> But that it still the wonted mead shall bear.'

"The bard then plays the ever welcome air, ' Neaill ghubh a Deirdre,', (the Lamentation of Deirdre for the sons of Usnach.)   He thus awakens the attention of the entire audience, and sings—

> ' Oh ! to hear my true love singing,
> Sweet as sounds of trumpets ringing ;
> Like the sway of ocean swelling,
> Roll'd his deep voice round our dwelling ;'—

this being one of the many verses of the Lamentation which had such a hold on the imaginations of the Irish that it was popular for nearly a thousand years.   The interest of the story consists mainly in its frequent examples of magnanimity and fortitude, and in the exalted idea which it gives us of ancient honour.

"The ladies then retire.

"After a time the chieftain host orders the hall to be cleared for dancing.

"The servants remove the table, and with the branch of an oak sweep the rushes off the floor."

"More likely whins," (furze,) interrupted Agnes, " as there is not a tree to be seen anywhere about this."

"You forget, young lady, that at Ballymagarry (about a mile distant) there was a large wood of oaks.

"When all was in readiness, we may imagine the

lovely and noble dames entering this hall escorted by
the chieftains. The harpers and pipers take their
places, and commence playing the music suitable
for dancing the graceful solemn minuet. Cannot
you almost fancy you see the stately dames, with
their slow, measured steps, and long, solemn curtsies,
and their stalwart partners making low bows, and
striving to emulate them in slow steps and dignified
demeanour ? "

"Alas! alas !" cried Lucy, "I can see nothing but
bare tumbledown old walls. Oh, how I wish I could
conjure up Edward and Hector ! Come along, girls,
and leave Mary and John to imagine whatever they
like about this deserted dismal old building. Come
and we 'll see if even a bird builds a nest here, or a
flower blooms." And off she tripped, improvising
and singing as she went—

> " And this Dunluce is
>   Which no other use is,
>   But for people to look at and walk inside.
>   And a tower that 's round, O,
>   And quite renowned, O ;
>   It's Mava Roe's room,
>   And swept by her broom,
>   And I care not what there is beside."

Bessie and Agnes followed Lucy, and the cousins
Mary and John were left alone. "Now," said the
latter, " that we are rid of those frivolous girls, " I 'll
read to you a poem which is applicable to what we
have just been talking about ; it is a translation from
the German, and is entitled ' The Minstrel.' " Then

producing a book from his pocket, he read as follows :—

> " ' From chain-drawn bridge to castle gate,
>   What sounds approach our dwelling ?
> Go summon to our hall of state
>   The harp with rapture swelling.'
> The monarch spake—the stripling page
> Straight usher'd in a man of age.
> ' All hail ! thou hoary minstrel.'

> " ' And hail to you, ye ladies bright !
>   Ye knights renown'd in story !
> A host of stars, a world of light !
>   A galaxy of glory !
> No time, I ween, is this to raise
> Mine eyes to meet the mingled blaze
> That darts on one poor minstrel.'

> " The old man closed his aching eyes,
>   But soon took heart and chanted ;
> Each maid looked down in modest wise,
>   Each warrior gazed undaunted.
> Uprose the king and call'd amain,
>   What ho ! bring forth a golden chain,
> To grace the reverend minstrel.'

> Gramercy ! Sire—thy chain of gold,
>   To freeborn bard ill-suited,
> Reserve for knight or baron bold,
>   In feats of arms reputed.
> Yon chancellor, with cares of state
> Though weighed, may better bear the weight
> Than I, a merry minstrel.

> " ' The birds that warble on the bough
>   No fee or favour covet ;
> The love of song is meed enow
>   To those who truly love it.
> Yet might I crave a boon, be mine
> The jovial cup and sparkling wine,
> Fit largess for the minstrel.'

"Deeply he drain'd the rich carouse,
  Till head and heart were glowing.
'A blessing on your royal house,
  With bounty overflowing!
All good be thine; and when 'tis given,
Remember me, and be to heaven
As grateful as the minstrel.'"

John and Mary then went over the ruins regularly, picturing to their fertile imaginations the scenes that might have occurred in ages past. "And this is all that remains of the kitchen," they said; "what a state of terror they must all have been in when, during a terrific tempest, the rock split, and the cook and eight assistants, who were busily engaged in preparing dinner, were precipitated into the yawning gulf below! All perished except a tinker, who, it is said, was seated in this window recess mending a pot. To this day it retains the name of the 'Tinker's Window.'

"So alarmed were the inmates that they removed to the mainland. This occurred about the middle of the seventeenth century; and the castle, being uninhabited, has been suffered to go to decay, and become the ruin we now see it."

"Mr John! Mr John! Ladies! where are you?" resounded through the deserted walls.

"Here we are," said Lucy; and there she was, seated on a fragment of a wall, with Agnes beside her. They had collected a quantity of a bright blue flower, a species of crane's bill, (*Geranium pratense,*) indigenous to the place; they were adorning their heads with it, "to be dressed," as they said, "to meet the grandees of the castle."

"Oh, ladies, come away!" said Mrs Moore; "and where is Mr John and the other lady? the potatoes are boiled, and dinner is ready."

"Oh! Mrs Moore, you need not ask them to come," said Lucy. "John and Mary have been imagining so many banquets, they will not require any dinner."

"Don't calculate so fast, Miss Chatterbox; the fresh air of the Atlantic has given me a good appetite, and I daresay Mary feels hungry also."

After dinner, John complied with the request of the party, and read the legend which he had heard from Granny Garland: it follows in next chapter.

CHAPTER XVI.

STERNEST among the stern chieftains of the age was M'Quillan Dhu, the stalwart, dark-visaged, heavy-browed lord of the fortress castle of Dunluce, and the wide extent of territory belonging to it. He ruled over his dependants and clansmen with an iron will and despotic sway; "Whom he would he kept alive, and whom he would he slew."

Yonder rising ground, instead of being as now covered with peaceful sheep and lambs, was then bare of grass; the soil trodden down by the trampling of heavy feet; and the surface raised in rough hillocks by erecting the gallows; it was no unusual thing to see several naked bodies dangling and swinging to and fro in the gale on the Gallows Hill.

Resentful and implacable, M'Quillan was constantly at variance with the neighbouring chieftains; Ishmael-like, " his hand was against every man, and every man's hand against him."

Rather more than a year after his marriage he returned to Dunluce early on a spring morning from a foray on the tribe of the O'Cahans, whom he had routed, carrying off with him numerous herds of cattle, and other valuable property.

K

Rushing hastily over the drawbridge, and without giving notice of his approach, he abruptly entered his wife's apartment. There on a couch lay the lady, pale as a statue, and beside her a babe of a few days old. Raising herself up, and looking lovingly at her husband, and then casting her eyes down tenderly on her infant, she exclaimed, (with all a young mother's pride,) " Is she not lovely ? and a true M'Quillan too! look, my lord, at her long black hair. I have named her after your lady mother Mava. Sheelah already calls her the Lady Mava Dhu,* to distinguish her from our niece, who is now known throughout the castle as Mava Roe." †

The lady, carried away by her feelings, had given vent to her natural emotions without noticing the gloomy looks of her lord, who abruptly interrupted her by saying in a loud stern voice, " Enough, I don't want to hear or see anything more of the girl ; curse her sex ; if it had been a boy ;" and turning away, the heartless father strode out of the chamber.

Although unused to kindness, and having frequently had experience of M'Quillan's savage temper, the poor gentle lady felt crushed by this cruel conduct, and swooned away. Her attendants used every means for her recovery, but the blow had fallen heavily on her ; she was completely stunned, and could not be brought to consciousness ; for hours she seemed to hang between life and death. At length the babe wept, and the old nurse Sheelah, lifting her up, placed her in the lady's arms. Nature prevailed ; the

* Dhu, Anglice, black.   † Roe, Anglice, red.

presence and voice of her infant recalled her senses, and opening her eyes with a bewildered look, then casting a most melancholy loving glance on the weeping babe, she burst into a torrent of tears.

The heart sorrow that was consuming the poor mother seemed to be communicated to her infant, as she seldom ceased wailing piteously day or night.

M'Quillan never came to see his wife or child ; if, when passing the apartment, he heard the cries, he would mutter imprecations, wish the brat was dead, and go out of hearing.

Summer, with its bright long days and sunny hours, passed unheeded and unenjoyed by either mother or child ; when the days began to shorten, the lady was one morning gazing listlessly out of her chamber window, rousing herself, as if from a lethargy, she said, (pointing to where the swallows were assembling on the towers previous to their departure,) " Look, Sheelah, our darling Mava came with the swallows and she'll go with them." " Whisht, my darling lady, the saints forbid ; plase God, the Lady Mava Dhu will be spared to us, and we'll all see happy days yet."

" Never, oh never, Sheelah! Pray that I'll not be long after her."

A few days afterwards the child died. M'Quillan at this time was absent on one of his warlike expeditions. A messenger was sent to tell him of what had taken place. He had been unsuccessful, and was in one of his savage moods.

" Tell my lady," he said fiercely, " I have matters of more consequence to attend to than to return to bury the girl ; it can be managed without me." The poor mother was saved the anguish of receiving the cruel message, her gentle spirit had breathed its last before the bearer had returned to the castle ; she was not long parted from her beloved babe, and one coffin contained the bodies of both. " Lovely in life, in their death they were not divided."

The chieftain was again sent to, and informed that he was not only childless, but wifeless. He received the intelligence in silence, and returned accompanied by all his attendants. His kinsmen assembled at the castle, where a funeral feast and wake was held ; the family vault was opened in the burying-ground, and the coffin deposited in it.

M'Quillan never mentioned the names of either wife or child afterwards, but became even more gloomy and reserved than he had heretofore been. His dependants dreaded to be in his presence, and even the wolf-dog, which was his constant companion, cowered at his look.

Mava Roe, his kinsman's orphan daughter, (now six years old,) alone feared him not ; instinctively she felt pity for her unhappy friend, and though often repulsed, returned again to him, and by her child-ish artless ways, and infantine prattle, soothed and amused him ; so that by degrees the hardened nature of the chief seemed to soften when in her presence.

Joyous as the larks which soared above her head, she might often be seen at early dawn tripping about Gort-na-Ban, with basket on arm, collecting mush-rooms ; again her light sylph-like form was reflected

in the rock pools below the castle, where she was
wont to collect the many beautiful weeds which vege-
tate there, or are thrown in from deeper waters.

Accompanied by her beloved spaniel, she would
dart off to the sandy beach, and there following the
receding wave, run away from the incoming billow;
the bark of the spaniel, and the merry ringing laughter of the child blending together, proving how much
enjoyment both had.

As she grew older she was fond of riding; and
sometimes when M'Quillan's black steed was being
caparisoned for the chase, she would beg that her
Rathlin pony, Shoanan, might be got ready, that
she might accompany him.

The maiden's presence among the rough, uncouth,
stern men was as when the glorious sunshine breaks
forth from under the dark clouds over the madly
dashing billows, lighting up the ocean, and making
the scene less awful; like Una and the lion she subdued, by her innocence and fearlessness, these semi-
barbarous men.

M'Quillan did not now so often give way to his
fierce passions; but occasionally his savage temper
manifested itself, showing that the volcano only
smouldered, and might break out afresh any moment; as his foster-brother said, "When the chief is
in his dark moods, it is like trying to walk on the
edge of a sword to attempt to please him."

Years rolled on, and Mava, strengthened by the
bracing breezes, and tenderly cared for and tended
by Sheelah, was now verging on womanhood; a love-

able, artless, beautiful maiden.   Acts of benevolence,
love, and kindness seemed to constitute the essence
of her nature.   To take gifts of fruit and dainties to
the children, the aged, and the sick, was a source of
real pleasure to her, and her visits were hailed with
rapture by all around.   Kindliness and love beamed
in her eyes, and her lovely radiant smile cheered the
most melancholy, and roused the care-worn and de-
spondent.   "Here comes our darling Lady Mava
Roe," the children would shout with glee ; and
"*cead mille failthe*" was on every lip, or echoed in
every heart.   The young men and maidens called
her Coluv na harriche, (Dove of the rocks,) and gazed
at her as if she were an angelic being.   The old
people called her Geal mo veha, (Light of my life,)
and declared that the Lady Mava's presence was a
cordial; that it revived them like basking in the summer's sunshine on the top of Long Gilbert cave, and
that her voice soothed them as did the ripple of the
waves among the pebbles on the beach below.

Imaginary or real insults soon led to quarrels between M'Quillan and his neighbours.   The chieftains
united and assembled together, determined to crush
the power of the proud Lord of Dunluce, and humble
his ambitious views.

An engagement took place, and after great blood-
shed on each side, M'Quillan Dhu and his followers
came off victorious, carrying with them, besides large
herds of cattle, several youths, sons and kinsmen of
the principal chieftains, who were to be retained as
hostages till a certain sum of silver and gold, and a

number of garments, were paid for their ransom.
They were treated as became their rank; but from
the time they were taken over the drawbridge they
were not permitted to leave the castle, where they
remained for several weeks. During this time they
were thrown into daily contact with Mava.

One of the youths, Reginald O'Cahan, attracted
her attention, he was so different from any one else
she had ever seen; for although manly in his bearing
and frank in his manner, he was gentle and unselfish.
He had been a page in France at the court of Francis
I., and had acquired accomplishments unknown to his
present companions. Being gifted with a sweet voice,
he beguiled the hours of his captivity by singing the
songs of " La Belle France," accompanying them on
his lute; even M'Quillan's gloom was occasionally
dispelled by hearing the lively strains or touching
melodies which in the freshness of his young heart he
poured forth.

Weeks passed away; the stipulated ransom was
paid, the hostages were delivered up, and they left
the castle.

Poor Mava now felt as if a pall had been cast over
every object around; she no longer rambled about
the cliffs or rode through the country, but wandered
listlessly through the castle, or sat silently looking
out on the ocean.

The change in the Lady Mava was visible to all;
but Sheelah, her faithful nurse, alone guessed the
cause of her darling's altered looks and abstracted
manner.

Hoping to change her thoughts and stimulate her to exertion, she detailed how much misery her absence from visiting her poor sick and infirm dependants would occasion. By this appeal to her benevolence and sympathy Mava was roused from her apathy, and went in and out among her people as formerly.

One sultry morning Mava rode off, accompanied by Sheelah's son, Paudeen, carrying a plentiful supply of articles suited to the wants of her dependants. Many were the fervent blessings invoked on the lovely, gracious, and graceful maiden, whose glowing face and eyes, lighted up with smiles, or moistened with tears, showed the lively interest which she still took in the joys or sorrows of her humble friends.

"Paudeen," said she, (when all their stores were exhausted,) " return to the castle and tell nurse that I have gone for a ride on the strand; I'll be back for dinner." So saying she started off at a smart trot in that direction. As she was passing the Wishing Arch a figure stepped out. Could she believe it? Yes; surely it was Reginald who approached towards her.

The tell-tale blushes which suffused her countenance, and her hesitating manner, betrayed the interest she felt, and her gratification at again seeing him; nor could Reginald conceal his joy at meeting her. Just then a flash of lightning, succeeded by a loud peal of thunder, passed over their heads, and reverberated like a discharge of artillery among the cliffs and caverns of the white rocks.

Reginald led the pony under the arch, and in a

short time he had, in ardent words, poured forth his tale of love; and Mava had laid her head on his shoulder; had wept, smiled, and allowed herself to be clasped in her lover's arms, forgetful alike of the angry warfare of the elements and the irreconcilable enmity which existed between the M'Quillans and O'Cahans.

It was then arranged between the lovers that the Wishing Arch should be the place of meeting as often as Reginald could get away without exciting the suspicion of his kinsmen.

Mava did not arrive at the castle till late in the afternoon, but the storm accounted for her delay. Sheelah was delighted to see from that day, by Mava's heightened colour and improved spirits, that she was becoming more like her former self; nor had she again to be urged to ride about. Shoanan was often ordered out for a trot along the strand, and there frequently the happy, loving, youthful pair spent many a blissful hour; nor was their meeting known or even suspected by any of the members of either clan.

The Lord of Dunluce had been absent for some weeks on a hunting expedition in the territory of his kinsman Rory Oge M'Quillan. He returned home, accompanied by his host and a large assemblage of friends and adherents, to keep high holiday at the castle.

Mava always disliked to have to associate with these savage men, but now she felt a stronger repugnance towards them, and her heart recoiled from hav-

ing to encounter the gaze of Rory Oge, whose looks
on a former visit caused her to shudder; now she
loathed his very name.

Throughout the greater part of the night the loud
laugh, the coarse voice, and all the sounds of revelry
and carouse might be heard through the castle, drowning the noise of the loud breakers which dashed
against its adamantine foundations, and making even
the noisy blustering wind without seem gentle compared to the tumultuous din within the walls.

After a few hours' sleep the revellers arose at daybreak, and prepared to go fox-hunting in the vicinity
of Dunmull.

As Mava had accompanied them on former occasions, it was fully expected she would do so now; but
she gave orders that her steed should not be caparisoned or brought out.

When M'Quillan heard this, and came to ask why
she was not coming, she gave an evasive answer, begging to be excused, on which the old dark frown returned to the chieftain's brow; and with a fierce
glance he left her, and flinging himself on his powerful steed, accompanied by his numerous party, rode off.

Another night of orgies succeeded the fox-hunt.

Next morning Mava was summoned into her kinsman's presence, and there presented to Rory Oge as
her destined husband.

Transfixed with horror for some minutes, she stood
silent and motionless as if spell-bound; then glancing
wildly at the chiefs, she fell on her knees, and clasping her hands above her head, with a gasp wailed

forth most piteously, " I cannot ; I will not ; I implore you not to ask me ; " then, overcome by the effort, she dropped fainting at their feet.

Rory Oge left that day, and the Lord of Dunluce paced the ramparts like a caged lion, muttering curses both loud and deep on the maiden for attempting to gainsay his will. The idea of her loving another never entered his mind. Rory Oge had not thought so, and placed spies about, who soon reported having seen Reginald disguised wandering about the castle. He had been disappointed at not meeting Mava at the usual trysting-place, and fearing something had occurred, (he knew not what,) he ventured about the precincts of the castle, and through the garrulity of the dependants learned what had occurred.

A messenger from Rory soon informed M'Quillan of the true state of the case. "So, so !" he hissed between his teeth, and striking his clenched fist against the palm of his left hand, " I now find what causes the minx to refuse to marry her kinsman ; but by the bones of holy St Patrick she 'll have to be his wife ; never, never shall she wed another, and that other an O'Cahan. Ole do curp agus anam, (bad luck to them body and soul.) "

Next morning Mava was told that there was no alternative ; she must within a year become Rory Oge's bride.

" I 'll suffer death first," she passionately exclaimed.

" We 'll see," said the grim chieftain, " when you spend a week in the lock-up tower in solitary confinement, whether you will gainsay my wishes."

" Welcome imprisonment, or even death," wailed forth the poor maiden ; "anything is preferable to being married to a man I hate and despise."

M'Quillan's savage nature broke forth in all its fury, and catching the trembling girl by her arm, he dragged her along to the tower, pushed her in, closed the door, calling down curses on her and her lover, whose name in his wrath he had allowed to escape his lips. Turning the key in the massive lock, he flung it to the warder, and strode over the draw-bridge, hoping to meet Reginald, on whom he would have wreaked his vengeance.

The inmates of the castle were awe-stricken at the cruelty practised on their darling lady, but M'Quillan was known to be relentless ; even Sheelah dared not interfere. All she could accomplish was permission to remove a couch and some other necessary articles of furniture and apparel to the tower. When this was done, she was told that Mava must occupy the tower alone, as no one would be permitted to speak to her but the chieftain himself.

Wearily passed the days, and more wearily the nights. No one came near her but the warder and an attendant, who at stated times brought her food, but did not utter a word ; willingly would they have assured her of the sorrow which they and all about the castle felt for her, but they feared the wrath of their stern lord, and only by looks could express the sympathy they felt for her unhappy condition.

A week passed over, M'Quillan appeared before her, and demanded what answer would be sent to

Rory Oge. " Death, my lord, before I consent to be his wife."

" Rash girl, you have decided for yourself; but leave this tower you never shall till you accept of the hand of your noble kinsman."

" Yes, my chief, I have decided ; prison, death, anything but wed Rory Oge."

" Be it so ; I 'll humble your pride, you wantwit ; you 'll not have any one to wait on you ; you 'll have to perform the most menial offices for yourself ; " and seizing a broom which was at the entrance door, he flung it at the terrified girl, exclaiming, " There, sweep your chamber if you prefer it to becoming an honoured lady."

The night which succeeded this interview was passed by poor Mava in an agony of spirit; she dreaded that M'Quillan would take summary vengeance on her lover.

Bitter were the tears she shed ; filled with such sorrowful thoughts she could not sleep during the silent watches of the night.

Just as the morning star appeared, she thought she heard a noise in the chamber below, as if some one was sweeping it, and rousing herself up to listen, distinctly heard the floor being swept, and the motion of the broom, accompanied by the following words, chanted in a low voice :—

> " Sweet lady sleep,
> No longer weep,
> For Reginald's good fairy
> Will ply the broom,
> And clean the room,

So that dust or soil,
Of menial toil,
Shall never stain the hand
Of the fairest in the land,
The lovely Lady Mava."

Soothed by these words, and lulled by the monotonous chant, she dropt over asleep, and all her sorrows were forgotten ; in her dreams she stood with Reginald under the Wishing Arch, and enjoyed all the happiness and rapture which two young loving hearts experience when in each other's society.   When she awoke it was bright daylight ; she was refreshed both in body and mind.   How sweet it was to think that she was watched over and cared for by Reginald ; this consoling thought quite revived her almost exhausted hopeless spirit, so that the day did not pass over so wearily.

When night came on and she retired to her couch, she slept soundly until just before daybreak, when she heard the broom at work, and the chant repeated as before.

On the third day M'Quillan again visited her, and seeing the chamber clean, and Mava looking more resigned, thought he had succeeded in bringing her round to accede to his wishes ; he did not address her, but merely glanced around, shook his head, muttered, " It is well," and left the tower.

During the day she commenced to sew at a white garment, which occupation helped to pass the time away.

After the lapse of a few days the maiden was again visited by her guardian, who, observing her engaged sewing, said, "I am glad, Mava, to see you making your bridal robe."

"You mistake, my lord," she replied; "say rather my shroud."

With a mocking laugh, he echoed, "Shroud," and hastily left her.

It was most galling to the proud chief to be thus thwarted by a girl; but he still hoped to make her subservient to his will.

Allowing a week to pass over, he again came to her, and in peremptory tones addressed her: "Mava, I say this is my final visit to you, to demand your compliance with my wishes to wed your noble kinsman."

To this she made no reply, but bent her head low over her work. Her silence exasperated M'Quillan, who tauntingly observed, "Perhaps your bridal dress is not yet completed."

"Oh yes, my shroud is now quite ready."

The melancholy tones in which these words were uttered sunk like an arrow into his heart, causing him to feel that they were prophetic. Seeing that his efforts to make her change her determination were of no avail, he did not again visit her; but her last words were constantly present to his mind, and he became a prey to remorse. He thought of his dead wife, of his babe whom he had scarcely looked at. Then the recollection of Mava's artless, winning ways, her sprightly manner, and her lovely form, the picture of health and happiness; and what was she now?—pale, dejected, and hopeless.

Then the recollection of Reginald's frank, youthful countenance, his manly bearing, and the soothing influence his music had in calming down his own angry passions ; truly the youth and maiden seemed fitted for each other, and were equals by birth, but how could he give his consent for her to be united to the kinsman of his deadliest foe ? How submit to confess he had been conquered by her ? Besides, by yielding to her wishes he would bring on himself the vengeance of Rory for breaking faith with him.

After a struggle, the stern man relented, and he formed a [plan to allow her (seemingly without his knowledge) to escape with her lover.

A message was sent to Reginald, as if from Mava, begging of him to come to the castle next evening ; that M'Quillan would be absent, and she was prepared to elope with him. This was unexpected and joyful news to Reginald, who promised to take a boat there to carry her off.

Mava knew nothing of this in her solitary prison ; she had heard the tramp and clangour of armed men that morning, and looking out had seen M'Quillan depart, as if for a lengthened absence.

A sudden terror seized her ; perhaps he was going to capture Reginald, kill him, or bring her beloved and hang him on the Gallows Hill just opposite. Or, even worse, was he going to bring the hated Rory, and by violence force her to be married to him ? " But sooner than be united to him, I 'll throw myself headlong from the top of the tower into the ocean beneath." These harrowing thoughts took complete possession of her mind ; she felt an instinctive knowledge of some dreadful coming event ; and as life had now no hope for her, she only looked forward to death as a conclusion to her sorrows.

Occupied with these sad thoughts, she arrayed herself in the white robe, and stood gazing out on the mighty deep, at that time agitated by a coming storm. A boat then appeared in view, breasting the stormy billows. As it neared the land, she thought, "How like is that figure at the helm to my Reginald ! Can it be possible ? or do my eyes deceive me ? Surely it is Reginald !"

As the boat approached nearer to the castle, she was then certain it could be no other ; her heart throbbed violently, and the certainty that her lover was near her infused fresh vigour into her frame, and hope returned into her bosom.

Presently the key turned in the lock ; the door opened, and a muffled figure bade her follow him.

"Where, and to whom am I to go ?"

"The Lord Reginald waits in the cave beneath the castle ; it was he who sent me."

She needed no further words, but sped on towards the cave, and down the rough-hewn steps, her white dress fluttering in the breeze.

With what transports did the lovers meet ! Every sorrow and fear were swallowed up in the bliss of being again united.

"Dearest, there is danger in delay. We must start at once ;" and lifting her tenderly, Reginald carried her into the boat, saying the Lady Mava deserved a

L

nobler escort, and stooping over her, imprinted a long kiss on her marble brow, and whispered, " Muirnin Maebhi mo mhile stoirin, * we 'll fly to France, and love and happiness are in store for us." So spake youth, love, and hope ; but, alas ! fate had willed it otherwise.

Anxious to know if his plans had succeeded, M'Quillan had returned unattended and disguised, so as to escape notice. He was informed by the warder that, obeying his instructions, he had unlocked the door of the tower, and escorted the Lady Mava to the subterranean cavern, where the Lord Reginald had brought a boat, in which she went off with him more than half an hour ago.

M'Quillan cast an anxious, troubled glance towards the sky, and then down at the foaming billows.

" Phelim," asked he, " what think ye of the weather ? "

" Angry, my lord."

" Angry, ay angry," muttered the chief; " another prophecy."

Standing on the top of the highest tower, M'Quillan's eyes were riveted on the frail bark which, impelled by four strong rowers, strove to make way against the wind and tide. The dark figure at the helm he well knew was Reginald, and at his feet lay a white object ; this was undoubtedly Mava.

" The shroud," he exclaimed ; and ever and anon as the boat sunk in the trough of the waves he held in

* Anglice, " Darling Mava, my thousand treasures."

his breath, and when it surmounted the crest of the billow he heaved a sigh of relief; but night was quickly coming on, and if the boat could not make way past the White Rocks before darkness set in, her doom was sealed.

The gale increased, the waves rose mountains high, and dashed in fury against the cliffs, and surged back with an angry roar as if in wrath at not being able to surmount or overturn these adamantine walls which form a barrier, and seem to say to the billows, " Thus far shalt thou come, and here shall thy proud waves be stayed."

But fiercer and more tumultuous than the elements were the emotions which raged within the bosom of the Lord of Dunluce.

How impotent he felt. What availed his power now ? The only beings he ever felt love or compassion for were now in that boat.

Kneeling at her lover's feet was the gentle, lovely girl ; as a sacrifice to his pride he had sent her forth to meet a watery grave or be dashed to pieces against the rocks.

Beating his breast, he exclaimed wildly, " The shroud, the shroud ! angry, ay angry ; but I 'll save her ;" and so saying dashed over the drawbridge and down the steep path to the bay, where the boats were drawn up on the beach ; the force of strong arms soon shoved them into the water ; but when the men attempted to make way against the foaming ocean, all their efforts were of no avail ; the oars were dashed out of their hands, and the boats thrown like drift-weed against the rocks; others were swamped; and awful beyond description was the scene.

The shouts of the drowning mingled with the roar of the waves and winds, and above the noise of all rose the loud voice of Dunluce's unhappy lord, commanding, threatening, promising, cursing, and occasionally muttering, "Angry, angry, ay angry. The shroud is quite ready now,"—her last words.

Foiled in their efforts to launch the boats, they resorted to the cliffs overlooking the white caves, but there a heart-rending sight met their view; the oars had been dashed out of the strong hands of the rowers; the boat was now unmanageable; the tide was setting in towards the land; she drifted towards it, and must inevitably be dashed to pieces against the iron-bound coast.

White was the blinding spray which surged over and against the rocks, and white the foaming waves which threatened every moment to engulph the frail bark in their depths; but whiter than all to M'Quillan's gaze seemed the object which leaned against the dark figure at the stern.

Cresting a gigantic wave, the boat remained there for a few moments, (to the chief it seemed hours;) plainly he saw the maiden stretch up her hands towards heaven in the attitude he had before seen her when she implored him not to ask her to wed the man she detested. All this now came clearly before his recollection. "My injured, my loved Mava, oh forgive me," he shouted in agonising tones; and to his ear the tempest seemed to reply, " The shroud is quite ready now."

The next moment all was out of sight ; the waves had swamped the boat, it was sunk in the depths of the ocean ; presently in the vortex of the seething waves appeared a dark speck, a vivid glance of sheet-lightning now shot over the waters, revealing with unmistakable minuteness the exact contour of Reginald's countenance ; with one arm he buffeted the waves, and on the other hung Mava, her long bright tresses floating like golden seaweed on the upheaving billows ; as if indued with supernatural strength he swam towards the land, and when thrown back, re-doubled his efforts until he had nearly gained the shore ; but a fearful wave dashed him against a rock and fractured his skull. Mava's fragile figure was then carried off by the rebound of the wave till, met by another, it was drifted further and further away. " Save her ! oh, save her !" was the agonising cry of the chieftain ; " half of my possessions I'll give to the man who will restore my injured Mava to my arms."

But powerless as his threats and commands had been, so were the offers of his wealth.

Resolute men were there, who from hardihood or love of gain, and some from compassion and for the sake of the lady so dearly loved, had clambered down the rocks, or been let down with ropes to the beach below ; but the tide was then at its height, the water filled the caves, and dashed the pebbles against their roofs and sides ; it was then dark and blowing a hurricane, so that torches were extinguished, and human aid was of no avail.

M'Quillan remained on the strand all night, battling with the tempest, and often repeating, " Angry, ay angry. The shroud is now ready."

Next morning at dawn Reginald's body was found, but Lady Mava's never. The sea has not yet given up its dead !

To this day it is firmly believed by some of the members of the family that Mava Roe, clad in her shroud, appears previous to the death of a true descendant of the M'Quillans, uttering her last words which were borne across the stormy billows, " The shroud is ready now."

Reginald's good fairy still plies her broom, but the chant has never again been heard ; it is for ever silent !

CHAPTER XVII.

DURING the next week Edward rode over on Rodger to Dunluce, and on his arrival was heartily greeted by Lucy, who was in ecstasies at seeing both. Edward's glee was equal to Lucy's on rejoining them.

Oh what happiness the young people now enjoy! but a cloud appears in the horizon, which will burst over this joyous party; however let us

> " Check not in its gladness
> The young heart's wild glow,
> For the hour of sadness
> Soon, alas! 'twill know."

but rather

> " Cherish youth's gay laughter
> Ere it learn to mourn;
> For such tones hereafter
> Never can return."

So we shall not anticipate sorrow, but rather dwell on those happy days when all was bright, and tinged with hope and "Love's young dream." The happiness of the little circle was further increased and prolonged on being joined by Mr Rutherford and Margaret.

The Giant's Causeway had not yet been visited

and it was arranged they should all go, accompanied by cousin Mary, who, from having heard so much of this great natural curiosity, was most anxious to see it, and to hear it described by her uncle and cousin John.

When the party came to the head-land overlooking the Causeway, the young people exclaimed in disappointed tones, "And is that what we came so far to see."

"I expected," said Mr Rutherford, "what would be your feelings, as from this there is nothing strikingly grand; but let us proceed along the path, made at the expense of the Earl of Bristol in the early part of this century. The walk forms a terrace underneath the cliffs, and leads to where the basaltic formation is uncovered; those conical hills are called 'the Steuchans' or 'Stookins,' from being shaped like stooks of grain."

"And," said John, "there is the rock which from its resemblance to an old woman wrapped in a cloak, and the hood over her head, is called the Giant's Grandmother."

"Is she the banshee of this place?" asked the youngsters.

"Oh no," was the reply; "you must remember that this is the region of the GIANTS. There," pointing across the bay, "is the grand causeway, which stretches upwards of seven hundred feet into the sea; the guides aver that it is the pathway Finn MacCoul constructed for the Scotch giant to come across to fight him."

Here they were joined by M'Mullan the guide,[*] who took up the description saying, "Yer honour forgot to tell the leddies that after Finn had gi'en the Scotch giant a good 'lickin''[†] an' sent him back to his own country with a skinful o' broken bones, he then sunk the middle part o' the causey, an' jist left the bit at Fingal's Cave in Scotland standin' to be a mimorandum to the Scotch giant of what Finn cud do if he was timpt' by him again. They say he was a mighty man entirely, bein' the hoyte o' half a score o' the cliverest men now-a-days—fifteen cupids high, a colledge gintleman said he was; so yer riverence will aptly know how mony feet that is."

"Farther round we shall see the Giant's Loom, Wash-basin, Organ, Chair, &c., but here we are at the 'Giant's Well;' we must taste the water which bubbles up between the rocks; it is delightfully pure, and has been pronounced by scientific men to be. 'the lightest water known.'"

"Let us go and have a chat with old Lillie, who has

---

[*] The manners, speech, and character of the guides are completely changed within the last fifty years.

Formerly they told legends, improvised doggrel rhymes, and related all kinds of impossible and improbable stories. A judicious writer of the present time, Mrs S. C. Hall, observes the difference between them and the Kerry and Wicklow guides. "The Northern guides," she remarks, "are people of knowledge--geologists—learned in the names of stones—conversant with stratas and basalts; stiff and steady; observant and particular; they are remarkable for the exactness and minutiæ of their details; they talk with a profound air of hexagons and octagons, and have the mystified look of philosophers."

[†] Anglice, beating or castigation.

charge of the well; she sells the water, but gives 'a drop of the crathur' out of the bottle beside her for nothing."

The young people had to partake of the water, as there were certain virtues consequent on doing so, and penalties attached if neglected; of course these rules were of a ludicrous character, and provoked general mirth.

"Lillie," said John, "when I was here before, you told me a story about Adam Morning; will you tell it now to the ladies?"

"Och, your honour and ladies, sure I'll do that. Adam tuk the farm above of 'The Aird,' but he had no luck with it ava'. The first year the wind blasted all his crop; the second year it was the same; and the third was little better. He had a son who was a clean cliver boy; he wasn't long married till he was seized by a press-gang, an' taken aff on boord a man-o'-war. His father and mother had hard times o' it, an' young Davy's wife was brought to bed of a son; and not long after Adam and his wife were climbing up the path from the bay below, with loads of rack on their backs to burn for kelp, the rope giv way, and Adam fell down nearly three hundred feet into the say, and was both kilt and drownded. Shortly after, Davy's vessel was paid aff, an' he brought home lashins o' gran' things frae foreign parts. Folk here said money wud hae been o' more sarvice nor watches an' shoe-buckles an' sich like; but he aye said guineas wud hae been stolen frae him, an' that he'd barter them for what he wanted.

Ye may be sure he was raal sorry at his father's death, but he set himsel' to labour the lan', hopin' to make a better o' it. When Armoy fair cam roun' he went there an' bought a horse for a watch an' other di-dies, but poor Davy was fairly taen in, the horse was sae auld an' stiff, that it was no use ava in the dour, clay land o' 'The Aird.' Next fair he tuk the horse an' swapped it for another, gieing the rest o' his prizes for boot. But when he brought it hame, it was as muckle too young as the ither was too auld, but Davy laughed an' said every day wud mend that fault."

"What a doleful tale," exclaimed the girls. "Oh," said Lucy, "I'd rather hear one ending well like the old stories, and they all lived happily together, and may we all be far happier."

"Well, Miss, and so they did; Davy and his wife get on geyly thegither; he still keeps up his heart and goes about singing,

> 'We hae aye been provided for
> An' sae wull we yet;'

his craps are no to say bad, an' young Adam is one o' the boys ye'll meet on the Causey yonder sellin' 'space-a-mens.' "*

* For a dozen years or more, and till within a few days of his death, this Adam was the guardian of the well, and will be remembered by those who have visited the Causeway lately as having for his stock-in-trade the story of his grandfather's death, as well as a bottle of the genuine Bushmills whisky. He only died, aged eighty-five, in the autumn of 1864; his photographic portrait, in stereographs and cartes of the Giant's Well, has been taken by tourists to all parts of the world: at this time he was called "Old Adam."

"Uncle," said Mary, "do explain to us how it comes that these rocks are so regular in form, looking as if they were chiselled by the art of man, and yet of such extent as to be beyond his power to make."

"Yes, girl," replied Mr Rutherford, "your remarks are correct; the army of Xerxes, with Archimedes to guide them, could not have constructed it; in the Grand Causeway alone it has been calculated there are forty thousand columns of prismatic shapes, principally hexagonal or pentagonal, the latter being the most frequent; there are others with four, three, seven, and eight sides, but only one with nine. The columns, you will perceive, fit in so closely to each other, that there would not even be room for 'the sharp blade of Luno's sword' to penetrate between them. You may remember, John, in Ossian's Poems that Luno was smith or armourer to Fingal, who 'tis thought was identical with the traditional architect of this place under the name of Finn MacCoul, or MacCumhal.

"Dr Drummond," said John, "in his poem on the 'Giant's Causeway,' (just published before I left Dublin,) expresses the same ideas—

> ' A far-projecting, firm basaltic way
> Of clustering columns, wedged in dense array,
> With skill so like, yet so surpassing art,
> With such design, so just in every part,
> That reason pauses, doubtful if it stand
> The work of mortal or immortal hand.'

I have the book in my pocket, and if you all promise

(Lucy and Edward included) to be an attentive audience, I will read you some extracts before we return to Dunluce."

Mr Rutherford then explained that the word "basalt" is, by some writers, derived from a Hebrew word signifying iron, or baked, or burned. Pliny describes it as a rock of iron colour and hardness.

"The celebrated statue of Memnon, said to emit musical sounds when struck by the first rays of the rising sun, was formed of this rock.

"You may also observe, girls, that these columns are in joints, the concave and convex fitting into each other; the columns vary in shape in a greater or less degree, so that a joint, if taken off one, would not fit on any other. You also see the concave is indented with a groove near the circumference, and furnished with a projection from one of its sides or angles, by which it is so closely locked to the ball of its corresponding stone that a separation is not effected without a fracture of that projection."

All the party now became interested, and declared that after all they thought it a wonderful place, although there was nothing to be seen but rocks, sea, and bold headlands.

"Yes, my children," said Mr Rutherford, "the Giant's Causeway itself is comparatively small and insignificant; its chief importance is derived from the surrounding scenery, and from association with its creative cause. Sedate and majestic, its characteristics are not to be developed by a rapid glance, but require attentive examination; and to have its

beauty comprehended, the whole must be considered
in detail, and visited frequently."

Here the guide, pointing to several large rocks unlike the rest, said, " They're the Giant's marvels, yer
riverence. A pheelosophee gintleman (I disremem-
ber his name just now) tould me as how the Causay
was made by big boulders like thae (whin-stone he
ca'd them) bein' all melted, and that when they
cooled an' hardened they made the six-a-gons, an'
all the other shaped stones ; so it's like these are the
cinders, the same as the big lumps left in the lime-
kilns at the White Rocks, when the kiln has done
burning."

The gentlemen smiled at this description, and
Mary and Margaret applied to them for a more
authentic and scientific explanation, but were told it
would take a long time to discuss the distinct and
opposite theories of the Plutonian and Neptunian
systems, the former ascribing the formation of basalt
to fire, and the latter to water; but books would be
supplied to them to read fully about it on their return
home.

" But," said one of the young people, " I see mother,
Agnes, and Cousin Bessie preparing for our pic-nic
beneath the columns of ' The Loom,' so we had better
proceed there at once."

Among all the many joyous parties which, before
and since, have rested themselves on the seats provided by nature for their accommodation, a happier
and merrier group could not have been found ; each
was happy in themselves, and pleased with each

other's society. No care for the future, or regret for
the past, dimmed the enjoyment of the young people ;
so the laugh and jest went merrily round.

After the repast the young people were starting off
abruptly, but were recalled by Mr Rutherford.

"You have forgotten," said he, "to wait until
thanks were returned after our meal. Oh ! how
often, like the lepers in the Scriptures, do we call
upon the Lord when in trial and affliction, but when
in health, comfort, and prosperity we forget to render thanks to Him for all the benefits He has conferred upon us ! True, we are encouraged to call
upon Him in the day of trouble, and He has promised to hear us ; but we are also told that he who
'offereth praise glorifieth God.' Let us not imitate
the nine lepers, but rather follow the example of the
one who returned to thank and bless the Saviour
—'And in all things, whether we eat or drink, or
whatsoever we do, let us do all to the glory of God.'"

Then rising off his rocky seat, and reverently un-
covering his head, Mr Rutherford thanked God fervently for supplying the bodily wants of himself and
friends, and prayed that they all might "so pass
through things temporal, that finally they lost not
the things eternal."

They were then joined by a troop of guides to
assist in clearing up, which they did most efficiently,
saving the trouble of carrying away fragments.

While the process of packing up was going on
under the supervision of Mr and Mrs Rutherford, the
youngsters strolled round Port Noffer Bay to see the

Giant's Organ, and get a closer view of the headlands called "The Chimney Tops," which the guide told them had been fired at by some of the vessels of the Spanish Armada, who mistook them for the chimneys of Dunluce Castle.

"An' a brave tall chimley for a house one o' them wud be," said M'Mullan, "as it is forty-five feet high."

"Here, I think," said John, "is where Mrs Susanna Drury took one of her sketches. Her drawings are considered very correct : they have been exhibited in Dublin, and a premium awarded to her for them by the Society for the Encouragement of Art.*

The "Sheep-path" was then to be clambered. This is a zigzag footpath up the face of the cliff, which is upwards of three hundred feet high, and nearly per-

* The two original drawings, taken in 1736, were in the possession of Dr Baring of Trinity College ; at his death they passed into the hands of a gentleman in the neighbourhood of the Giant's Causeway, who still retains them. After being exhibited in Dublin they were sent to London to be engraved ; but the vessel they were in was seized by a French privateer, which was on the look-out for a survey of Ireland, taken by General Valency. The pictures were lost sight of for a time, but afterwards recovered and engraved by Vivares in London. A pair of the original engravings are still to be seen in the Dublin Museum. In 1837 Mr Hodgson of Belfast found the copper-plates in London ; modernised the costumes of figures in the foreground of these pictures, and republished them. In 1851 the east view was again reproduced, and exhibited in London. Being a contribution from Ireland to the Exhibition, the artist was desirous to make it thoroughly Irish in all its details. It was a facsimile of the engraving worked by an Irishwoman on Irish linen with the ravellings of crape and fine black silk, and framed in Irish oak. It was awarded a prize medal. At the New York World's Fair, 1853, it also obtained a medal, and narrowly escaped destruction there. The picture had not long been removed, when the Exhibition building took fire, and in an incredibly short time the whole structure and its contents were destroyed.

pendicular. The ascent is tiresome; but young,
active limbs, and cheerful dispositions, are not deterred by the prospect of fatigue.

Grasping at the rocks to gain a steady footing,
stumbling, catching at the grass, or going on all-fours,
elicited many a laugh and jest. But when the height
was gained, the trouble of ascending was forgotten in
the contemplation of the matchless bays and bold
headlands which presented themselves to view.

"Oh, how glorious!" exclaimed the whole party;
"why, this is grander than the Causeway." "Shure,
yer honour and leddyships," said M'Mullan, "it's all
the Giant's Causay, an' the biggest half too; but the
most part of the leddys that come here are fear'd to
climb, an' the gentlemen either won't quit the leddies,
or else won't fash themselves by goin';—but yees
shud take a boat to the caves, an' go all roun' an' see
the 'Pleaskin Bay,' an' 'Head,' an' all the rest o' the
curosities o' the place."

"I thought," interrupted Mary, pointing to a head-
land with basaltic columns, "that this was Pleaskin."

"Och! na, yer leddyship, Pleaskin has three rows
of columns in the face o' it; it's farther roun', an' so
is 'The King an' his Nobles,' 'The Priest an' his
Flock,' an' 'The Nurse an' Child Rocks,' an' iver so
many more."

"M'Mullan, do tell us something about the rocks
you've named," said Lucy; "are there not some
legends about them?"

"Well, Alick, my nevy, knows more o' thae stories

M

nor I do; he's sae glib at them, he's called Alick M'Cock, but I'll just tell yees one I remimber; it's about 'The Nurse an' Child.'

"Ye see one o' the giants that lived here in the ould ancient times had a wife that had no weans; an' as he natrally enough wished to hae childer, an' aften said he wished he had another wife that wud have a son, this fretted his wife, an' what does she do but purtend she was in the family-way; an' when her time come she got the midwife to bring her a boy child, an' pass it aff for her own. The giant was quare an' plased; but somehow he tuk it into his head that the wean wasn't like him, an' as his wife didn't suckle it, an' niver bothered herself much about it, he got mighty onaisy, an' at last went to ask a witch wife how he'd find out if it was his own son or not. So she tells him to bid his wife take the babby in her arrums, an' go an' sit on a rock she pointed out to him, an' for him to tak a han'ful o' san' an' throw it in her face, an' say, 'For the truth;' an' if it's not your wean, says she, her an' it'll be turned into stone, says she; but be shure an' not let on till her what ye're doin' it for, says she. So he comes an' tells her to take her son, an' go an' sit where he bid her. She was both proud and lazy, an' says she, the nurse may take him. But he up and tells her she was bound to obey him. An' as he was in a towerin' passion, threatened to give her a clout on the lug* if she did not do as he bid her. An' aff she had to go, an' him followin' her all the while; an' when she

* A box on the ear.

sat down on the rock he threw a han'ful o' san' at her, an' repated the words 'For the truth,' as the witch-wife had tould him, an' at onest she turned into stone, with the babby in her arms, an' so they remain till this day."

"Served her right!" said John.

"Well done, M'Mullan," echoed from all the party; "Alick M'Cock could not have done better."

"Tell me," said Edward, "where are the giants now? did you ever see them, M'Mullan?"

"Well, I can't say I iver did, barrin' in a dhrame; "ye see, yer honour, them things that are out o' natur' never lasts."

"But," pertinaciously insisted Edward, "when was the very last giant seen here?"

"Och, an' it's myself can tell yez; shure it was the hermit that lived in Portcoon Cave ayont there; ye see he was coortin' a joyentess that lived in Port-rush, an' a furriner came in atween them, an' married her, an' tuk her away to France; an' it was towld how that her man put her in a show-box, an' ex-hibited her in Lunnon and other furrin parts. The poor desaved joyent tuk it sore to heart, and shut himself up in Portcoon Cave, an vowed he'd not taste food brought to him by mortial hands; but the sales, the craturs, tuk pity on him and brought him mate an' as they are not mortials, but lives whiles in the say, an' whiles on the lan', he ate it from them; an' then he thought better of starvin' himsel' to death, tuk heart again, an' went about doin' good, and died in his bed beside Port-na-Spania yonder ahint us, an' was burried at Mount Sandy, near Cowlrane, where his grave is to be seen to this day." *

"Look," said John, "there is father waving his handkerchief to attract our attention ; he beckons us to return by the headlands ; he, mother, and hampers are in motion, so we had better walk along and meet them."

"How little they look," said Agnes ; "and the grand Causeway and Stookans seem so small from this height."

"And the sheep down there," said Lucy, "don't look bigger than Mrs Moore's Manx cat."

Jesting in this way the happy party walked along, and rejoined Mr and Mrs Rutherford at Port-na-baw.

"Your nephew," said Mr R., addressing M'Mullan, "tells me that this bay is called Port-na-baw, but cannot tell what the name is derived from. Can you inform me ?"

"Shure it 's not becoming in me to larn yer riverence ; but I ax yer pardin, ye hae dootless forgot more nor iver the likes o' me learned. Yer riverence will call to yer remimberance that Finn MacCoull

---

* Notwithstanding that an Irishman is generally believed to have a sixth sense, viz., nonsense, yet in the midst of seeming lies there may be a grain of truth, as the extract which follows, copied from one of the Sloane MSS. in the British Museum will prove :—" I James Paris saw a woman in Ireland in 1696, who was born at Portrush, not far from the wonderful Causeway, in the most northern part of Ireland. She was then twenty-three years old, and stood seven feet high without shoes or head clothes, very well shaped, with a very handsome face. In the year 1701 she was at Montpellier in Languedoc, in France, at the time of the fair, where I saw her again being shown for money, as she had been before in London."

was tuk prisoner by King Cormac MacArt, and no money could ransom him; for the ould bla'guard concocted a plan by which he thought he wud hev Finn all'ays in his power. So when Finn's friends (an' they were many) come to inquire what was the sum the king wanted for his release, he wudn't ask no money on no tarms; but, says he, 'I'll let him free whenever ye bring me two and two, male and faymale,' says he, 'of ivvery bird an' baste throughout all Ireland,' says he.

"But the ould villain was sore surprised when, a year and a day after, who shud appear at the Castle o' Tara but Finn's foster-brother, Cailte MacRonain. 'King Cormac,' says he, 'ye'll hae to relase Finn at onest; for on the green ye'll fin' two and two of ivvery bird and baste to be had throughout all the len'th an' bredth o' the lan'.'

"So the ould daysaver had nothing for it but to give him up. An' Finn, when he got back to his own country, he set about making stone effigies of different bastes, to place as mimerandums all round his possessions; for, says he, when I am dead and gone, I'd like all them that comes afther me to hear tell o' the love o' my brother, an' the mighty deed he done for me, to be a moral to all ginirations. Yon big stone cow was then put up, an' the bay called Na Baw, being the Irish for cow, as yer riverence knows right well. Just then the Scotch joyent Benandonner sent Finn word, that if it wasn't for wetting hisself he'd swim over and fight him. Finn then tuk to makin' the Causay; an' when he had it done, the Scotch joyent cum over dry-shod to get a good thrashin', as all the world knows.   Finn guv it to him in raal Irish style."

The party then sat down to rest, and after each (and frequently all together) had told their adventures since they had left "the Loom," it was proposed that, as a finale, John should read what he had promised out of Dr Drummond's poem.

He at once acceded, only remarking, "The difficulty will be in making selections."

"Well, give us the parts which you think applicable to what we've seen to-day," said his father; "we can read all the poem again."

He read as follows :—

> " Come, lonely genius of my natal shore,
> From cave, or bower, wild glen, or mountain hoar ;
> And while by ocean's rugged bounds I muse,
> Thy solemn influence o'er my soul diffuse.
> With joy I hail thy visionary form,
> Rough, dark, august, and clad in night and storm.
> To me more dear thy rocky realm by far,
> The cliff, the whirlwind, and the billowy war,
> Than e'en the loveliest scenes which Flora yields,
> Her myrtle bowers, or incense-breathing fields.
> Oh thou, whose soul the muse's lore inspires,
> Whose bosom science warms, or genius fires,
> If nature charm thee in her wildest forms,
> Throned on the cliff, 'midst cataracts and storms ;
> Or with surpassing harmony array'd,
> In pillar'd mole or towering colonnade,
> Seek Dalriada's wild romantic shore,
> Wind through her valleys, and her capes explore.
> Let Folly's sons to lands far distant roam,
> And praise the charms of every clime but home ;
> Yet sure such scenes can Dalriada boast,
> As please the painter and the poet most.

Swift torrents foaming down the mountain side,
Rocks that in clouds grotesque their summits hide,
Gigantic pyramids, embattled steeps,
Bastions and temples nodding o'er the deeps,
Aërial bridges o'er vast fissures thrown ;
Triumphal arches, gods of living stone,
Æolian anthems, thunder-rifted spires,
And all the wonders of volcanic fires.
Here broken, shatter'd, in confusion dread,
Towers, bridges, arches, gods, and temples spread,
Stupendous wrecks, where awful wildness reigns.
From Albin oft, when darkness veil'd the pole,
Swift o'er the surge the tartan'd plunderers stole,
And Erin's vales with purple torrents ran,
Beneath the claymores of the murd'rous clan ;
Till Cumhal's son to Dalriada's coast,
Led the tall squadrons of his Finnian host,
Where his bold thought the wondrous plan designed,
The proud conception of a giant mind,
To bridge the ocean for the march of war,
And wheel round Albin's shores his conquering car.
Deep in the dreary caves of ocean lie
The ponderous ruins, far from mortal eye ;
Yet each abutment of the structure stands,
A proud memorial of the giant bands,
Through earth's extended realms renowned afar,
As great in peace and terrible in war.
Dark o'er the foam-white waves
The giant pier the war of tempests braves ;
A far-projecting, firm basaltic way
Of clustering columns, wedged in dense array ;
With skill so like, yet so surpassing art,
With such design, so just in every part,
That reason pauses, doubtful if it stand   .
The work of mortal or immortal hand.
The sportive fancy of th' untutored swain,
To wonder prone, and slave to terror's reign ;
Unskilled to search how Nature's plastic hand
Moulds the rough rock, and form the solid land ;
To Fion, ruler of the giant line,
Ascribes the glory of the grand design ;

> And fondly dreams, though reason spurn the thought,
> That human power the massy fabric wrought.' "

During the time John was reading, the bright rays of the setting sun shed a golden radiance over the scene, causing each rock, headland, and promontory, with the various strata, to stand out prominently.

"See," said Mary, "even the dull, prosaic granite, whinstone, and adamantine cliffs are lighted up and warmed, as if sympathising with the writer who appreciated and admired them so justly."

"My children," said Mr Rutherford, "admiration of the works of the Creator is enjoyable, but the Christian who, by faith in the Saviour, has been adopted into the family of God, can appropriate all he sees to himself, and say, 'My Father made them all.' "

"What a glorious sunset," remarked Mrs Rutherford ; "often, when gazing on such brilliantly-tinted clouds, have I repeated—

> ' When day with farewell beam delays
> Among the opening clouds of even,
> And we can almost think we gaze
> Through golden vistas into heaven ;
> Those rays that make the sun's decline
> So bright, so glorious, Lord, are Thine !' "

"I have frequently heard those words repeated by you, mother," said Margaret, "but never realised them as I do now ; and look, there is also a golden pathway across the sea leading to the golden vista."

"And so it will be with us, my dear daughter, if, in passing over 'the waves of this troublesome world,' we keep our eyes steadfastly fixed on the 'Sun of Righteousness'; our pathway will be lighted up till we finally enter the glorious mansions prepared for those who loved Him."

With reluctance the happy party turned their steps towards Dunluce, all agreeing that, instead of thinking the Causeway dull and uninteresting, as they had pronounced it on the first view, they now declared that it was a most wonderful place, and that they hoped to visit it again and again, as they felt they had only seen a portion of its wonders.

The Giant's Causeway.

CHAPTER XVIII.

JULY came to an end, and the party must return home. The invalids were greatly benefited; but some of the young people did not like the idea of parting. John began to think of Mary in more than a cousinly way; whilst she acknowledged to herself that she experienced towards him a warmer feeling than gratitude warranted in return for the instructions he gave, and the information he imparted to her; but they were both young; he had to return home, and thence back again to college; and she to resume her home duties at the " Royal Arms," Ballynacraig.

Edward's uncle came and took him away to London, so the last day of the month was a sorrowful one. But whether in sorrow or in joy, time will speed on.

Lucy grieved greatly at his departure, but the variety of the journey cheered her up. She felt his absence more on her return home; indeed his departure was universally felt and regretted. Mr Rutherford missed his pupil, and began to suffer from ennui.

At this juncture two events happened which roused up the spirits of the inmates of Thornbrae, and afforded them occupation. The rector of the ad-

joining parish met with an accident, and was obliged
to look out for a curate. Mr Rutherford being ab-
solved from his vow, (as his mother was dead,) applied
for the appointment, and the rector gladly accepted
of his services. This was the first event. The second
was the arrival of a piano, (or spinnet, as it was more
generally called then,) as a present from Edward's
uncles to the Misses Rutherford. Margaret did not
care for music, and had ample employment in assisting her father in compiling his sermons, looking out
texts, references, &c., and visiting the parishioners;
but Agnes and Lucy spent all their leisure time
learning to play on the spinnet. "In my Cottage by a
Wood," "Rousseau's Dream," "Auld Lang Syne,"
"Home, sweet Home," "Nae Luck about the House,"
&c. &c., were to be heard from morning till night re-
sounding through the cottage.

John had returned to college. Hilary (we beg his
pardon, the young doctor) was getting into repute as
a successful practitioner, and was employed occasionally at the Hall, when their regular medical attendant
was not at hand. During these visits Lady Southend, who felt interested in him on account of knowing
his father, now formed a favourable opinion of him
for his own sake. A niece of her ladyship's being in
a delicate state of health, was ordered to go to Madeira for the winter. Dr Rutherford was offered a
large fee if he would accompany the lady and her
mother there. The proposal was acceded to, and we
shall leave him *en route* to that lovely island.

Edward became a prime favourite with his uncles.

He often wrote to Thornbrae, and in his unsophisticated, affectionate manner, "begged to be remembered to every man, woman, and child about the place." Rodger the pony was not forgotten, and many of the other animals mentioned ; even the pigs were thought of with regard. He inquired if the pig which Jamie had pronounced "a beauty" still retained its charms ? &c. &c.

Winter and spring passed over ; John had returned from college, bringing with him a flute, and a collection of Dibdin's songs, and he and his sister practised duets together. In July a letter came from Edward, announcing his intention of visiting his old friends, and remaining with them during the month of August. This news was received with general joy ; many preparations were made for his reception, and the days and hours calculated till his arrival. All about Thornbrae was in a flutter of excitement from early morning of the day Edward was expected to arrive ; and although it was not likely he could reach his destination till the evening, yet every sound was eagerly listened to during the day. The wish prompted the hope that the winds and waves had proved favourable, and wafted him to the green isle in a shorter time than it usually took to accomplish a voyage from London to Belfast.

Every one had something to do to afford pleasure, and give a welcome to their visitor ; so that the day was spent in quite an unsettled manner by all the inmates. Lucy and John in vain attempted to practise "Black-eyed Susan ;" Agnes to read ; Margaret to sew ;

even Mr Rutherford could not continue at his writing
or reading for any length of time. Hector seemed
to comprehend what was going on, as at the slightest
noise he roused himself up, wagged his tail, and
rushed out towards the avenue; then returning quietly,
looked up in Lucy's face, and laid himself down in
his accustomed place at the door of her apartment;
which it will be remembered was off the sitting-room,
and which opened into " The Young Lady's Flower
Knot," (as it was called,) a sweet spot filled with gay
flowers, and redolent of the perfumes of mignonette,
stocks, &c. This parterre was cultivated entirely
by the girls, assisted by John, and on the present
occasion had received more than ordinary care, so as
to do honour and afford gratification to the expected
guest, and the choicest flowers had been culled to
adorn Edward's chambers.

Mrs Rutherford was the only member of the family
who kept on the even tenor of her way, attending to
her household duties as usual; fortunately it was Margaret's week to assist her mother in housekeeping, as
she was less excited than her other sisters. Hour after
hour passed away; at length, just as the sun was
tinging the landscape with its departing golden rays,
Hector pricked up his ears and darted out. The
noise of wheels was then heard, and again a rush was
made to the door. A post-chaise was coming quickly
up the avenue; out of the open window appeared
Edward's happy face, and before the chaise stopped
he had dashed out, kissing and hugging all the party.

Welcome! welcome! resounded from every tongue,

Hector all the time jumping and barking vociferously. Lucy, who had been the foremost to rush and embrace Edward, now drew back blushing, when she looked at his tall manly form and altered appearance. Twelve months had indeed made a great difference, and transformed the slight beardless youth into a full-grown whiskered man ; with self-possessed manners and polished address ; his warm expressions of joy, and bright loving glances, showed how delighted he was to be again in the midst of his old friends and playmates.

Reassured by his manner, Lucy's shyness wore off, and the party were so happy in their mutual reminiscences, that when the time arrived for evening prayers, they could scarcely credit that it was so late.

Next morning proved that in Edward's absence he had been thinking of his friends, as was shown by the care he had taken in selecting and procuring gifts for them.

Each seemed to think he had known their wishes and anticipated their wants. The gifts consisted of books, music, stuffed birds, shells, a paroquet, canary, and a pair of doves, (the latter for Lucy,) a brass collar with Hector's name engraved on it, a bridle for Rodger, and pipes and tobacco for Jamie, and sundry other gifts for his friends, the men, women, and children about the place. Many a hearty grasp of the hand, and fervent " God bless yer honour for minding us an' the childer when ye were over the say. Oh, to think o' the likes o' us gettin' presents all the way from Lunnon :" these and similar remarks quite repaid Edward for his generosity.

CHAPTER XIX.

SHORTLY after Edward's arrival, a letter was received from Mary Wilson, in which she mentioned that her eldest sister Nannie was in rather delicate health, and her mother would be glad, if convenient to Aunt Rutherford, to send her for change of air to Thornbrae. "Write at once Margaret, my dear," said Mrs Rutherford, saying, "we shall be most happy to see Nannie, and hope she'll be benefited by the change." "And say," interrupted Edward, "for Mary to accompany her; we'll then have to take pilgrimages to all the old remains of antiquity. Cousin Mary always ferrets out such things wherever she goes; she and John talk as if they were the age of Methuselah, and had witnessed events which occurred during centuries long past."

The invitation was given, and gladly accepted by Nanny and Mary Wilson. A day or two after their arrival, a visit was proposed to Tullyhogue, formerly the crowning place of the kings of Ulster, situated near Dungannon.

"How do you intend going, children?" asked Mr Rutherford; "it is too far for the girls to walk : will you take the car?"

"Oh, no!" exclaimed they, "it must be a regular

gipsy party; it will be greater fun to take only a
horse and Rodger, and 'ride and tye.'"

Next morning the young people started early to
have a long day. Lucy and Cousin Nanny rode on
Rodger by turns, the other three girls rode alternately
behind John or Edward on a pillion : hung over the
horse's neck was the saddle-bags containing refreshments. Let us follow the happy group until they
arrive at the circular rath of Tullyhogue : the horses'
bridles are thrown over one of the upright stones ; the
party seat themselves, and partake of the viands they
have brought with them.

Edward afterwards mounted on one of the large
stones, and addressing John, said, "In the times of
the monarchs of Ireland each king and chief had a
bard who sung the glories of their ancestors, and
handed down their deeds from one generation to
another ; it is a pity you had not been alive then,
you might have been chief bard to the great O'Neill,
as you can relate so many tales of bygone days, and
events which would supply matter for many a minstrel's theme. Imagine that I am the O'Nial More
and these the ladies of the court, and tell us about
the grand kings, chieftains, knights, and warriors,
from whom all true-born Irishmen claim to be lineally
descended from time immemorial."

"Well, my gracious liege, when you command I
shall cheerfully obey. Our enemies have traduced us
by saying that

> ' Our ancient, but ignoble blood
> Has run through scoundrels since the flood ; '

but I shall prove to you, most high and mighty monarch, and these fair maidens, whose sweet faces are beaming so inspiringly on me, that we are descended from a race of kings, and kings have descended from us, if we would attempt to say anything else, this royal sacred circle, stone inscriptions, and undecaying seats for the nobles would contradict me."

"But the minstrel has no harp," exclaimed the youngsters.

"Alas! alas!" said John,

> " 'Mute, mute the harp! for ever lost the art
> Which roused to rapture each Milesian heart;
> Cold, cold the hands whose thrilling touch sublime,
> Caught the rapt ear, and stay'd the flight of time.'

My friend, Rory Dall O'Cathain, who was the author of some of the most beautiful strains that ever sounded on the harp of Erin, was obliged to flee to Scotland on the downfall of the great O'Neill, and he, a descendant of the sub-king, or chief subject of O'Neill, was compelled to travel from house to house among the nobility and chieftains, where he was received partly as a guest, and partly as a minstrel, requiting their hospitality by the exercise of an art he had acquired as an accomplishment in better days; he was there known by the name of Rory Dall Morrison. Among the visits made by him to the houses of the Scottish nobility, he called at Eglinton Castle. Lady Eglinton not being aware of his rank, affronted his Irish pride by demanding a tune in a peremptory manner. O'Cahan, though blind, poor, and houseless, refused, and left the castle.

N

"Her ladyship afterwards understanding who he was, sought a reconciliation, which was readily effected.

" This incident gave rise to the composition by him of the favourite tune ' Da Mihi Manum,' or ' Give me your hand,' the fame of which afterwards spread throughout Scotland, and reaching the ears of Charles II., induced him to send for the illustrious composer and musician to court. Delighted with his performance, the king walked towards him, and laid his hand familiarly on his shoulder. One of the courtiers present remarking the honour thus conferred upon him, the minstrel replied, ' a greater than King Charles has had his hand on my shoulder.'

" ' Who was that man ? ' said the king.

" ' The O'Neill, sire,' replied Rory Dall, standing up.

" In his latter days he was reduced to very indigent circumstances, and died in the house of a family named Robertson, of Lude, to whom he bequeathed his harp and silver tuning-fork ; the harp had been a present to the minstrel from the unfortunate Mary Queen of Scots."

" Then, as the voice of minstrelsy is mute," said Mary, who longed to hear an authentic account of these really curious antiquarian remains, " John can describe the place without so much circumlocution. Edward, please don't interrupt John in his recital." This request was seconded by Margaret, whose curiosity was also aroused.

" Well," said Edward, jumping off the stone, and flinging himself down at Lucy's feet, " I have to descend from my throne, being deposed by Queen

Mary; after all I am not the first monarch who was glad to cast aside state, and throw himself at the feet of youth and beauty."

"Edward, is there a Blarney Stone in London," said Lucy?

"John, pray do let us know something about this remarkable place," interrupted Mary and Margaret; "we will listen to you, so don't heed the chatter of the rest."

He then told them that in this circular enclosure there formerly stood a stone chair called "Leac na Kiogh," (the stone of the kings,) in which the monarchs of Ulster were crowned and invested with authority. The customs observed at the inauguration were curious, and are graphically described in part of a poem which I shall now repeat to you:—

' Unsandall'd he stands on the foot-dinted rock,
　Like a pillar-stone fix'd against every shock;
　Round, round is the Rath on a far-seeing hill,
　Like his blemishless honour, and vigilant will.
　The greybeards are telling how chiefs by the score
　Have been crown'd on "The stone of the kings" heretofore,
　While crowded, yet order'd, within its green ring
　Are the dynasts and priests round "The true Irish king."

' The chronicler read him the laws of the clan,
　And pledged him to bide by their blessing and ban;
　His sheen and his sword are unbuckled to show
　That they only were meant for a foreigner foe.
　A white willow wand has been put in his hand—
　A type of pure, upright, and gentle command—
　While hierarchs are blessing, the slipper they fling,
　And O'Cahan proclaims him a true Irish king!'

"Casting the slipper as a token of submission is evidently of Eastern origin; the Scriptures refer to it in several places, as 'Over Edom will I cast my shoe.' This symbol of sovereignty was performed by the highest chief, or sub-king, and was considered a highly honourable office."

" This was the origin probably," said Agnes, " of its being considered lucky to throw a slipper after a bridal party, or any one going on a journey ; when you are going, Edward, we'll all throw our slippers at you."

" Oh no, not *at* me, but *after* me."

" But, John," chimed in Mary and Margaret at the same time, "let us hear more about the kings of Ulster."

" I shall only tell you now of the last king, Con O'Nial ; he had taken up arms against Henry VIII., by whose troops he was defeated, and obliged to re-treat to one of his fortresses ; soon after he submitted to the English authority, took the oath of allegiance, renounced the title of king, and the name of O'Nial ; for this submission he was created Earl of Tyr-Owen.

" His son Shane, who was a man of great physical strength, indomitable courage, and of a most ambi-tious mind, stirred up the chiefs to rebellion. After his father's death he made more strenuous exertions, and aimed at recovering the forfeited sovereignty of Ulster ; but being worsted in several encounters with the British troops, he was finally driven into his stronghold of Dungannon by the Lord-Deputy Sus-sex, and compelled to be at peace, but he would not tender his submission to any one but to Elizabeth in person. Perhaps Shane thought he would make a favourable impression on the maiden Queen. Certainly his style, bearing, and retinue, were more like a conqueror, or an independent prince, than a vassal, and one who came to make concessions to the British crown. Escorted by five hundred galloglasses armed with battle-axes, and preceded by a piper, O'Neill marched about ; with surprise the English gazed on the stalwart men attired in shaggy cloaks made out of the undressed skins of animals, yellow shirts, and short tunics. When O'Neill appeared before Her Majesty his followers must have contrasted strongly with her body-guard ; the costume of the beef-eaters being so much ornamented, their close cut hair, and low-crowned hats, hose, and rosetted shoes, made the long uncovered curling locks and bare limbs of the Irish more conspicuous. Elizabeth received Shane most graciously ; terms were made with him, and his submission was considered of so much importance that a printed proclamation was issued and circulated throughout all England. He became the warm friend and zealous champion of Elizabeth ; but this did not continue long, as he again rebelled and was a constant source of trouble and annoyance to the Queen and the British Government. After his death by assassination, his successor, Hugh O'Neill, resisted the power of the English ; at length he was subdued by Lord-Deputy Mountjoy, who took possession of this place and broke in pieces the inauguration chair. O'Neill fled to the Continent ; a reward was offered for his apprehension, but he escaped to Rome, where he abode till, enfeebled by age, he died, blind, and in poverty."

"It is now my time," said Edward, "to tell you I saw the coronation chair of the kings of England in Westminster Abbey ; it has a stone under the seat which was brought from Scone, on it the Scotch used to crown their kings."

"But, Edward," interrupted John, "that stone was in Ireland previous to being in Scotland."

"Hear ! hear !" echoed the party.

"Farther," continued he, "it was brought to this country from Egypt, and it is said to be the pillar on which Jacob rested his head at Luz."

"Oh !" exclaimed Edward, "I never thought you were such a story-teller till now ; how can you make out it was in Ireland ?"

"Scotia was formerly the name of part of Ireland," replied John.

"Well, well, you 'll tell us anything after that."

"John is right," interposed Mary ; "it is well authenticated that the inhabitants of Ulster went over to Scotland and founded a kingdom which they named Scotia, after the country they had left. Afterwards this name was usurped by the whole territory, and Erin got the name it now bears."

"The tradition is," resumed John, "that this stone was brought over by the Phœnicians, who came to Ireland upwards of a thousand years before the Christian era."

"I do recollect," said Edward, "that the Phœnicians came to Cornwall to trade in tin ; I suppose they must have brought the big stone for ballast."

"Oh !" exclaimed both Mary and Margaret.

" Edward, you would do away with all romance ; and," continued the latter, " you may remember father telling us that it is presumed that Ireland was the Hieron of the Greeks, hence called Ierne, at same time reading to us lines from Festus Avienus, written in the fourteenth century, which he translated,

> ' But hence the sun's diurnal race,
>   To reach that western sacred place,
>   By the ancients " Holy Island " named,
>   Where dwells the Irish race so famed.' "

" You all remember," resumed John, " that when Jacob awoke after his wonderful dream, as related in the 28th chap. of Genesis, ' he took the stone which had been his pillow, and set it up as a pillar, and poured oil on the top of it, and called the place Bethel' (or House of God.)   Tradition further tells that this stone was taken away from Bethel by the tribe of Joseph, when they destroyed the city of Bethel and its inhabitants, it being a current belief among the Jews that whoever possessed this stone would be especially blessed, and be king or chief. On the first destruction of Jerusalem, some of the royal family of Judah escaped and sought an asylum beyond the seas, taking this precious stone with them.

" We next hear of its being in Gallicia, whence the exiles came to Ireland, bringing the relic with them, and founded a kingdom.

" Many centuries afterwards Fergus king of Ulster went, with his brother's permission, to found a king-dom in Scotland.   He determined not to go without the sacred stone, and on his brother's refusing to allow it to be removed out of his dominions, Fergus stole it, and established a kingdom in Scotland, where his descendants afterwards reigned, and were crowned sitting on that stone. It was afterwards enclosed in a wooden chair, and this prophetic distich engraven on it :

'If fate deceive not, where this stone is found,
The Scots shall monarchs of that realm be crowned.'

"It was placed in the Abbey of Scone, and the Scottish kings were crowned on it till it was removed by Edward I. to its present situation in Westminster Abbey. The tradition is, that in whatever country this relic is, the sovereign must be descended from the Dalriadic line. This prophecy was fulfilled in the person of James I. of England, who was lineally descended from Fergus ; consequently our royal family trace their descent from the same source."

"Truly," said Edward, "in the present state of affairs, I don't think our Britannic Majesty George III. would acknowledge his Irish friends, or think it any compliment or honour to be descended from them ; but the lengthened shadows thrown by the stones around, should remind us of our promise not to keep Nannie out after sunset, so exeunt the O'Nial More and all his regal court."

A few days afterwards, the young men took their fishing-rods and walked to Lough Neagh, some miles distant, accompanied by the girls. This lake ranks among the largest in Europe, and as the mythological account of its formation is curious it shall here be introduced. The Isle of Man being the exact size and shape of Lough Neagh, there is a tradition that the soil which forms the island was taken out of the part of Ulster which is now covered by the waters of this lake. The story runs that a giant who resided in this locality was disgusted and grieved by the wickedness of the inhabitants, and fearing the fulfilment of a prophecy that the water of a fountain in the neighbourhood if left uncovered would overflow the country, and drown the people for their crimes, he determined to remove his family to Scotland. His grandmother being of a nervous temperament refused to go, fearing the sea voyage. At her solicitation he remained, until Fin MacCoul had completed the road across to Scotland, which from the remains still to be seen at the " Giant's Causeway," Rathlin, and Staffa, puts Macadam quite in the shade. Perhaps in these go-a-head days some descendant of Ossian or Fin MacCoul may repair it. The "grand chemin" being finished, the giant's family and suite started on their travels. Previous to leaving, the grandmother determined to take with her some of the Irish earth which had been blessed by St Patrick, so as to preserve her in her new abode from toads and serpents; accordingly she lifted a lapful, and succeeded in carrying it half-way to Scotland; her apron-string then broke, the earth fell out, and her grandson, being in an irascible mood, and impatient to get to his journey's end, would not wait to allow it to be collected, and thus the Isle of Man was formed.

Shortly after this family of giants left Ireland, the catastrophe occurred which they had dreaded ; the district was inundated, and the water, rushing into the excavation made by the giantess, constitutes now the deepest part of Lough Neagh. Caxton, who wrote in 1497, gives the following quaint description of the event :—

" There were men in this contre that were of evyle lyving, and there was a well in ye lande in grete revrence of olde tyme, and always coured, and yf it were left uncoured, ye well wolde rise and drowne all ye lande, and so id hoped yd a woman bente to ye well for to fetche water, and hyed her fasd to her childe yd wypd in ye cradele, and left ye well uncoured, when ye well sprynged so fastly yd drowned ye woman and her childe, and made all ye contre a lake and fishpond. For to prove this it is a grete argument," continues Caxton, " that when the wedder is clear, fysshers of yd waters see in ye grounde under ye water, round towers and hyghe shapen steeples, and churches of yd lande."

This tradition was familiar to all the party, but did not recur to their memory until it was recalled by Margaret saying to John, " In the volume of poems which you brought me from Dublin, the allusion made to the legend connected with this lake is beautifully expressed :

' On Lough Neagh's banks as the fisherman strays,
   In the cold clear eve's declining,
   He sees the round towers of other days,
   In the waves beneath him shining.

Thus shall memory oft in dreams sublime,
Catch a glimpse of the days that are over,
Thus sighing, look through the waves of time,
For the long faded glories they cover.'"

" What a pity," said Edward, " that, in confirmation of the story, some of the submerged inhabitants have not been cast ashore, as the water of the lake, from its highly petrifying qualities, doubtless turned them all into stone."

When the weather did not permit excursions or out-of-door amusements, books, games, and music made the days pass quickly over.

Edward's taste for music had been cultivated, and his naturally good voice improved by instruction and practice. Lucy and he sang duets, and their voices harmonised well together. Edward had experienced that "absence makes the heart grow fonder." He also saw plainly that Lucy loved him with all the warmth of her young loving nature; and as he was the acknowledged heir of his uncles, and had their consent to woo and win her as his bride, he declared his attachment to Mr and Mrs Rutherford, who could not withhold their consent. But, on account of Lucy's youth, it was stipulated that a year should elapse without naming a time for the marriage to take place. " Lucy," said Edward, after this interview had taken place, " Shakespeare has said, ' the course of true love never yet did run smooth,' but ours is a contradiction to it; all is bright before us; we have no stern fathers or grim relations to run counter to our wishes. Your father grasped me warmly by the hand, said he had long loved me, and henceforth he would expect me to love him in return as a son, which indeed I would be, when I was the husband of his youngest pet, his darling Lucy. And your mother looked so lovingly at me, that I rushed towards her, and gave her a hearty kiss. I felt inclined to give her half a dozen; but her stately distant manner repelled me, so I must make up for it by giving them to my own darling, my Cush-la-machree."

Fie, fie! some of my readers may say. Well, I suppose this was not the first kiss, nor yet the last, the lovers indulged in; and, in the words of Burns, Edward could say,

> " The golden hours on angels wings
>   Flew o'er me and my dearie ; "

so that the month seemed to come too quickly to an end.

> " Then wi mony a vow and lock'd embrace,
>   Their parting was fu' tender."

Thus, full of love and hope, the lovers parted; Edward promising to write often, and to inform the inmates of Thornbrae of his arrival immediately after he reached London.

CHAPTER XX.

THE fortnight which succeeded Edward's departure from Thornbrae passed wearily to all the inmates ; the hours which before sped so quickly, now seemed to linger on leaden wings. Lucy, more than any of the rest, felt the change, and anxiously looked out for the expected letter, but it did not arrive. Another week elapsed, and still no letter from Edward ; but one came instead from Mr Charles Talbot, addressed to Mr Rutherford, inquiring when Edward left, and wondering what occasioned him to be so long in reaching London.

As the cause of the delay could not be understood by Mr Rutherford, he determined to go to Belfast, and ascertain further particulars respecting the departure of the vessel, previous to replying to the letter. On inquiring at Belfast, he found that " The Blooming Sally " was the name of the vessel which Edward had sailed in ; that she had left the port on the 2d of September, bound for London, and had not been heard of since ; but as a storm had arisen shortly after she put to sea, and several vessels had been obliged to take refuge in Belfast Lough, some had been disabled, and were still in Garmoyle Roads, undergoing repairs. It was therefore thought that "The Blooming Sally" had ran into some of the Scotch ports till the gale was over, and she might by this time have arrived at her destination. Mr Rutherford wrote these particulars to the Messrs Talbot, hoping that ere it reached London, Edward had arrived there.

This news cheered Lucy, who always looked on the brightest side; and though from day to day no letter came, yet hoped against hope; but when another fortnight passed over, and brought no tidings, the sickness of hope deferred began to show itself on poor Lucy's pale face and altered looks; she often burst into tears, and then rousing herself up, endeavoured to play on the spinnet; but when she attempted to sing, she fairly broke down, and was obliged to stop. Her laugh was seldom heard, and then it sounded so unlike her former ringing happy laugh; it only proved that

> "A beam o'er the face of the waters may glow,
> While the tide runs in darkness and coldness below;
> So the cheek may be tinged with a warm sunny smile,
> Though the sad heart to ruin runs coldly the while."

At length a black-edged letter arrived from the Messrs Talbot; they also had hoped against hope, and now wrote to say that "the vessel must have been lost at sea in the storm after she left Belfast, as every inquiry had been instituted, and there was now no prospect of her ever being heard of." They therefore mourned their nephew as dead; it was a sad blow to them, as he was the prop of their declining years, and in him all their hopes had centred ; but they must bow to the will of God in taking away the young and hopeful and sparing themselves, who were past the meridian of life. They begged Lucy would accept their warmest sympathy, and hoped that time would gradually bring her round to bear with patience this her first affliction."

Mr Rutherford's utterance was frequently choked while reading the foregoing ; John groaned aloud ; Bessie cried bitterly and audibly ; Mrs Rutherford and Margaret wept silently with looks bent on Lucy, who, with eyes distended and lips apart, eagerly devoured each word. At the conclusion of the last sentence, she passionately exclaimed, " Bear with patience ; no, I 'll not. What mockery to talk of patience to me, and acquiescing in the will of God ; it is easy for old people to preach ; they cannot feel as I do ; my heart will break. Oh, was ever any one so afflicted as I am ! "

All were spell-bound at poor Lucy's violent outburst ; her mother came gently to her side, took her hand, and led her like a child to her own apartment.

Convulsive sobs agitated her whole frame. Mrs Rutherford laid her on the bed, and allowed her to unburden her pent-up feelings by giving vent to lamentations, without attempting to restrain or console her, otherwise than by a pressure of the hand, and weeping silently beside her. At length tears came to her relief.

Then came the agonising question—" Mother, you and father often speak of the goodness of God to all

His creatures, and that He loves to see them happy ; if so, why am I afflicted thus ? Oh ! why was Edward, who was so good, taken away ? Why must I bear all this ? If He is a God of love, why does He afflict those who love ?—does He dislike us to feel love in our hearts ? "

" Forbear, oh forbear, my child, to talk in such a rash manner. God is love, and does not forbid our loving, if we do not put the creature in the place of the Creator ; but if our love becomes idolatry, then our idol is laid prostrate, and we are made to feel that our affections should be ordered aright, and brought into subjection to His law, which says, ' Thou shalt have no other gods but me.' "

" O mother, I did idolise Edward ; he was bound up with my very life. I cannot live now that he is taken from me ; or if I can survive, my life will ever be a burden to me ; I am miserable, and never will be otherwise ; nothing will ever make me happy again."

" Lucy, my child, how your impious words shock and harrow my feelings, by awakening recollections, and opening up wounds in my heart which I thought time had entirely healed. I shall now relate to you circumstances which your father alone has heard from me. Listen attentively, my child, to what your mother has endured, and if, from the recital of her sufferings, you learn to submit to the will of God, I shall not regret the agony I feel while disclosing my woes to you."

" But, mother, you are so calm and gentle, you could never have suffered or felt as I do."

"Lucy, I was once as impulsive, ardent, and impatient as you are."

"O mother, could you ever have been so?"

"Even so, my child. You have heard I was married before; but you never knew I had, in addition to my husband, lost two children; you never heard me say I had been in America. But all this occurred to me, and more. I told you I was impulsive and impatient; I was also wilful. Perhaps if I had had a mother to counsel me I might have escaped much sorrow; but being left an orphan at an early age, and living with my mother's brother, who was a widower, I was left greatly to myself. William, my cousin, was two years my senior; we were seldom away from each other. We loved, and thought it but natural we should; but my uncle, when he observed our affection for each other, forbade William to think of marrying me. His consent, he said, he would never give; it was unlucky for cousins to be united; it was always sure to turn out badly, and a great deal to that effect. In vain William tried to reason with him; nothing would make him accede to our wishes. At length we both told him he might as well do so, as we were determined to be united. I had a small sum of money which had been left me by my mother. I demanded it from my uncle, telling him that after William and I were married we would go to America. To this my uncle angrily replied, 'You'll get your money, and I'll see you married before you and William leave this house; but I'll not give him one penny, so you may take

O

your own way, and abide the consequences.' William was only nineteen, and I seventeen years old. He thought if we went to America he and I would be able to have a comfortable home there, picturing to ourselves a long life of happiness. Alas! how little did we know what was before us. I need not dwell on the discomforts we had to endure, not only on our voyage, but before and after we got located in a farm in the backwoods. My first-born, my darling Bessie, was born without any one near me but my husband, who was as kind as husband could be; but oh, in nature's agony, I felt it hard not to have one of my own sex beside me. Notwithstanding all my trials, I was happy in the love of my husband, in ministering to the wants of my child, and attending to my household duties. Our crops were good and remunerative—the woods were being cleared around us— several settlers had located in our neighbourhood; so that, when my Willie was born, I not only had a doctor, but a kind female friend with me, and a servant to attend me. Then followed a brief happy season; all seemed cheery, hopeful, and prosperous. One night we were awoke out of our peaceful slumbers by the whoop of the Indians. The glare of light and crackling sounds soon made us aware that the hut was burning about us. My husband rushed out. I followed with my infant in my arms in time to see three savages attack him with their tomahawks. Just then the roof of the hut fell in. I fled; I knew not the way I took, nor how I managed to reach a place of refuge; but when I recovered my senses, I was lying prostrate at the door of a log hut on a clearing about three miles distant. I remained in a state of stupor for I know not how long; when I awoke to consciousness, words cannot express my agony in realising the events of that awful night. I had seen my husband murdered before my eyes; and my child, my first-born, my darling Bessie, entombed in the burning flames. My proud heart rose in rebellion against my Maker. I blasphemed His holy name, reproaching Him for bringing such overwhelming calamities on me; appealing to Him that as He had poured all the vials of His wrath on my devoted head, and withered all my joys, He would end my misery by taking me out of this world. Thus by my want of submission I mocked the great and mighty Being who had called me into existence, and further provoked His wrath against me. Oh what a hard lot I thought was mine! bereft of husband and child, I refused to be comforted; even my infant's smiles and caresses failed to soften my obdurate heart; further sufferings had to be endured before I submitted to the chastening rod. The friends to whose kindness I was indebted for a shelter were shocked at my impiety. I was even ungrateful to them, and often spoke reproachfully and hastily when they attempted to console me. At length I believe they thought I was mad. Truly my reason was perverted, my mind unenlightened, and my heart unrenewed by the softening influences of grace. A letter at length arrived addressed to my husband; it was from a lawyer, informing him of his father's death suddenly, and begging to know if he would return, and what was to be done with the property, &c.

" Here was a cause for thankfulness—a prospect of a home and provision for myself and child ; but I did not feel so. I dreaded going home, and hoped I 'd die on the passage. What signified a home and the means of living comfortably to me, now bereft, as I said, of all hope, and without prospect of any happiness ?

" In this awful state of mind I went on board ship to return to my native land. When ten days at sea my babe sickened. My mother's feelings were then aroused. As day by day he grew worse, my heart yearned affectionately over him ; and when I found the disease was small-pox, and likely to prove fatal, I prayed, I entreated, I implored God to spare him. I acknowledged that I had sinned in saying I had been deprived of every comfort while my child had been spared me, vowing that if this last object of affection were not taken from me, I would never again repine ; but death called away my child, and his body was committed to a watery grave.

" By this bereavement my eyes were opened to see the enormity of the crime I had committed in not humbling myself at first, and submitting to the trials my heavenly Father had thought fit to lay on me. I felt that by my rebellion I had challenged Him to assert His power to do as it seemed right with the creatures He had formed. I then saw His goodness and long-suffering mercy in not acceding to my wish of being taken out of this world till I had been brought to acknowledge that He ordereth all things wisely and for our everlasting well-being ; that ' He knoweth best what is for our good ;' that we must all bear the cross laid on us here, if we would wear the crown hereafter.

" I learned to think of my husband and babes as angels in heaven. I would not, if I could, recall them to earth. I still remember them with love, and hope to be welcomed by them in the regions of bliss, where sorrow, tears, and parting are unknown ; and I trust your dear father, you, my Lucy, and all my other children, will also be there, to sing the praises of redeeming love, and to acknowledge that all our sufferings on earth were wisely permitted, and see the reason why we were called upon to bear them.

" Pause, my dear child, before you again entertain such hard thoughts of God ; do not permit your tongue, which was given you to praise Him, to mock Him with your reproaches ; be assured ' He is too wise to err, too good to be unkind.' Learn from your mother's example to look for consolation where it alone is to be found ; humble yourself, and pray to be enabled, not only to say, but to feel, ' Father, Thy will be done.' "

During this recital poor Lucy had forgotten her own affliction, had raised herself up in bed, and gazed intently at her mother. When she had concluded the last sentence, she jumped hastily off the bed, threw herself into her arms, exclaiming, " Forgive me, oh forgive me, my darling mother, for giving you so much pain. Indeed, indeed I will try to control my feelings, and shall pray to God to assist me to resign myself to this trying dispensation ; and I hope I'll be enabled to prove to you that your confidence has not been misplaced, in relating to me your griefs, and that I will endeavour to profit by your advice."

"I pray, my child, that you may be strengthened in your good resolutions. I shall now leave you for a little, to bring you a cup of tea. Your father, the girls, and John will be anxious to hear how you are. You know we all sympathise with you, and bear a part of your grief. Between your father, you, and I, there is now a bond of union. We alone are the repositories of the early sufferings, sins, and trials of your mother."

When left alone, Lucy pondered deeply on her mother's words, and the knowledge that others were called upon to suffer trials and afflictions assuaged her grief. Strange it is that we are prone to think no sorrow is equal to our own, and when we hear of a greater we take comfort from the knowledge ; but such is human nature. Presently Mrs Rutherford returned with tea, and found poor Lucy in a more composed frame of mind ; but after a time her lamentations broke out afresh.

"My child, why will you grieve so immoderately ? Have you not many comforts left ? Why will you distress me so much by seeing you thus. I shall assist you to undress ; and when you lie down, I shall sit beside your bed. It is better Agnes should not come to you to-night. You must, indeed you must not allow your unruly tongue to give utterance to such rebellious expressions."

" Mother, I will indeed try to restrain my feelings; but it is so hard to bear the thought that dear Edward was engulfed in a watery grave. Oh, it would not have been so bad if he had died, and been buried where I could have gone to mourn over his dear remains."

" Again," urged Mrs Rutherford, " you are upbraiding God, and you are proving your selfish nature in wounding and grieving me. Do you forget already what I told you of my suffering?"

" Pardon, oh pardon me, my beloved mother. Will you sit by me, and sing some of the verses you often sang to me when I had the measles, and was so wayward and fretful? Your sweet voice used to lull me to sleep then, and it would now, I am sure, soothe and quiet my agitation. Kiss me, darling mother."

She then laid her head on the pillow, and closed her eyes. Mrs Rutherford bent over and caressed her like an infant, and in her low musical voice sang—

" Sweet baby, sleep! what ails my dear,
    What ails my darling thus to cry?
Be still, my child, and lend thine ear
    To hear me sing thy lullaby.
My pretty lamb forbear to weep,
Be still, my dear ; sweet baby, sleep.

" A little infant once was He,
    And strength in weakness then was laid
Upon His virgin mother's knee,
    That power to thee might be convey'd.
Sweet baby, then forbear to weep,
Be still, my babe ; sweet baby, sleep.

" In this thy frailty and thy need
    He friends and helpers doth prepare,
Which thee shall cherish, clothe, and feed,
    For of thy weal they tender are.
Sweet baby, then forbear to weep;
Be still, my babe; sweet baby, sleep.

" The King of kings, when He was born,
    Had not so much for outward ease;
By Him such dressings were not worn,
    Nor such-like swaddling-clothes as these.
Sweet baby, then forbear to weep;
Be still, my babe; sweet baby, sleep.

" Within a manger lodged thy Lord,
    Where oxen lay, and asses fed;
Warm rooms we do to thee afford,
    An easy cradle, or a bed.
Sweet baby, then forbear to weep;
Be still, my babe; sweet baby, sleep.

" The wants that He did then sustain
    Have purchased wealth, my babe, for thee;
And by His torments and His pain,
    Thy rest and ease securèd be.
My baby, then forbear to weep;
Be still, my babe; sweet baby, sleep."

During the time Mrs Rutherford was singing these
verses, she rejoiced to find poor Lucy had fallen
asleep.

CHAPTER XXI.

OFTEN during that night did the anxious mother come on tip-toe to watch over her child, who slept; but it was evident from her restlessness, muttered words and sobs, that even in her slumbers her sorrow was not forgotten.

Next morning poor Lucy was in an utter state of prostration; her nervous system had undergone a complete shock. For many days she remained in this state; every sound in the house was hushed, and every face was pale with anxiety about her.

After many weary days and nights of watching and tending, Mrs Rutherford's care was rewarded by hearing Lucy say, while a sweet smile played over her young, pale face, "Mother, dearest mother, I am better, the bitterness is passed away."

"Thank God, my child," responded Mrs Rutherford, stooping down and kissing her warmly.

"I'll not grieve you any more with my querulousness or with my sinful remarks, mother. I have vowed to God here on my bed of agonising suffering, that until I can say in sincerity, and with all my heart and soul, 'Father, Thy will be done,' I'll not speak from this day a single word on any subject to any one."

" O Lucy, Lucy, I thought you said the bitterness was passed."

" And so it is, mother; but as I find I cannot control my tongue, I am determined, with God's assistance, not to speak at all, till I can have more command over it."

Mrs Rutherford was quite stunned with Lucy's resolution, but having a deep sense of the sanctity of a vow, replied, " I am grieved, my child, to find you have been so hasty in your resolution, as 'conversation is the nourisher of content;' however, if you have made a vow to God, I shall not throw any hindrance in the way of your fulfilling it. It will be a sad trial to your father, John, and your sisters, but we will all pray that your mind may soon be brought into the way of peace."

When the tidings were conveyed to the family they all felt, as Mrs Rutherford had said, that another affliction had fallen on them ; but they also regarded the sanctity of a vow made to God, and they were obliged to submit.

Having for many weeks been precluded from holding any intercourse with Lucy, or even entering her chamber, owing to the nervous state she was reduced to, they did not at first realise the privation it would be to them all not to be able to have an interchange of thoughts with her, and to be replied to by her sweet ringing voice.

The winter had passed over wearily to the inmates of Thornbrae ; John did not go to college, but remained moping indoors, or walked about the fields ;

Mary and Agnes attended to the household duties mechanically and silently; Mrs Rutherford was seldom absent from Lucy's chamber; Mr Rutherford had his parish or farm duties to attend to ; and perhaps of all the family he was least affected by the gloom which hung over the cottage.

When Lucy's resolution was communicated to her father, he was in truth surprised ; he had hoped that her former volatile youthful spirits had not altogether forsaken her, and that time, the great consoler, would assuage her sorrow, and trusted that her grief would soon exhaust itself ; but he now feared that the course she was taking would cause her mind to prey more on her bereavement ; however, he thought it best to acquiesce cheerfully, fearing if chided it would agitate her, and only more strongly confirm her in her determination.

During her illness he had always, previous to retiring to rest for the night, gone and knelt down at her bedside, silently imploring God to give her peace, and if His will, to restore her to health, and grant her resignation.

Lucy seldom observed him, but latterly she had murmured " Father " or " Good-night," and sometimes held out her hand, or turned round on the pillow to have a kiss imprinted on her forehead or lips.

On entering as usual, on the evening of the day she had declared what was her intention, he was surprised to see her stretch out both arms to embrace him, and with a bright pleading look say in firm, but gentle tones, "Father, I hope you are not angry with me for

the vow I have made. O father, pray that I may
be forgiven for the sinful feelings which prompted
me to give utterance to such reproaches, and for daring to blaspheme with my tongue, accusing God of
want of love and injustice towards me ; won't you
bear with me, dearest father, I have been the cause of
great sorrow and anxiety to you, and through my
selfish recrimination harrowed the feelings of the best
of mothers."

"May God bless and forgive you, my dear Lucy,
and pour down His Spirit to enlighten your understanding, to apply to your case the many promises of
consolation He has given in His Word to those who
call upon Him in the day of trouble. I would much
rather you had not taken a vow of silence, as grief is
only nurtured by it ; but I trust it will not be long till
my child will gratify her father by joining in the
morning and evening hymns of praise."

"My dear father, if that will comfort you, so soon
as I am able to rejoin the family circle at prayers, I
shall as formerly sing and play."

Mr Rutherford then knelt down, and repeated, in a
voice almost inaudible from emotion, "Almighty God,
our heavenly Father, who of His great mercy has
promised forgiveness of sins to all them that with
hearty repentance and true faith turn unto Him,
have mercy upon you ; pardon and deliver you from
all your sins ; confirm and strengthen you in all goodness, and bring you to everlasting life ; through Jesus
Christ our Lord." To which Lucy fervently responded,
Amen. Father and child embraced affectionately, and

this was the last word she uttered for many many months.

Although Mr and Mrs Rutherford had alone of all the family access to Lucy's chamber, Hector had always found an opportunity of slipping in, and gazing wistfully at the bed ; he seemed to comprehend that there was something wrong. When Lucy felt so much better as to be able to stretch out her hand to him, he licked it in a quiet subdued manner, and looked at her sympathisingly and pitifully. As spring advanced, and Lucy gained strength to go for a walk in the garden, leaning on the arm of some of the family, Hector was always her attendant ; but with measured pace, so unlike his former rapid motions and playful gambols, he followed her slow footsteps, quietly and sedately, often turning, and with earnest, trustful gaze, sought to be recognised by his beloved young mistress. John took especial care of Lucy's flower knot, for which he was rewarded by a pressure of the hand, a sweet smile, or a gentle pat on the shoulders from Lucy, when he was stooping down, tending her dearly loved flowers.

Her canary, parroquet, and the doves which Edward had given her, were removed from her apartment when she first became ill ; but as she got convalescent they were brought back again. Agnes had carefully attended to them, but Lucy was able to take charge of them herself during the summer; and as she gained strength daily, it was hoped before winter she would gladden them further by joining in their conversation. Christmas, however, came and passed over, also the

New Year, but further than singing at the morning
and evening devotions her voice was not heard. She
seldom looked unhappy, and was constantly occupied
attending to her birds, reading, or working ; and many
a blessing was invoked by the old women of the parish on the dear afflicted young lady for the warm
garments she had made, and sent with her sisters to
them.

At first she retired to her room when any one
except the family were present ; but when the next
spring came round, she began to attend church regularly on Sundays, shook hands with and nodded to
her friends whom she met there, and afterwards remained in the room when they visited Thornbrae.

The family for a time had not addressed their
conversation to her, but now they did so, and she
listened, and in return smiled or bowed her head, or
waved her hand, in token of assent or otherwise, so
that her load of sorrow seemed gradually to be wearing away, and her health quite restored. But her
appearance was greatly changed ; her elastic step,
bright colour, rounded cheeks, sparkling eyes, and
luxuriant curls, were gone ; the illness had caused
her hair to fall off, so that it was cut short, and she
was obliged to wear a cap ; her white teeth, and occasional sweet smile, were all that remained to remind
any one of the former Hebe-like beauty of Thornbrae.
Again spring came round, bringing its lovely flowers,
and sweetly singing birds ; but she who had been as
blooming as the flowers, and her voice as sweet and
joy-inspiring as the lark, now more resembled the

drooping snowdrop, and her sweet voice was still silent, as, with the exception of singing the morning and evening hymns, she uttered not a word.

During the summer Lucy spent the greater part of the day in an arbour formed of laburnum and lilac trees, wreathed over with honeysuckle and eglantine ; it was at the foot of the garden, which was at some distance from the house. One day towards the end of August Mrs Rutherford was going in that direction, and heard a voice as if in prayer ; she knew it was Lucy's. Breathlessly she listened, and heard her pouring out her soul to God, thanking Him for mercifully sparing her till she had accomplished her vow, and could now with heart and tongue acknowledge the loving-kindness and justice of God, and meekly and uncomplainingly say, "Father, Thy will be done."

Mrs Rutherford turned away with tears of joy overflowing her eyes ; sought her husband, who was in another part of the garden, to convey the cheering intelligence that their child had obtained consolation, and was now resigned to the will of her heavenly Father.

Presently Lucy approached, bearing traces of tears on her cheeks, but with a calm expression in her eyes, and a sweet smile illuminating her pale features. She embraced her parents, saying, " By the grace of God I will praise the Lord with my best member, and with my tongue, which reproached my God, I can now say it was in wisdom and in mercy He afflicted me ; that He ordereth all things wisely, and hath a right to do as He pleaseth with His creatures on earth.   Before I was afflicted I went astray, but now His consolations rejoice my soul ; like Thomas à Kempis, I have found silence my best friend, and prayer its auxiliary." Entering the house she met her sisters, and warmly embraced and thanked them for all their forbearance and love.

When John drew near the house on his return in the evening, the unusual sound of the spinnet attracted his attention, and pausing before entering the room he was rejoiced to hear Lucy sing to the air of " The Sicilian Mariners Hymn,"

> " Now my soul its triumph raises,
> Bless Jehovah's gracious care;
> He will not disdain my praises,
> For His grace has heard my prayer.
> He has all His power reveal'd,
> He my strength, and He my shield ;
> When in faith on Him I waited,
> Then the Lord to help me sped.
> Now my heart with joy elated,
> Now my tongue His praise shall spread."

John this season returned to college, and the inmates of Thornbrae spent the winter occupied with their various duties.   Mr Rutherford had his parish and the farm to attend to, and Mrs Rutherford, the thrifty housewife,

> " O'er house and o'er home
> Behold her preside !
> With prudence she governs,
> And orders and aids,
> Exhorts or upbraids,
> Rebuking the boys
> And instructing the maids."

The girls enlivened the time with books, and music, and occasionally visiting and being visited by friends ; among whom none more heartily rejoiced in Lucy's recovery to health and spirits than her uncle, aunt, and cousins, the Wilsons of Ballynacraig, but in Lucy's presence they never referred to her former period of silence.

CHAPTER XXII.

WE must now follow Hilary to Madeira, and see what he is about. It is upwards of three years since we left him going there as medical attendant to the Honble. Mrs V——.

His treatment was most judicious, and under his care the invalid reached Madeira in improved health. He received the warmest thanks and a large fee from the lady's mother, accompanied by a request that he would remain their guest as long as he pleased.

Botany was a science in which Hilary (or rather we should style him Dr Rutherford) specially delighted ; here was a good opportunity for gratifying his taste by collecting specimens. The salubrious climate of Madeira, with its undulating surface of alternate hill and dale causing so many different aspects, is favourable to the growth of plants belonging both to the tropical and temperate zones ; it is therefore an ample and most varied field for botanical study and research. Week after week slipped away in his favourite pursuit without his feeling the lapse of time. Often had he come to Funchal with the determination of returning home, but on hearing of rare plants which were to be had in other parts of the island, he was induced to visit those localities to procure them.

He had always a hearty welcome at the Honble. Mrs V——'s, where he was sure to meet with agreeable society. On one of these occasions he was introduced to an officer and his lady who had come from India to recruit their health. They told him that a number of their friends were only remaining in Madeira till they could get a ship in which there would be a medical man. Here was an opportunity for Hilary to accompany them, and be well remunerated for his services. It had been his most anxious wish to go botanising on the Neilgherry Hills, but the expense of the voyage had hitherto prevented him from attempting to do so. Arrangements were made with the first merchant vessel which called at Madeira, to convey the party to Madras. Nothing of consequence occurred on the voyage ; all arrived safely. Hilary shortly afterwards left on his botanising expedition, throwing his whole energies of both body and mind into the pursuit, caring not for fatigue nor danger, if rewarded by the acquisition of a fresh specimen. "What a waste of time and labour !" some of my readers will exclaim ; but as the wisest of men has said, " In all labour there is profit," and it literally turned out so with our friend. His botanical researches had discovered many hitherto unknown plants, which were highly valuable to the sciences of chemistry and medicine. A botanic garden was then forming in Calcutta : he was appointed curator and general manager.

One day he was walking about the gardens superintending some work going on, when his attention

was arrested by a sailor stopping not far from where
he stood, and exclaiming, " By all that's lovely, a
shamrock ! Oh what would I not give to be again
on the green sod of dear Ireland !" Something in
the tone of the sailor's voice struck Hilary as not un-
familiar to his ear ; so, stepping up to him, he said,
" Friend, it seems to give you pleasure to recognise
that little plant ; are you an Irishman, as well as
myself?" During this introduction the stranger
looked wildly at the speaker, then gasped forth,
" Hilary, am I so changed that you do not know
me ?"

"No, oh no, Edward !" and rushing forward, they
grasped each other's hands most heartily and warmly,
and for some minutes neither was able to speak a
word. Hilary first recovered his composure, and
said, " But where have you been for so long, Edward ?
We thought you were dead."

" I 'll tell you all," replied the sailor, (who my
readers doubtless have recognised as Edward Talbot ;)
"but tell me, are they all well at Thornbrae ? Is
Lucy"—— here emotion choked his utterance.

" All are well, and all will be right when you go
home."

Hilary then took him by the arm and led him into
his house, where he partook of some refreshment,
during which there were frequent interrogatory questions on either side ; but in cases of this kind, where
the feelings have been so excited, little lucid information was given or received by either party : sufficient, however, was told to let Edward know how

deeply his loss was mourned ; how poor Lucy had
suffered ; how long and severe was her trial, till she
could acquiesce in submission to her fate. "And,"
said Hilary, "they write me, 'she is so changed I
would not recognise her to be the Lucy I remember.'
Her beautiful luxuriant curls had to be cut off, and
she is quite pale and thin "——

"But no matter," interrupted Edward, "how
changed she is in appearance, her heart is still the
same ; her love for me has not changed."

Edward then told his friend, that after leaving Belfast Lough the vessel had encountered a gale, which
was so severe as to completely disable the " Blooming Sally." " While in this condition they were seized
by a French vessel which was hovering off the coast
of Ireland. Perhaps they expected to take on board
some of the disaffected persons who were going to
communicate with the French government about
sending supplies, to enable Ireland to become a re-
public ; or perhaps, as we were at war with France,
we were seized as a prize. At any rate we were un-
able to do anything but submit to be towed into
the harbour of Brest. On arrival there the captain
and crew were taken ashore, guarded by gensdarme ;
I suppose they were taken to prison, as I never saw
any of them again.

" I was the only passenger on board, and I must
have been regarded as a personage of some importance, probably a spy, as a double guard of gensdarme were sent with me, and I was taken to prison.
My pockets were then examined, and every article of

my apparel underwent a strict scrutiny, but papers
or anything treasonable were not found on me.
Words cannot, dear Hilary, give you the slightest
conception of the agony I endured, when I found
myself a prisoner in a country we were at war with,
whose language I scarcely knew a word of, and not
having any one to whom I could apply to assist me,
to make my case known, or communicate with my
friends at home.

"Previous to leaving the vessel, the captain of
'The Blooming Sally' had kept up my spirits by
telling me that all we had to fear was imprisonment
for a few weeks; that then there would be an ex-
change of prisoners, and we would be sent to London.
He had no idea, however, we would be separated.
Several days passed over. You remember my hasty
impetuous temper when I was thwarted in anything,
and here I had no Lucy to check me with her sweet
look; nor your dear mother, with her gentle voice, to
whisper, 'Better is he who ruleth his spirit than he
that taketh a city;' or, 'The patient in spirit is better
than the proud in spirit;' or, 'Anger resteth in the
bosom of fools,' Edward.

"My pent-up passions vented themselves furiously.
I shouted, stamped, raved, flung my arms about, tore
my hair, knocked my head against my prison walls;
in fact, acted like a maniac. But at last I could
struggle no longer; I was seized with brain fever,
and what occurred while I was in this state, or how
long it lasted, I know not. My first remembrance
was being conscious of suffering great bodily pain:

then gradually I remembered where I was ; and as I saw no hope of release, I contemplated the prospect of my death with satisfaction. Often did I murmur Lucy's name ; and I thought if I could get a letter conveyed to her, telling her that, in my last moments I still remembered her, it would soothe my departing spirit. But notwithstanding all my affliction, I daily got better. I then formed the resolution that I would endeavour to acquire as much of the language as my situation would permit, hoping it would aid me to escape. I listened attentively to every word, and this diverted my mind. I found that I was in the hospital connected with the prison. As I got convalescent, I was allowed to walk in a courtyard where there were other invalids. We were not prohibited from speaking to each other ; and I took every opportunity of entering into conversation with my companions ; but they were of the lower classes, and I could learn little from them. Just as I was about to yield to despondency again, a happy circumstance occurred, which roused me. The daughter of the jailer, a child of about ten years old, came out frequently to sit with her book, or work in the courtyard. I assisted her to wind her silks, fastened her embroidery in the frame, and in many other little ways made myself agreeable to her. I told her English words, and she, in return, told me French. She lent me books, and made me feel happier, more cheerful, and hopeful. She was an only child, and motherless. Her father was devotedly attached to her ; it gratified him to perceive the progress his child was

making in acquiring the English language; he purchased her books, and she became regularly my
pupil. I soon—thanks to your dear father for ground-
ing me so well in Latin—gained a knowledge of
French, so that I could converse tolerably well. M.
le Borde informed me that, as I had no documentary
or other evidence to prove that I was otherwise than
what the captain said, (a passenger,) I might have been
allowed to depart when the vessel and prisoners were
exchanged; but fever had prevented me accompanying them when they left. That the English were
still at war with France; that Bonaparte was carrying all before him by force of arms in Europe; that
he entertained a great hatred to the English, and
cherished the hope of invading and humbling the
power of England; so there was little hope for me to
get free.

"Among the various topics of conversation M. le
Borde and I entered into, freemasonry was introduced. I don't think you ever heard I had joined
their society shortly after I went to London. My
uncles thought it was very foolish; but now it
proved the best thing ever happened to me. I communicated to M. le Borde that I was one of that
fraternity, and at once recognised him as a brother
freemason. Here was indeed a grand discovery.
From this time I was treated as a friend, and given
to understand that, if opportunity offered, proofs of
brotherly affection would not be wanting. Shortly
after this, while seated with Lisette, giving her the
daily lesson, we were interrupted by Monsieur le

Borde dancing into the room where we were sitting,
singing, at the same time, his usual song, the subject
of which had at first amused me greatly—it being a
description of the death and burial of the Duke of
Marlborough, and I had rendered it into English. It
had been introduced to notice by the peasant nurse of
the Dauphin singing it while rocking the royal cradle ;
and Marie Antoinette having been struck by the sim-
plicity of the words, the singularity of the refrain, and
the melodiousness of the air, felt interested in it, and
frequently sang it ; and hence Marlborough became
the fashionable air in the state apartments of Versailles.
Being caught up by the attendants, it was then sung in
the kitchens and stables. From the court, it was adopted
by the tradespeople of Paris, and passed thence from
town to town, till it was heard all over France. Even the
revolution, the fall of the Bastile, and the Marseillaise
hymn, were insufficient to smother the sounds of that
never-ceasing song. It is even told of Bonaparte
that, despite his general antipathy to music, he often,
when getting on horseback to start on a campaign, sang,

> ' Marlborough s'en va-t-en guerre,
> Mironton, Mironton, Mirontaine ;
> Marlborough s'en va-t-en guerre,
> Ne sait quand reviendra,
> Ne sait quand reviendra,
> Ne sait quand reviendra.'

"It was wafted over to England, where it soon
became as popular as in France ; you know it as
Malbrook. From hearing the air so frequently, it
fell unheeded on my ear ; but when Monsieur, after

pirouetting round me several times with great vi-
vacity, and more than his usual share of shrugs and
grimaces, stopped opposite me, and sang,

> ' Monsieur de Marlborough est mort,
> Mironton, Mironton, Mirontaine ;
> Monsieur de Marlborough est mort,
> Est mort et enterré,
> Est mort et enterré,
> Est mort et enterré,'

I wondered what could have excited him so much,
and endeavoured to interrupt him ; but he still continued in his mock-heroic style—*Ecoutez Anglais*—

> ' I 've noting more to say,
> Mironton, Mironton, Mirontaine,
> I 've noting more to say ;
> Von't you say 'tis 'nuff ?
> Von't you say 'tis 'nuff ?
> Von't you say 'tis 'nuff ?'

" ' Hold, hold, my dear friend,' said I, ' it is truly
enough.   What does this all mean ?'

" Lisette was dismissed, and after grimaces and
gesticulations, I heard what had caused all this
tumultuous joy.

" I then learned that the doctor who had the supervision of the prison had been ordered off to join the
army in Italy ; that he was to be replaced by a young
man from one of the medical colleges in Paris ; that
the said youth should have been here before his prede-
cessor left ; but he had not made his appearance yet ;
that the doctor was so hurried on leaving, he had
omitted to wait to see the particulars registered of
those who had died during the night, but had merely

signed his name, and left Monsieur le Borde to fill up the description of the deceased.

"Here again his spirits got up, he caught me in his arms, shed tears, vowed he'd never forget me ; but it would break his heart to part with Monsieur Talbô, &c. &c.

"'But,' said I, 'what has all this to do with me, my friend ?'

"'Everything, mon Dieu! You no comprehend? I write you what you call mort ; you go to your own enterrement n'est ce pas aussi à l'enterrement des defuncts to the cimetière outside la prison ; mon Dieu! you walk away, leave pauvre moi et Lisette au desespoir.'

"Here was an unexpected prospect of deliverance. I need scarcely say I was elated ; but when I thought over the many difficulties in the way of my getting out of the country, and the dread of being unsuccessful, it checked my ardour.

"I communicated to Monsieur le Borde my fears as to the result of my escape.

"'Ah, bah!' replied he ; 'Monsieur Talbô ne vous affligez pas ; à cœur vaillant rien d'impossible! Je donne une lettre pour un ami, un franc maçon à L'Aigle d'Or près le quai ; à table-d'hôte vous voyez plusieurs capitaines peut-être donnez-vous une traversée.'

"'But,' interrupted I, 'there will not be any vessels for England. Oh, this horrid war, what affliction is it not bringing on thousands, as well as on me!'

"Here I was stopped by Monsieur le Borde reminding me we had little time to spare; that the funeral was to take place in the evening, and that I must be ready to accompany it.

"I need scarcely say I was rejoiced at the prospect of regaining my freedom. I caught the spirit of my kind friend the jailer, and felt quite elated. I pictured to myself the happiness of returning home, the pleasure of getting to Thornbrae, the joy of meeting all, and of clasping my beloved Lucy in my arms. I had few preparations to make, as the clothes which had been in my portmanteau were nearly worn out; besides, I could not carry anything with me but a change of linen and my toilet requisites. My watch had not been taken from me, and my purse still contained eleven guineas. I offered these to Monsieur le Borde, but he indignantly refused them. 'Monsieur Talbô, ne vous inquiétez pas. A la bonne heure! Mon ami et le vôtre qui fait partie de la fraternité pourra peut-être obtenir l'argent français en échange de la monnaie anglaise. Voici la lettre; il n'est pas difficile de découvrir l'Aigle d'Or; c'est un càfé sur le quai.'

"He then produced a workman's blouse for me to wear. He further explained that, when I accompanied the funeral, the sentinels would think I was either one of the undertaker's men, or a workman who had been employed about the prison.

"Poor Lisette! I dare not see her to say farewell. She could not be told of our plans, so I was obliged to allow her to think I was unkind. Monsieur le Borde I hoped to see again; but it grieved me greatly to think of parting without the hope of ever again meeting the dear child who had first soothed my agitated feelings, and been as a ray of hope and life illuminating my prison. However, I had been obliged to submit to greater trials than this; so hastily embracing my kind friend, I stationed myself in a passage near where the coffins were to be carried out. When they were passing, I joined the procession, and with a throbbing heart followed through the inner, and then through the outer gates of the prison, and gained the street. Oh, with what different feelings I found myself here again; I almost felt inclined to kiss the ground I trod on. When I had entered the prison, I had taken no notice of the streets we passed along from the vessel, as my heart was too full. I now dreaded asking any questions, lest I should attract attention; so I walked on silently, pursuing the direction Monsieur le Borde had told me, and presently found myself at L'Aigle d'Or. I stepped in, and seating myself at a table, called *le garçon* to bring me *une petite verre cau-de-vie.* Presently the maître d'hotel came beside where I was seated. I presented my letter, accompanying it with the masonic sign. He motioned me to follow him to his bureau. ' This is rather a troublesome commission, my friend, M. le Borde has given me, but we 'll see what can be done. You must lie here *perdu.* But have you no other dress, my friend ?'

"' Oh yes!' I replied; 'under this blouse are ordinary garments.'

"For three days I was doomed to experience the sickness of heart consequent on hope deferred; but on the fourth, worthy Monsieur Dubois informed me that he had a prospect of getting me taken by a captain who was going to the East Indies.

"'Oh! can you not get me sent nearer home?' exclaimed I.

"'My friend must bear in mind that, if he would get into any of the European ports at this moment, he could not get out of a French vessel to England; but from Calcutta there likely will be a chance.'

"I had no alternative but to submit myself wholly to his direction. Shortly afterwards I was introduced to the captain of the vessel, who agreed to take me, on condition I would work for my passage. This I gladly consented to; and I gave him the contents of my purse to pay the maître d'hotel and my outfit.

"Previous to leaving Brest, I had the gratification of seeing my kind and ever-to-be-remembered friend, Monsieur le Borde; but the pleasure was deeply mingled with pain at having to bid him adieu. I wished so much to have seen Lisette, but prudence forbade it; and as the only recompense I could make her for my seeming unkindness in leaving her without a parting word, I requested her father to convey to her, with my best wishes for her welfare, the only trinket I possessed. You may remember the locket I had, which contained a lock of my mother's hair, to which I had added a curl of dear Lucy's just previous to leaving Thornbrae. On my return, when I had declared my love, and she promised to become my wife, I wished her to accept the locket; but she playfully refused, saying, 'I'll not take it till I get the owner along with it ;' but now she 'll have to do without the locket when she gets myself.

"See, here is the hair I took out of it. I have worn it next my heart, notwithstanding that I parted with what it was contained in.

"My night of darkness and grief seems now to have passed away, and a bright morning of joy dawning on me. Rejoice with me, my dear Hilary, for the Lord has heard my desires. Oh let us therefore praise Him for His goodness, and declare the wonders that He hath done, and still doeth, for the children of men."

Hilary gladly supplied Edward with the means of purchasing clothes and all other necessaries for his homeward voyage.

The firm of the Messrs Talbot being well known, there was no difficulty in getting a passage in a vessel bound to England.

With mingled feelings of sorrow and joy, Edward departed, bearing with him the love and best wishes of Hilary, also a large packet of letters to be posted on his arrival in England.

The voyage was long; to Edward it seemed interminable. There were not any other passengers, and the captain and mate were unsocial and uneducated men ; so he was left to his own thoughts and resources.

When with Hilary it made him feel that he was not so far away from Thornbrae and his beloved Lucy. But now that he was so situated as not to be able to talk about her, and mention her loved name, his spirits became dull ; and as day after day the vessel was becalmed, he experienced the bitterness of hope deferred.

Oh how he rejoiced when the vessel got into the trade winds, and the heaving of the log told the good news that they were making ten knots an hour! But there were still thousands of miles between him and his destination. Often did he contrast the slow flight of time now with the seemingly short fleeting month which he last spent at Thornbrae. Like an imprisoned bird he chafed at his confinement; he even felt more miserable than he did while in the prison at Brest; here he had no Lisette to revive and cheer his lonely hours. There was no alternative but patience, which, we already have seen, was not a virtue Edward possessed. One weary week after another passed away. The Cape of Good Hope was at length reached; this was a tangible proof of being homeward bound, and raised his drooping spirits for a time.

From this the voyage was speedy; and having got well through the Bay of Biscay, England was neared, and the cry of "land a-head" greeted Edward's delighted ear. Then came a revulsion of feeling. What if Lucy had drooped under her trial, and was now so far exhausted as to be sinking into an early grave? Or oh, torturing thought, she might already be dead!

The Channel gales were then encountered; and after three days beating up under contrary winds, the long-wished-for port was reached. The Messrs Talbot received Edward as if risen from the dead; his return gladdened their hearts, and seemed to infuse new life into their veins.

Hilary's letter to his father was posted immediately, Edward followed it the next day, love and ardent hope throbbing in every pulse; but as it will take him six days, or perhaps longer, to reach Thornbrac, we shall leave him on his journey, and in next chapter learn what is going on in the abode where Edward's hopes and wishes centred.

CHAPTER XXIII.

ALL at the cottage was going on in the usual routine. Mr Rutherford had ample occupation in his duties as a curate, and in the supervision of the farm. John had not yet decided on his choice of a profession, and spent his time in going about the farm, reading, and riding, or walking with his mother and sisters. The girls were constantly occupied, either in assisting their mother in the household management, in sewing for themselves and the poor, in visiting or receiving visits from their friends, and in ministering to the wants of the sick and afflicted.

Nor was the culture of their tastes and minds forgotten; music and drawing, books, and conversations on literary and scientific subjects, formed a pleasing part of their occupations. To use Woolner's words:

> "A cool repose lay grateful through the place;
> And pleasant duties, promptly, truly done;
> And every service, touch'd with hidden springs,
> Oil'd with intelligence, moved smoothly round."

John returned one evening from Slievedhu, bringing a letter to his father, addressed in well-known writing. It was from Hilary, whose letters were always most welcome. He was not only regarded with affection, but looked up to with pride by every member of the family as being talented and clever. All were soon assembled, and every eye riveted on Mr Rutherford, who read as follows :—

" BOTANIC GARDENS, CALCUTTA, 13*th October* 17—.

" MY DEAR FATHER,—The wish of my heart has been realised. I am now enjoying to the fullest extent the pursuit of my two favourite studies, botany and medicine, (and remuneratively too,) as I am in receipt of a salary of 8000 rupees yearly, besides a free house, perquisites, and permission to practise as a physician whenever it does not interfere with my duties as curator here.

" I know it will rejoice you all to hear this ; and selfish though it may seem, I write it first. I trust this will find you *all* quite well. I now come to news which will make you all happy. Our dear Lucy's trials are over. Edward has most unexpectedly turned up ; he is now beside me ; and is just about to sail for England, and takes this to post to you. I leave him to tell his adventures. Where his heart is, he will soon appear in *propria persona.*"

Here a deep sigh from Lucy arrested general attention. She was ashy pale, and instantly swooned away. John laid her on a couch, and restoratives were applied ; presently she recovered, and, with a hesitating voice, asked, " Can I credit my senses ; did Hilary write my beloved Edward was alive, and would soon be here ?"

Congratulations and caresses soon assured her that

it was true, and that all around participated in her happiness. Then, bursting into tears, and burying her head in her mother's bosom, she murmured, "Blessed be God, who hath not turned away my prayer, nor His mercy from me, for He hath delivered me out of trouble, and put gladness in my heart. Bless the Lord, O my soul."

Two days afterwards Edward arrived ; but as our readers are already acquainted with his adventures, we need not recapitulate them as he did to the inmates of Thornbrae.

Hilary had told Edward that Lucy's appearance was altered, but still he could not imagine that such a change was possible. He had left her a blooming, sprightly young girl ; now she was pale and thin, and looking so much older ; her fair, wavy, luxuriant hair had been cut off during her illness ; it had grown darker, and she now wore it plainly braided ; her manner was subdued and quiet, and her expression melancholy. But changed though she was, Edward thought her more beautiful than before. Her sweet smile still remained the same ; and when her eyes rested on Edward, they beamed with tenderness and love. He would have wished her to look more robust, but he was hopeful that now that he had returned, the blushes of health might again overspread her countenance. It was arranged that they should be married on the first of August, the anniversary of the day Edward had left Thornbrae four years ago ; to them it seemed an age, so many events had occurred within that period.

It was now the middle of July, and all were engaged in preparations for the coming event. The sun shone brightly on the wedding party as they walked to church, accompanied by Margaret, Agnes, John, and their cousins, Nannie, Mary, Francis, and James Wilson. This was the whole bridal party ; and although not merry or joyous, they were perhaps happier in reality than where jest and mirth prevail.

Edward looked with pride and tenderness at Lucy, who confidingly and lovingly leant on his arm. Mr Rutherford had walked on before them, and in his surplice received the party at the church. The service was read by him in a solemn, impressive manner ; but when he came to the words, " Almighty God, who at the beginning did create our first parents, Adam and Eve, and did sanctify and join them together in marriage, pour upon you the riches of His grace, sanctify and bless you, that ye may please Him both in body and soul, and live together in holy love unto your lives' end. Amen," the feelings of the father nearly choked his utterance ; but a glance at Edward convinced him that he would be a true and faithful husband to his Lucy, and that instead of losing he was gaining a child.

On returning from church, Mrs Rutherford received the party in her gentle kind manner, and Edward was so overjoyed, that he forgot her stately bearing, and this time kissed her over and over again to the great amusement of the young folks.

After luncheon, a post-chaise arrived from Slieve-dhu to convey the happy pair to Belfast. Mrs

Rutherford up to this time had kept calm, but now the mother's feelings proved too strong to be repressed ; there had been a greater bond of union and sympathy between her and Lucy than the rest of the family were aware of, and she wept piteously at the thought of parting.

Mary Wilson seeing her aunt so affected hastily pulled off her slipper and flung it at Edward when he was entering the chaise ; this provoked a general outburst of laughter. Edward turned round and said, " Miss Mary, I bargained with you at Tullyhoge that you were only to fling the token of sovereignty after me, but here you have hit your liege lord on his august shoulders."

London was safely reached ; Edward and his bride were received by their uncles Talbot in the kindest and most cordial manner, and everything that affection could devise and wealth procure was bestowed on their niece Mrs Talbot.

It afforded them the greatest pleasure to observe a marked improvement in her appearance from week to week ; but as they feared the effects of the November fogs on her still delicate constitution, they suggested to Edward to go to Madeira for the winter, and this falling in with Edward's own wishes, the young couple sailed for that lovely island early in the month of October, and after a pleasant passage arrived safely.

Bowles had not at that time penned the lines that " the woods of Madeira trembled to a kiss ;" if ever woods did so, their vibrating might now have been visible, as sure we are a kiss was often exchanged between Lucy and Edward there.

One day after Lucy's marriage, Mr Rutherford and his son John were returning from Slievedhu, and Mr Rutherford proposed coming a short cut across the fields. The conversation at first was on the happy termination of Edward and Lucy's sorrows; John, who had relapsed into silence for some time, said abruptly, "Father, don't you think Mary Wilson would make a good wife ?"

Mr Rutherford, who had noticed the growing love between the cousins, would rather it had been other-wise, as he had more ambitious views for his son; but fearing that opposition would only strengthen their affection, he had avoided speaking on the subject, hoping that it was merely a youthful fancy, because they had been thrown so much together, and that it would vanish when John got into the society of other girls, and Mary, when he was absent, might be addressed by some other suitor. This feeling caused him to reply curtly, " Perhaps she would."

" Perhaps," echoed John; "could there be any doubt of it ?"

" Certainly there would," was the reply; " Mary's temper would not do with every one."

" I do not think, father, she has a bad temper."

" Well, I did not say she had a bad temper, but she is hasty and impulsive, and from being unaccustomed to restraint, and having unlimited control at home, she could not be expected to be a submissive wife, and it is not every man she would suit on that account."

" Oh, is that all ?" said John ; " I am sure Mary and I would not disagree."

This was, Mr Rutherford thought, drawing too much towards the subject he wished to avoid, which caused him to answer petulantly, "Of course all girls are good-tempered before they are married, but what makes all the bad wives ? I presume the husbands must all be to blame ; but we are wasting time on this useless subject ; I came this way expressly to talk to you on a more important matter. It has annoyed and grieved both your mother and me greatly that you have not attended to your studies, or made the progress we expected you would have done, and you are so wavering in the choice of a profession ; you are now come to manhood, and it is exceedingly foolish in you not to decide on the course of life you mean to pursue. Hilary did not act as you have done ; he had completed his studies, and entered on his profession, before he was your age."

John felt that he deserved reproof, but urged that grief for Edward's supposed death and Lucy's unhappy state had unsettled his mind for study, but he was determined to act differently for the future.

CHAPTER XXIV.

THE parish of Termonabrack at this time became vacant by the death of the incumbent; the living was a good one; it was in the gift of the Southend family, who still esteemed their former tutor, and remembering their promise to him, they at once offered him the living, saying that perhaps after a time his son John might succeed him in the parish.

The Bishop of Derry had promised his interest in getting Mr Rutherford appointed dean, (on the demise of the present dean,) to whom there could not, in their opinion, be a more worthy successor than their late tutor. Here were now the early dreams of Alexander Rutherford about to be realised; this would also decide John in adopting a profession, about which he was unsettled. Mrs Rutherford felt sorry at the prospect of leaving Thornbrae, and so did Margaret and Agnes; but youth is generally fond of change, and the prospect appeared a pleasant one. The parsonage was large, the neighbourhood had many resident gentry, who were sociable, and their position higher, so that there would be more visiting, consequently more variety for the girls, who, since Lucy's marriage, felt occasionally dull; so with feelings of sorrow, softened by hopes of the future, Thornbrae was left in charge of Jamie M'Gwiggan and family, and all hands were busy fitting up the parsonage to be ready to receive visitors ; but although we have seen Mrs Rutherford's card basket, it is not our intention to give a list of her visitors, the motives which caused the visits, the conversations which took place then, and the observations made afterwards, and the "Thought I to myself," and "Did you remark the dress or address of so and so?" who was thought genteel, who vulgar, and the hundred and one other topics generally discussed and descanted on in similar circumstances. Suffice it to say, all went on satisfactorily at Termonabrack parsonage, and the family began to think it was home, and time passed pleasantly.

Lucy came to pay a visit at the parsonage. Her renewed health and spirits were a source of great plea-sure to them all, and the looks, words, and actions of baby Charles Francis were duly registered and com-mented on. There never was such a child ! so good ! so handsome ! so intelligent ! During the six weeks he was at the parsonage he was the principal personage. He was the alpha and omega of everything ; each one in the house seemed to think they were guilty of some misdemeanour if they attempted to settle to do anything but attend his little lordship. It was now a usual sight to see John on all fours, on the lawn, with Margaret on one side and Agnes on the other, hold-ing the baby on his back, while Lucy sat on the grass beside Hector, who, though not sobered by trials,

yet by age was made sedate and quiet ; while Mr and
Mrs Rutherford would stand, arm in arm, on the hall
door steps watching the happy group,—Mr Rutherford
reiterating the feelings generally expressed by grand-
parents : " I never thought I would feel so foolishly
fond of a child.   Why, I love him as dearly as I do
Lucy !" and Mrs Rutherford's sweet smile and pressure
of the hand re-echoed her husband's sentiments.

Edward now joined the party, and after a short sojourn, he, wife, and child, accompanied by Agnes,
returned home.   Margaret being the eldest should
have gone to London, but her father said he could
not spare her till he got better settled in the parish ;
and as John was obliged to go back to college to
finish his course of studies, preparatory to taking
orders in the Established Church, Mr Rutherford had
to visit Thornbrae occasionally, but in another year
he could dispense with her services for a time.   " But
who knoweth what a day or an hour may bring
forth ?" and yet we plan what we will do next year,
or for many years to come.

At this time the Episcopalian, or church established
by law in Ireland, engrossed a great part of the pro-
fits and honours of the country, besides a large share
of the landed property.

The majority of the peasantry of Ireland were
Roman Catholics, and in a state of wretchedness and
poverty.   The payment of tithes to support a church
which was so opposed to their wishes and belief in
every way, and from which they believed they did
not derive any benefit, either spiritually or tempo-

rally, became a very great hardship and burden, and was the cause of numberless outbreaks in various parts of the country. This feeling of discontent had been rankling in the minds of the people, and year by year it gained strength. As the poverty of the country increased, the payment of tithes and church rates became more obnoxious to the lower classes, as they were the most numerous tithe-payers.

The bailiffs who collected the tithes and church rates were generally persons of low character, coarse and brutal in their manners and language. They spoke in a taunting way to the persons they came to, demanding payment in a peremptory, overbearing manner; and if their demands were not immediately complied with, threats of distraining and driving off the cattle were held out, and in too many instances carried into effect without more than a day or two's delay after the refusal of payment.

If the sum demanded by the collector was not paid immediately, either from absolute want of cash, absence from home, or a wish to give him the trouble of calling again, threats, supplemented with oaths and opprobrious epithets, which led to abusive retorts and imprecations, and most frequently ended in the tithe collector's being beaten, or thrown into, or dragged through, a bog hole. Then followed the capture by soldiers of the offending parties,—a trial before one or two magistrates, (if trial it could be called, where no witnesses were allowed except on the one side.)

A committal to jail for some months might be the

penalty, or the offenders were confined in the stocks, to be pelted and hooted at by the rabble, who were urged on by the soldiers and tithe proctors.

The clergy were often strangers in Ireland, who had got their livings, not for their virtues or their knowledge. They felt no interest in the people, and looked down on them as serfs and inferior beings. The clergymen as a body were far from zealous in the observance of their duties, being more addicted to the pleasures of the table, hunting, shooting, gambling, &c., but were strict in demanding the full amount of their tithes and incumbents' dues, and, in many instances, permitted and encouraged payment to be enforced in a most insulting, aggravating manner. It was, moreover, a very great grievance to the small farmers to have their fields ridden over by the hunting parson and his associates, or the fences broken to accommodate them when out shooting, or riding steeple-chases through the country ; and when they happened to meet the owner of the farm there was too frequently a haughty bearing, and proud, insolent manner displayed towards him, and on his part he felt neither respect nor esteem for the parsons, who were looked upon as heretics and robbers ; and as the farms were so small, and the tenants miserably poor, it cannot be denied that it was sufficient to rouse them to resist payment out of their little stock which they had earned by their hard labour. It was indeed a hardship for them to have to support men in luxury, while they had great difficulty to keep themselves and families in food which the parsons would not have

considered fit in quality or sufficient in quantity to
feed their hounds. Added to this, the overbearing
pride of many of the incumbents exasperated their
poor parishioners to retort disrespectfully, to curse
them, (not always inaudibly,) and to feel a deep-
rooted hatred, which in many instances led them to
take a terrible revenge.

The parish of which Mr Rutherford was now the
rector was owned principally by extensive landed proprietors, and was chiefly used by them for pasturage,
which according to the tithe laws were not chargeable
with incumbents' dues; these landowners rented off
small patches of land which were cultivated principally by Dissenters and Catholics, and it aggravated
their feelings to be obliged to pay tithes for the crops
which by their hard labour they had raised on their
smalls farms, or for a cottier, who had only one rood
of potatoes, which was all a family from seven to
twelve persons had to subsist on during the winter,
to be compelled to give a tithe of them, while the
large owners were exempt from payment for their
pasture lands.

John had redeemed his promise, had studied closely,
obtained his degree at Trinity College, taken orders,
and was now the recognised curate of Termonabrack,
assisting his father in all his parish duties, as well as in
superintending the farm at Thornbrae. Occasionally
he went to see his cousins at Ballynacraig ; but they
did not come so frequently to the parsonage as they
had to Thornbrae. A kind of tacit understanding
seemed to have sprung up between them, that the

rector and his family considered they were now in a position, and moving in a circle above their relatives, who kept an inn. This change was felt by both parties, though not openly expressed, and led to an estrangement between them. John felt it keenly; but it only made him love Mary more dearly. He met with many matrons who had shown him plainly that they would not object to having him for a son-in-law, and whose daughters gave him to understand, by winning smiles and looks, that if wooed they could be won. Still his heart was his cousin Mary's; and now that he was curate, with the prospect of being rector when his father would get a larger parish, or succeed to the Deanery of Derry, he determined to ask his father's consent to marry her, and live for the present at Thornbrae.

Mr Rutherford scarcely knew how to refuse; but as Mary had a number of admirers, he hoped by delaying the union she might be induced to accept some one else; besides, he wished to get his two daughters married to persons of rank and position, and thought it would militate against them if their brother, who was so caressed by all the families in the neighbourhood, should marry beneath his present rank. He did not however think it prudent to acquaint his son with all these motives, but pleaded that as he was younger than his sisters it would make them seem old if he married before they were settled in life, urging as encouragement for delay that Mary and he were both young, and could wait for some time; he was induced to adopt this mode of reasoning, having ascertained from John that he had never spoken openly of love to his cousin.

John was therefore reluctantly compelled to accede to his father's wishes; but as he was devotedly attached to his sisters he expressed himself willing to submit to any personal hardship, rather than do anything to be a hindrance to their forming eligible matrimonial alliances.

CHAPTER XXV.

FOR some years before the late incumbent's death, he had great difficulty in getting even a part of his tithes and church rates paid, and when Mr Rutherford succeeded him in the parish of Termonabrack, it was an additional cause of discontent, as the Dissenters, who disliked the family for leaving their communion, united with their Catholic neighbours to resist the payment of tithes even with more obstinacy and determination than they had displayed on former occasions. It was with great difficulty that a part of the tithes and dues were got the first year of Mr Rutherford's incumbency; the second year the receipts were less, and the opposition more strong and more openly expressed.

Previous to the third harvest a letter was received by Mr Rutherford signed by all the Catholic and dissenting parishioners in the form of a " Round robin," couched in respectful but strong language, that unless the parson would send to the fields and remove the grain, (every tenth " stook" of which would be left for him,) they would not give tithes in any other way.

R

We have already seen that Mr Rutherford was not a man to be coerced into measures, and now that he had the law of the land to support him, backed by the influence of Lord Southend and the magistrates, he treated the proposal with scorn and silent contempt, and continued getting in his own abundant harvest at Thornbrae.

The parishioners with one accord left grain in each field, to be taken away by the rector ; but he seemed not to notice it, and when the season came round for raising the potato crop, a similar proposal and warning by the same parties was sent, but this also was unheeded, so that not only was the grain left to be blown about and go to loss, but the potatoes to rot in the fields. The letters being shown to the magistrates and influential gentlemen of the neighbourhood, it was universally agreed that it would be setting a dangerous precedent to allow the plebeian ranks to dictate and compel the clergy to come into their measures ; and they commended Mr Rutherford for withstanding these attempts, promising to uphold him with their influence, and assist him by the aid of a military force to collect the tithes to which by law he was entitled. Accordingly, when the time came round for the bailiff to call on the parishioners for the tithes, he went as usual to their houses, but accompanied this time by a detachment of soldiers to prevent him from being maltreated. In every case they were peremptorily refused payment, and no threats or abusive language could provoke in return more than a black withering look, a muttered imprecation, or where the more impulsive natures were roused by taunts, the reply was, "Do as you please, we have been so oppressed and wretched, we can't be worse."

The next step allowed by law was a complaint to be made of non-payment before two justices; this was done, and immediate steps taken against the defaulters. Each parishioner had summonses from the magistrates served on him to make his appearance before the bench, or in case of non-compliance there would be a warrant of distress issued to seize whatever was available to pay the demands. These summonses were unregarded by the parties on whom they were served; they well knew they would not get redress, so after the sitting of the magistrates on the appointed day, and when no defendants appeared, writs were issued against all the parties, and the tithe proctors and bailiffs, protected by a strong body of military, and accompanied by several magistrates, all well armed, proceeded to each farm and cottier house, and having brought with them carts, horses, and men, they seized and carried away grain and potatoes, or where those were not available, cattle and horses; the grain was carted to one of the rectory fields and the potatoes taken to another, the cattle and horses driven to Slievedhu, and impounded there to be held over till they were sold. For several days the seizures continued, the people during the time maintaining a dogged silence.

Almost all the parishioners of Termonabrack, and a large assemblage of persons, came to Slievedhu on the market-day to attend the sale of the horses and cattle, which had been advertised to be auctioned in the parson's name. A considerable force of soldiers were present with bayoneted muskets, charged with ball cartridge. Lord Southend's agent and several of his tenants were also there; the latter were the only bidders at the sale. It is useless to add that the cattle sold considerably below their value.

When the auction was over the pent up feelings of the poor sufferers could no longer be restrained; oaths, curses, and threats of vengeance, poured out vehemently, followed by a shower of stones among the cattle, which losing all restraint rushed madly among the people, scattering and knocking down the crowd in their fury. A magistrate present attempted to read the Riot Act, but groans and imprecations interrupted him. The English officer who had command of the soldiers, ordered them to fire among the crowd; six persons were shot dead on the spot, and a number wounded.

A scene now occurred which defies description; the frantic gestures of the crowd; the screams of despair uttered by the women and children; the groans of the wounded; the threats of defiance and vengeance; the explosions of the muskets; the commands from the officers; the orders from the magistrates, combined with the smoke, dust, and blood flowing on the pavement, made up a fearful picture.

Thirteen men were seized and dragged off to prison, and finally the crowd was dispersed, and driven at the point of the soldiers' bayonets for miles out of the town, amidst the horrid yells and lamentations of those who were compelled to leave the dead and dying; the former were allowed to remain where they were till coffins were provided for them; they were then thrown into a sunk ditch at the north end of the burying-ground attached to the church of Slievedhu, and slightly covered over with earth. During the dispersion of the crowd, many of the wounded were carried surreptitiously away by friends in the town, who tended and cared for them; some died of their wounds, others found means to get out of the country.

The wounded who had been left on the street were removed to a house which had been fitted up as a temporary hospital for the soldiers; their wounds were dressed, but several died, and those who survived were reserved to stand their trial by court-martial.

During this time the wretched insurgents returned to their miserable homes; many of them were deprived of a father, husband, or brother, and all had to mourn the death or imprisonment of a relative, friend, or neighbour. Is it, therefore, to be wondered at that vengeance should be the one prevailing feeling amongst them?

The soldiery, who had previously guarded the grain and potatoes in the rectory fields, had been taken away to Slievedhu in the morning, and, in the affray which occurred there, their former guardianship was forgotten. Here was now an opportunity for revenge.

That night the inmates of the parsonage were awoke by a crackling noise and lurid flames penetrating through the closely-barred shutters. At first they thought the house was on fire, but presently found it was the grain which had been stored in the field had been set on fire in several places at once, so that in half an hour all was consumed.

Next morning all that remained to be seen was a heap of black ashes. The field in which the potatoes had been was also rifled of its store; only a few remained scattered on the ground, and the marks of footsteps over the earth, and a potato dropped here and there, pointed out the direction in which they had been carried away to a bog, where they had been thrown into a deep pit filled with the morass water. The footprints on the soil proved that not only men with heavy shoes, but women with shoeless feet, girls, and even children, had lent their aid in this work of destruction.

The day appointed for the trial of the poor wretches (who had now sufficiently recovered so as to be able to attend the court) drew on. It was but too well known what would be their fate.

At this crisis, the following letter was addressed to Mr Rutherford, dropped into Slievedhu post-office, and duly received at Termonabrack parsonage :—
" Ye blackavised villain ; ye imp and lim' o' Sattan ; ye turn-coat robber ; ye murthering rapscallion ; we give ye du notis that if ye let the hair o' the head o' one o' the boys fall, that ye hav in limbo now, all

through yer extorshuns, we swear by the holy ✝ yer doom is writ below :

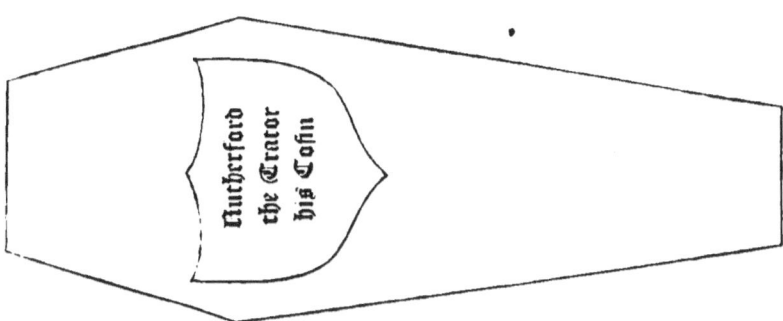

Rote and sined wi' the blud o' thim that 'll do for ye, if ye don't get a release for the boys that 's to come to a sham trial the day after the morro'.

"So min' yerself, we warn ye."

Reader, do not think this a fictitious epistle; the writer of these pages has seen numbers of letters in the same style, and even more strongly worded.

Tithes and church rates are now collected in a less obnoxious manner, so that outrages on this account are now happily unknown in Ireland. Party outrages have unfortunately of late broken forth; but it is to be hoped that the " memory of the pious, glorious, and immortal King William the Third " will not again call forth disgraceful scenes, such as were en-acted during the Belfast riots in August 1864. Oh ! when will the sons of Old Erin learn that their coun-try will never be peaceful, prosperous, and happy, until

party feelings and party colours are abandoned, and,
in the words of our national poet,

> " Till like the rainbow's light
> Thy various tints unite,
> And form in heaven's sight
> One arch of peace."

CHAPTER XXVI.

THE rector and his family had a very cheerless prospect for the future. Mrs Rutherford had always advised pacific measures, and submission rather than resistance, but was overborne by her husband, son, and Margaret. They all coincided in opinion that when the rebellious ones saw that they were the weaker party, and that the law was against them, they would be obliged to submit, and all would go on well afterwards; but if the insurgents should be allowed to escape unpunished now, it would only lead to a worse state of affairs in future.

When the day came round on which the prisoners were to be tried, it was necessary for Mr Rutherford and his son to attend personally. They examined the loading of the brace of pistols with which they were armed, to defend themselves; and they also carried heavily-loaded walking-sticks; but what would these avail, if they were attacked by a number of infuriated men. With tearful eyes and sorrowful hearts Mrs Rutherford and her two daughters saw them prepare to depart for Slievedhu.

While they are getting ready to depart, we shall describe the situation of the parsonage, as it will serve to elucidate events which follow.

A smooth level lawn of beautifully verdant sward stretched across the greater part of the front of the parsonage, and at one side a semicircular carriage drive swept along towards a massive iron gate, (hung between two strong stone pillars,) which opened on the highroad leading to Slievedhu. On one side of this avenue was a close plantation of trees, and on the other side a belt of evergreens about ten feet in width, behind which was a high, thick hawthorn hedge; at the end of this hedge, and nearly opposite the hall door, were two yew trees, and in front of them a weeping ash, under which was a rustic seat made of gnarled branches ornamented with fir cones. This had been constructed by John, shortly after the family had come to the parsonage, previous to Lucy's visit. It was a spot hitherto full of pleasant memories. Here Lucy had sat with her first-born in her lap, gazing on him with a young mother's radiant, loving looks; again Edward had been seated beside her, while Hector and baby rolled about on the grass at their feet, forming a picture of love and domestic happiness, suitable for the pen of a poet, or the pencil of an artist. Here the rector had sat during many a sultry afternoon, and while digesting his comfortable, plentiful dinner, digested the sermon he was to deliver in the church on the following Sunday to his flock; and here he and his beloved wife often held many a conference on family and domestic affairs; here the girls sat during the summer forenoons occupied with books or needlework, and occasionally on a summer evening "Black-eyed Susan," "Highland

Mary," or "My dark haired girl," might be heard proceeding from this spot. Of course these celebrated females did not appear in *propria persona*, but the pathetic airs which have immortalised their names, were played on the flute by John—"Master John" he was designated by the household and farm-servants, and "the curate" by the parishioners. Henceforth the pleasant memories of this place will be effaced by the recollection of the horrible events with which it was indelibly connected in the minds of the Rutherford family. However, let us not anticipate, but accompany the father and son on their walk down the avenue. Unmindful of the bright sunshine, the song of birds, the gay flowers, and the many objects in nature which usually called forth feelings and expressions of pleasure from both Mr Rutherford and John, they walked on absorbed in silence. When they came to the gate and emerged on the highroad leading to the town, they expected to see a number of persons, but the way was quite deserted, and they soon found that a short time previously a mounted troop of dragoons had chased every one away, and were now returning to station themselves at the entrance to Slievedhu.

The insurgents were sentenced by court-martial to be shot immediately. They were escorted by the dragoons to a field at one end of the town. The four unfortunate men were ordered to kneel down in a row, opposite to a file of soldiers; they were then blindfolded, and the word given, "Fire." When the smoke of the muskets cleared away, the work of destruction was found to have been done effectually, as in every case life was extinct, or the life-blood flowing so freely that recovery was impossible.

At this juncture the Mr Rutherfords had left Slieve-dhu, and were on the road returning home; but the volley of musketry too plainly revealed what had taken place. If possible, their return was even more melancholy than their morning walk had been. They both pondered how it would be best to com-municate the dreadful result of the trial to wife, mother, daughter, sisters; but, save by groans, a shake of the head, or a sympathising look, they seemed to forget each other's presence, and they walked mechanically and abstractedly along till they came nearly to the end of the avenue, when John hastened his pace, and ran on before his father, to announce to his mother and sisters their safe arrival. Just at the moment he had entered the hall, and was clasped in Agnes's arms, and about to be greeted in the same way by Margaret, the report of a gun was heard issuing from behind the arbour, and turning hastily round, to his exceeding horror, he saw his father fall prostrate on his face against the flight of stone steps. John bounded down and attempted to move him, but as latterly Mr Rutherford had got very stout, and poor John was so agitated he could not lift him, Margaret immediately joined him, and they succeeded in raising him up; but a glance was sufficient to show that the vital spark had fled. The fall against the steps had split his head open, his brains were scattered about, his nose smashed, and his face covered with blood, made him a most awful spectacle. By this time Agnes's screams and shouts of "murder" had brought the servants from the house and yard, and, with the assistance of two men, the mangled remains of the rector were carried into the parsonage. A messenger was instantly despatched to Slievedhu for a doctor.

During all this fearful scene, poor Mrs Rutherford did not scream or shed tears ; she seemed as if bewildered and horror-stricken, but, save a groan, no sound escaped her lips. Agnes wept and screamed alternately ; Margaret, for a time, did not seem to realise in its full extent what had . occurred, but walked about silently, wringing her hands, pressing her temples, and covering her eyes, as if to hide some horrid sight, then fainted away. The doctor just then arrived, and after administering some restoratives, left her, and accompanied John to examine his father's mutilated body. There was not the slightest sign of life. The fall, he said, had been sufficient to cause death ; the bullet had entered the left side close to the spine, pierced his heart, and lodged in the abdomen, causing the wounds to bleed inwardly.

Presently two magistrates arrived, escorted by a party of soldiers, to make an official examination of the spot where the murder had been committed, and, if possible, to gain some information which might lead to the discovery of the perpetrator of the bloody deed.

All that could be ascertained was what has already been told. They then proceeded to examine the spot from which the deadly shot was fired, and there they found lying on the ground, between the two yew trees, the murderous weapon, which, on examination, proved to be a double-barrelled gun, still containing an undischarged ball. The back of the rustic seat bore traces that it had been rested on it, and, from the flattened marks on the grass, the assassin had evidently knelt while he discharged the musket. Footmarks were traced to the road, and there lost.

On the gun being shown to John, he immediately recognised it as his, which he used occasionally when out with his volunteer corps. He had just cleaned and loaded it that morning, and left it in the harness-room adjoining the coach-house, intending to remove it to his sleeping apartment, where he kept it when not in use; but being called away, he neglected to do so, and had forgotten all about it till the circum-stance was painfully brought to his recollection by its now being produced.

It must have been carried away during the time the men were absent for dinner, as they affirmed, on oath, that they had not seen any one come into the yard, nor had they seen the gun, except in Master John's hands.

Of course the news spread rapidly over the country, and before noon the day following, Mary Wilson was with her aunt and cousins. Prompted by her warm affectionate heart, she wept and sympathised with the poor sufferers, and, with her ready willing hands, tended them, and made herself useful in discharging the last sad duties to an uncle she had so dearly loved, and now so sincerely lamented.

The houses of the disaffected parishioners were entered, and each individual questioned by the officers of justice when they had last seen the parson, but nothing could be elicited to lead to the discovery of the murderer. A reward of £500 was offered to any one who would give information that would lead to his apprehension, but all was in vain.

The parish was placed under martial-law, and a strict watch kept over all persons in it, in hopes that the delinquent would try to leave the country, and by that means fall into the hands of the authorities; but no clue was ever obtained to point out who had discharged the fatal shot.

Immediately after the funeral the heart-stricken family removed to Thornbrae; and oh! with what altered feelings did they again enter their former happy home.

In the time of happiness and comfort, Mrs Rutherford had often lifted up her heart in thankfulness to God for the many blessings He had bestowed on her; and now in the time of her sore trial and bereavement, she drew closer to her heavenly Father, relying implicitly on the promises given of drying up the mourner's tears, and being a husband to the widow, and a father to the fatherless. In this frame of mind she experienced consolation, which the world could not give or take away from her.

The living of Termonabrack was offered to John,

who at once decisively refused it, declaring that he would never officiate in that church again.

We shall for the present take leave of this mourning family, hoping that the soothing influences of time, and the consolations of religion, will calm and soften their grief, and enable them to bear with resignation their heavy trial.

CHAPTER XXVII.

IN addition to being in a good situation for a post-ing-house, Ballynacraig had weekly and monthly markets, half-yearly fairs, and was the centre of a good agricultural and flax-growing neighbourhood.

The linen buyers were a hardy set of robust men, who travelled about from one town to another in troops on horseback, with saddle-bags, containing gold to pay for their purchases, slung across their horses necks, and a valise containing their changes of shirts and toilet necessaries, strapped behind their saddles. They had not a covered market to purchase the linen webs in, but placed in the public street were high narrow tables with a step attached to stand on, so as to raise the buyer over the heads of the crowd who thronged round, and handed up their webs to be examined and valued. The buyer then marked each web he bought, and the seller took the goods away to where they were to be measured and paid for.

At the "Royal Arms" there was a large room which was used for this purpose; on each side were ranged tables, and the products of the wheel and loom paid in spade guineas and thirteens. Twopence each web was paid for the accommodation of the room; then there were refreshments which both buyer and seller

s

required, the substantial dinner after the business
of the day was over, the provender for the horses,
the sleeping accommodation, drink, &c. All this
was a considerable source of revenue to the "Royal
Arms," and gave the family and domestics ample
occupation; so that although there were no striking
incidents in their lives, there was such a constant
variety, that time slipped away almost impercep-
tibly.

We have already mentioned that Mrs Wilson's
health was delicate, and that Nannie was not energetic, therefore Mary had taken an active part in the
management of the house; her exertions were now
further taxed as her father's brother, who had attended
to the farm and posting department, died, and Mr
Wilson's time was so occupied that the entire management of the inn devolved on Mary. In this way
she was thrown among many strangers, and heard so
much of what were the topics of the time, that she was
quite *au courant du jour*.

Ireland at this period was in a state of ferment;
the misgovernment of many years began to make
itself known visibly. It was felt to be a great
grievance that Roman Catholics could not hold
leases of land, receive a liberal education, or be
represented at the bar or in parliament. The union
of all denominations and classes as volunteers in
defence of their native country, made a liberality
of sentiment, and a fraternity of feeling, which
caused a sympathy to be called forth that Roman
Catholics should be allowed equal privileges with

their Protestant fellow-countrymen. This universal
wish for emancipation was further fostered by a correspondence with friends in America, who had emigrated from Ireland, many of whom had taken part
in the war of independence.

But it is not our place to enter into a minute history
of the time preceding, and the rebellion of 1798, but
merely to narrate sufficient to make our story understood. Various societies had sprung up to organise
plans for the regeneration of their country; but these
associations either dissolved through quarrels among
the members or split up into other societies. "De-
fenders" were succeeded by "Hearts of Steel," they
again by "Hearts of Oak," "Right Boys," "White
Boys," and others; at the time we write about the
"United Irishmen" was the title the disaffected
took; and affairs got into such a turbulent state
that strong military reinforcements were quartered
all over the country. The "Royal Arms," from
having such good accommodation, seldom was without a number of the military billeted on them, much
to the annoyance of Mary, who sympathised with the
wrongs of her countrymen, whose thoughtless conduct
only brought punishment on themselves, increasing
instead of lessening their woes or mitigating their
grievances.

As the Habeas Corpus Act was suspended, and the
country under martial law, any suspicious or turbulent
person could be seized, imprisoned, flogged, or even
shot or hanged.

Then came the disarming of Ulster, when all firearms were obliged to be given up ; this the volunteers thought hard on them, as it was at their own cost they had supplied their arms and equipments. The seizure of a gun often so exasperated young men that they became disaffected against the government, joined the society of " United Irishmen," and with characteristic recklessness threw themselves into collision with the military.

Previous to matters coming to this state, Francis Wilson had finished his apprenticeship, and college courses. Had undergone a favourable examination, and got an appointment on board a man-of-war, which had gone out to the West Indies. His brother James was now with Dr Conway, the chief medical practitioner in Ballynacraig.

James was delicate in constitution, timid and reserved ; his brother Francis was quite different, being robust, candid,. and courageous. Often his parents were thankful that Francis had left home before Ulster was disarmed, fearing that the order to deliver up his prized volunteer musket would have irritated and roused him to become a disloyal subject.

Mary entered into his feelings ; she well knew how it would grieve her brother if, on his return home, he found that his gun had been taken away, so she determined to conceal it. Without making known her plans to any person, one moonlight night, when the officers and men had gone out to relieve guard, she carried the gun into the large room which they had just left, and placing it on a table, with a key opened the door of a room in which was stored linen webs; she carried them out two at a time, forming a pile on the table, which with the addition of a chair to stand on, raised her sufficiently high to open with the gun a trap door in the ceiling; she then shoved the gun across the rafters and closed the door, removed the chair, replaced the webs, and hurriedly left the apartment just as the military entered.

When the house was searched, and an old blunderbuss and a pistol taken possession of, the soldiers did not suspect that a gun was concealed just over their heads in the room which they occupied.

James Wilson had a fellow-apprentice at Dr Conway's named Andrew Gordon, his brother Henry, who was several years his senior, was nearly out of his apprenticeship with lawyer Conway, brother to the doctor. The father of these young men was the Reverend Andrew Gordon, the esteemed and respected minister of a Presbyterian congregation in the county Down; he was popular among all sects and denominations, and liberal and tolerant in his sentiments. Of course, as the manner of his persuasion is, he occasionally inveighed against Church and State, and warned and pointed out to his hearers the evils and errors of Popery and Prelacy; but he was on intimate terms with members of all creeds, paid his tithes regularly, went out to fish with the rector, and often dined in the parsonage; spent an evening occasionally with the priest, taking a glass of punch, and playing a game of backgammon with him.

He did not interfere in politics—in fact it was a subject on which he was rather indifferent and reticent.

His mind was not narrowed down by sectarian opinions; he thought that each individual of every denomination should be allowed to worship God according to the dictates of his own conscience. He wished heartily that instead of being estranged from one another, all Christians would emulate each other in love and good works, for Jesus Christ's sake. " Ireland," he often said, " will never be as she ought until Presbyterians, Episcopalians, and Roman Catholics, forget all their differences, and consider ' that they are only three leaves forming one shamrock.' "

Mr Gordon was indeed "a man to all the country dear and passing rich, (with a little over) forty pounds a year."

His meeting-house was in the town of S——, but he lived rather more than a mile out of the town, in a cottage, on a farm of thirty acres, which he got by his wife. At this time the Presbyterian Church in Ireland did not receive the *Regium Donum*, and Mr Gordon had little revenue coming in from his pew rents, (or stipend,) and having eight children, he was obliged to divide his attention between the pulpit, the farm, and the education of his children, which gave him ample occupation. Besides visiting the sick and other duties, there were christenings to attend in the houses of his flock, it not being at this period a rule of the Presbyterian Church that baptisms should take place only in the meeting-houses.

Marriages were also celebrated in the house of the bride, or among the poorer classes in the minister's house; there was no stated time of the day for the

ceremony to take place, nor any notice required ; so
that it was not an unusual occurrence for the clergyman to be roused out of his bed " to marry a couple ;"
the ceremony often being performed in the kitchen,
the minister in deshabille leaning against the dresser
while he joined a pair in the holy bands of matrimony ; for doing so a fee was given which was determined by the means, generosity, or warmth of feeling
of the bridegroom.

The cottage from time to time, as the family increased, required enlargement; in front it still retained
its former appearance ; but behind, from the additions
at various periods, and at all possible angles, it resembled a Chinese alphabetical character.

Mrs Gordon had been a celebrated beauty, but
hard work, and the care and anxiety attendant on
nursing and rearing a numerous family, had prematurely aged and worn her down, so that there was
little left to tell the tale of former beauty. Still intelligence beamed in her eyes, and although the pearly
teeth were gone, the kindly smile ever welcomed the
friend as of yore, so that the absence of the bloom
of youth was forgotten. She was truly a good
kind wife, and a devotedly attached Christian mother,
pointing out to her children the way to heaven, and
encouraging them, both by precept and example, to
walk in the ways of righteousness. Patrick Henry,
Mrs Gordon's brother, who had emigrated to America
before her marriage, had become a leading orator of
the time ; in eloquent soul-stirring words, and with
all the fire of an Irishman, he addressed the senators,

in a speech which, to the present day, is regarded as
a finished specimen of oratory, and still borne in remembrance by being inserted in books on elocution.

A strong attachment existed between brother and
sister ; they kept up a correspondence, and it was for
him that her eldest son was named, but Patrick being
then considered vulgar, it was dropped, and Henry
only used.

Mrs Gordon had a small fortune when she was married, but from time to time it had been encroached
on for apprenticing her two eldest sons, and other
exigencies, till only sufficient remained to fit out with
the strictest economy Andrew for the navy, and to
pay the fees, &c., for Henry to be sworn in an at-
torney.

Both boys were now nearly out of their apprenticeship ; Andrew had given great satisfaction to Dr
Conway, who had formerly been in the British navy,
and who had prepared his own sons and several other
lads for the service.

Henry had completed his apprenticeship creditably,
and was to accompany for the first time Mr Conway
to Dublin. Mary Wilson and Henry were often together ; they had mutual tastes. He read to her, lent
her books, and often attended her in walks or rides ; he
had many commissions to execute for her in Dublin,
purchase books, et cetera. It had been a pleasure for
Henry to read, and Mary to listen to " The Pleasures
of Hope," " She stoops to Conquer," and other publi-
cations of the day ; but on Henry's return from
Dublin all these were laid aside to read the speeches

of Grattan and Curran, some of which he had heard
delivered. These he read, and thought over so
frequently, that they became part of his daily conversation. Under these influences he formed acquaintance with some disaffected persons who easily
persuaded him to join the society of United Irishmen.
Being ardent and impulsive, he gave vent to his
sentiments incautiously, became suspected of disloyalty, and his movements watched.

One of the places of rendezvous was at an old stone
quarry, a little distance out of Ballynacraig, the time
of meeting being night, and the hour of assembling
varying according to the moonlight or other circumstances. On the evening that Mary hid her brother's
gun, and almost at the same hour Henry left Mr
Conway's, and had proceeded part of the way when
he became aware that he was dogged by two men
who kept in the shade ; he slackened his pace, they
did so too ; he stopped, they turned off as if going
away ; he then quickened his steps, and in a few
minutes heard footfalls again behind him. This
proved to him he was right in his suspicions, that the
persons following were actuated by a determination to
discover where he was going. Having now got within
a short distance of the quarry, and fearing least he
should betray where his associates were assembled, he
turned quickly round and encountered two soldiers,
who immediately commanded him to halt and show
his pass, permitting him to be out after the nine o'clock
beat of drum. He was then made prisoner, and taken
to the guard-house, where he was kept all night.

Next morning Mr Conway's house and Henry's sleeping-room were examined by the military, but nothing treasonable was found. He was then brought before the officers, and was addressed by the captain in a haughty, supercilious manner : " Give an account of yourself, you young rebel. What took you out last night ? and where were you going ? "

To this Henry merely replied by a contemptuous look at the assembled group. He was further addressed in a more threatening tone, and told by the officers that he was their prisoner, and that they had it in their power to compel him to tell what he was about.

Tauntingly he replied, asking them to prove that he was about any harm, and sarcastically asked them how his taking a solitary walk along a deserted road could make him a sufficiently noble object for them to show off their valour by heroically capturing him. He was then pronounced by them an unmistakable incorrigible rebel, and ordered to be imprisoned till sentence should be pronounced on him by court-martial.

A detachment of soldiers marched him off handcuffed to Dungannon, and lodged him in jail.

As Henry was a great favourite, not only with Mr Conway, but with the greater part of the inhabitants of Ballynacraig, his seizure and imprisonment caused universal sorrow.

Mary did not attempt to conceal the sympathy that she felt for him, and thinking that she could break the sad news to his father and mother in a less grating manner than if conveyed to them by the hundred tongues of rumour, which were sure to exaggerate, and perhaps make the circumstance appear in the worst possible light against Henry, she immediately sent off a messenger on horseback with a letter to Mr Gordon, detailing the events, and suggesting if he would appear along with his son at the trial, plead his youth, and the esteem and regard in which he was held by his master and all who knew him, he might perhaps escape the degradation of being flogged, and get off with a few days' imprisonment.

CHAPTER XXVIII

"OH, how altered and unlike dear Thornbrae!" thought Mary Wilson, (when riding up to the cottage to visit her aunt and cousins for the first time since their return to it;) "the very place seems gloomy, as if the sorrow within had cast a shade over everything without."

"How improved is this place!" thought a young man of the neighbourhood who was passing at the time; "the trees and shrubs have grown up, and it is such a bright, lovely spot; surely happiness, health, and contentment dwell here."

The contrast between the thoughts of each proves that the appreciation or admiration of objects is often caused either by the tone of feeling at the time, or the associations called forth when scenes and objects are gazed upon.

Mary missed being hailed by Lucy's joyous shout, "Oh, here is cousin Mary!" and the hearty "Welcome, welcome!" uttered by all assembled at the hall door. Her uncle, John, or Jamie M'Gwiggan, formerly was there to assist her off the pillion or side saddle, but now she was indebted to Denny M'Durk, one of her father's men, (who had accompanied her,) to help her to dismount.

The door was opened by Bessie, who showed she was heartily glad to see her cousin; but she looked so grave, aged, and careworn, as if sorrow had done the work of years.

"My aunt!"— exclaimed Mary, and hesitated, fearful to finish the sentence, "how is she, Margaret, and John?"

"You'll see them all presently," replied Bessie, and led her into the sitting-room. John was seated in an arm-chair; languidly he stretched out his thin hand, caught Mary's, and slowly imprinted a kiss on it, while a faint smile lit up his countenance. Though prepared by letters from Bessie and Margaret to see John altered, Mary could not imagine the change to be so great; her feelings overcame her, and she burst into tears. Poor John also wept like a babe.

Margaret now entered, supporting her mother. Both showed plainly by their looks that sorrow and bereavement had made sad havoc on their health. Every eye was bathed in tears. Scenes of former meetings passed rapidly and vividly before the memory of each; sobs and broken sentences were all that for some time could be heard.

Mrs Rutherford was the first to regain composure, in her usually kind manner she welcomed her niece, and thanked her for coming to see them, as she well knew her services were much required at home; asked particularly for her father, mother, and all the rest of the family. She had felt the shock of her husband's death more deeply than could be known by a casual observer, her manner being uniformly

quiet and gentle, she seldom gave utterance to her
feelings. We already know from her former life the
ordeal she had passed through before she attained to
a state of perfect resignation to the will of God in
all things. Human nature, however, would sometimes assert its rights ; and often were tears repressed
in society to be more freely indulged in when in the
solitude of her own chamber.

After a slight show of emotion, Margaret's force
of character fully displayed itself in struggling to
prove, not only to Mary now, but to all whom she
came in contact with previously, that she would not
succumb to adverse circumstances, nor would she
ever acknowledge that her father's death had been
caused by animosity to himself personally, but as-
cribed it to hatred of the system of levying the tithes,
and to the unsettled state of the country. As she so
closely resembled her father in energy and decision
of character, all the household looked up to her, as
they had done to him. Her mother, Bessie, and even
John leaned on her for counsel, consolation, and
assistance. Well would it have been for John had he
inherited stability and firmness of character like Margaret ; but instead of trials rousing him to combat
and bear up against them, he was so crushed and
prostrated as to become totally unfitted for either
bodily or mental exertion.

Mary's attention was now attracted to Hector, who
came to her, and testified his joy at seeing her. He
also was altered and subdued ; instead of his former
rapid pace and loud bark, he moved along slowly and

quietly. She found that he was Mrs Rutherford's constant attendant during the day, and her faithful guardian, lying at her bedroom door at night, or when she was confined there by illness.

Mary's presence and conversation on the startling events which were daily occurring began to excite John's attention, and had a wonderful effect in rousing him out of the lethargy into which he had sunk. He listened to the events which she related as passing around them, and from that time began to read the newspapers and take an interest in politics, so that her visit had a beneficial effect on him. Mrs Rutherford, Margaret, and Bessie were so pleased at the improvement in John's health and spirits, that they often proposed for him to accompany them, or go alone to Ballynacraig. Being in Mary's society awoke all his former love for her, which he thought he had (in obedience to his father's wishes) for ever banished from his heart. He determined for her sake to make every effort to overcome his morbid feelings, and shake off his weakness, still hoping that she would yet be his wife. Instead of moping about the house and farm, he began to visit Slievedhu occasionally, and so far succeeded in shaking off the incubus which was weighing him down as to mingle in the society of the neighbourhood.

Once a week, and sometimes oftener, John went on the ostensible pretence of inquiring how his aunt and cousins got on during such troublous times. Each visit only made him more aware that his happiness depended on being united to his cousin Mary ; but

as he thought it might hurt his mother's feelings to
broach such a subject at the present time, when the
wounds caused by the painful circumstance of his
father's death were still unhealed, he spoke of all at
Ballynacraig in general terms, and sometimes did not
mention his being there at all.

The embers of discontent which had smouldered
for so long in Ireland now burst into the lurid flames
of disloyalty and open rebellion.   The political cal-
dron hissed, bubbled, and boiled over, hoping to quench
the turmoil ; but still the country was disturbed by
outrages, and disaffection largely prevailed.   All classes
of the community were interested in the struggle, and
the inmates of Thornbrae, though steeped in sorrow,
were roused from brooding over their own trials by
the stirring events passing around them.   Although
John was deeply interested in the politics and startling incidents of daily occurrence he did not interfere
in them ; his mind regained its former healthy state,
and he was a comfort and solace to his mother and
sisters.

Our old friend Lucy, now Mrs Talbot, still resided
in London, and had a young family rising around
her ; but though blest with renewed health, a loving
husband, kind friends, and every comfort which
wealth could procure, she often grieved at being so
far away from her beloved mother and sisters ; and
as it was not thought safe to visit Ireland, she was
obliged to condole and comfort the inmates of Thornbrae by writing to them as frequently as possible.

Hilary still continued in Calcutta, increasing knowledge and amassing wealth, with the aim in view of returning home at no very distant day, and settling down for the remainder of his life in his native country.

" Then tell me why do Erin's sons in sorrow often mourn ?
  Tho' blest with wealth in foreign lands, their thoughts on home
      return ;
  Their love of country is the cause which they will freely own,
  They mope and pine for Erin's isle, as Erin was their home."

CHAPTER XXIX.

WHEN Henry was brought before the court-martial and interrogated if he was a United Irishman? where he was going when he was made prisoner? &c., he either gave evasive answers, bitter replies, or maintained a dogged silence.

Promises were made to him of escaping the punishment of flogging due to his being out at night without a pass, if he would reveal all he knew about the United Irishmen. This he indignantly refused, and in insolent language braved them to do their worst. The sentence was then passed on him to get fifty lashes in the market-place for the first offence, and on the following market-day ninety for his abusive language at the court-martial.

With feelings of the deepest sorrow Mr Gordon had read the letter from Mary, and he and Mrs Gordon agreeing with her suggestion, he at once prepared to act on it, and rode quickly and by the nearest route to reach Dungannon. But who can describe the anguish which wrung the heart of the father on hearing that his son had been flogged in the public market-place an hour before his arrival. At once he proceeded to the jail, expecting to gain admission to see his son; but the jailer could not permit him to do so without an order from the commanding officer.

He then went to the barracks, and was informed that Major P—— had gone to dine with the Honourable Mr W——, and on his return it would be too late to get an order for admission to the jail. Mr Gordon had no alternative but to wait till the morning. With a sorrowful heart he retraced his steps to the inn where he had left his horse. Entering into conversation with the landlord, he heard that the punishment inflicted on the youth (whose appearance and bearing had called forth great sympathy) was only a part of the sentence; that more lashes were to be given him on the next market-day.

At first it was not known that Mr Gordon was the father of the poor sufferer; but parental love soon betrayed relationship by the keen interest he took in all the particulars.

On making further inquiry, he heard that during the time Henry was undergoing flogging he suffered without allowing a moan to escape his lips. His fair smooth shoulders quivered when the lash was applied, but the most attentive observer could not detect a change of muscle in his rigid features, nor was the slightest groan of anguish uttered by him; but the vibration of the triangles he was tied to showed the tortures he was enduring.

After passing a sleepless night, Mr Gordon called at Major P——'s quarters, but was told he was at breakfast, and could not be seen until after parade.

Mr Gordon waylaid him in the street, and was waved off. "It was impossible for him to be detained at that hour."

After parade Mr Gordon was admitted to where the council of officers were sitting, and at once, in a peremptory manner, he was refused admission to his son. He then applied to one of the magistrates in the neighbourhood with whom he was acquainted, but was informed by him that he could not interfere with a court-martial case.

On the next market-day, at twelve o'clock, Henry was brought out of jail, escorted by a strong body of soldiers to the market-place. A hollow square was formed by the infantry, the outside rank standing with charged bayonets; the triangles were then set up inside the square, and Henry (stripped of coat, shirt, and waistcoat) bound to them. The army-surgeon, officers, corporal, drummer, and drum-major stood around and beside the prisoner.

The drummer beat a tattoo, then took off his coat, turned up his shirt sleeves, and having been handed the cat-o'-nine tails, commenced to inflict the lashes, the drum-major standing beside him calling out slowly each lash as it was administered. The first forty-five lashes did not elicit a word from the sufferer. Then came the corporal's time to give the remainder. At the first stroke Henry's blood began to flow, and after a few more lashes his shoulders were all one mass of blood and raw flesh. Still his strength and nerve held out, and although smothered groans could not be suppressed, his lips were sealed, but the final number had not been told when Henry fainted away. The surgeon applied restoratives, and pronounced he was not at that time able to bear any more flogging.

With blanched cheeks, compressed lips, and tottering limbs, Mr Gordon stood among the assembled crowd. As lash after lash resounded on his son's shoulders, a groan would escape his lips, or a shudder pass over his frame. For a few minutes there was a pause while the cat-o'-nine tails changed hands, and the doctor made his examination if the prisoner's strength was sufficient to bear more punishment. Mr Gordon breathed a sigh of relief; but when the corporal (who was a strong muscular man) took the lash into his hands, and he saw the first blow draw blood, his anguish could not be repressed, nor his voice silent any longer. With a piercing, heart-rending cry, he exclaimed, " My son ! my son ! would God I could suffer for you !" and frantically pushing through the crowd, ran a short distance, then fell fainting on the street, not far from the inn. He was carried into the house, and every attention paid to him ·by the landlord and landlady. How can words convey an idea of the harrowing torture endured by this poor father ; every stroke of the lash on his son seemed to lacerate his own flesh, to cut into his brain, and rend his heart. No wonder that fever succeeded such an awful ordeal. For some days Mr Gordon was insensible, then followed weakness and debility consequent on such a tension of the brain and nerves.

As conveyances often went from the Royal Arms

to Dungannon, Mary Wilson had frequent opportunities of hearing about Mr Gordon and Henry. When the former was thought able to bear the fatigue of the journey, Mary went in a post-chaise to bring him to Ballynacraig. Before leaving Dungannon she went to the prison, hoping to get an interview with Henry. Having failed in this, she gained admission to the jailer's wife, who took a hearty interest in the poor young man, felt deeply for his parents, and sympathised with Mary in her disappointment. From her she learnt that Henry had recognised his father among the crowd, and hearing his voice had quite overcome his courage. His shoulders and back were so lacerated, that he could not lie in bed; and only getting prison fare, his strength was fast sinking.

Mary handed her some guineas, accompanying the gift with a request that everything nourishing and strengthening should be given to Henry, and that intelligence should be conveyed to him of his father being better, and removed to Ballynacraig, where he would be sure to receive every care and attention.

Dr Conway exerted all his skill in bringing about Mr Gordon's recovery, which was greatly aided by the attendance of his son Andrew, and the sympathy and assistance of Mary. In a short time the poor sufferer was able to return home to his unhappy, almost heart-broken wife, who in his absence had prematurely brought a delicate babe into existence.

We have already mentioned that Mr Gordon had not hitherto taken any interest in politics, nor had he interfered or tampered with any of the laws of his country; but now "the iron had entered into his soul." He felt not only aggrieved, but deeply indignant at the treatment which he and his son had received. He joined the society of United Irishmen, and from being a passive, loyal British subject, became an active, fearless rebel, and cast off for ever fealty and subjection to the king of England and his government.

Mary Wilson also felt so exasperated that she urged her father to discontinue business, and by so doing get rid of the military being quartered there.

Mr Wilson was unwilling to compromise himself, as he was considered a staunch loyal subject. A large bill being now due to him by the military, and a statement of it having frequently been forwarded to Charlemont, and personal application made without its being liquidated, Mr Wilson began to think that Mary was right in wishing to close the inn. "Why," argued she, "should we have our substance wasted and our services given without remuneration?"

Still her father hesitated before giving his consent; but Mary was determined to effect her purpose, and an opportunity soon offered itself to her. The military who had for some time been quartered in Ballynacraig, were ordered off to another town. Mary took advantage of their absence, and previous to the arrival of the others, who were to replace them, got the sign of the "Royal Arms" removed off the front of the house, wrote notices that the business was given up, and pasted them on the closed gate and door.

Mr Wilson returned from his farm in the evening, and finding what was done, said, " Perhaps it may all turn out for the best," and being fatigued, after sowing oats all day, he retired early to bed.

Shortly after nightfall, the trampling of horses and the heavy tread of men announced the arrival of fresh troops. The street was quite deserted, as every one was afraid to be seen out at that hour. Presently the word " Halt " was heard, and the inn door was loudly knocked at, but no notice was taken of it. Again and again the knocking was repeated. Mary heard it, but determined to seem not to do so. Her father and mother were awoke out of their slumbers, and entreated her to open the door. " Wait a little, father ; leave all to me." After putting on a nightcap, and throwing a shawl about her, (to look as if just roused out of bed,) she went up-stairs, and opening the window, demanded why the house was so assailed ? " Is not this the Royal Arms ? How does it come that it is closed, and that there is no light or any accommodation for the king's troops ?" was the reply.

Mary hastily answered, " This *was* an inn ; but we have given up business now. Look at the notices on the door and gate ; we have taken down the sign ; it is now a private dwelling ; we are willing to accommodate the number of men billeted on us, but we have not accommodation for horses."

After a long parley and conversation, the military dispersed muttering vengeance on the inmates of the house. Two officers and six privates were billeted on them ere an hour had elapsed. Fires had then to be kindled and provisions cooked for them, which we may be sure was not done *con amore.*

When Henry was released out of prison, he proceeded immediately to Ballynacraig. Mr Conway was afraid to admit him into his house again, and many of his former acquaintances (though in their hearts sympathising with him) were also afraid to be seen in his society, or to receive him into their houses.

Mary Wilson, however, was not one who would forsake a friend in a time of trial, nor was she to be restrained from bestowing kindness from fear of persecution; by her Henry was received cordially, and Mr and Mrs Wilson taking pity on his dejected looks and emaciated appearance, invited him to remain with them till his health was improved, and till he would hear from his father. Henry's delicate health, and Mary's influence, deterred him from running the risk of venturing out of doors. The inn being closed made his presence there unnoticed ; and as he was not seen, it was supposed he had gone to his father's. Mary had been the sharer of his joys and pleasures, his sunshine in prosperity, his benefactor, solace, and comfort in affliction ; the prop and consoler of his father, she was now the star of hope and the ray of light to guide him. While in her presence he forgot all his former sufferings, and his gloomy prospects for the future; she was to him become inexpressibly dear. This he did not venture to tell her ; but love such as his, founded on esteem and gratitude, could not fail to make itself known by looks as expressive as words. To Mary he was also very dear; but she

did not acknowledge it to herself, ascribing her
regard for him to pity ; she only loved him she
thought in a brotherly way.

During this time the insurgents waxed bolder, and
the soldiery more harsh and precipitate in their
punishments.   Mary heard that Mr Gordon was now
an avowed rebel ; and as his influence and example
had strengthened many in rebellion, he was a marked
man by the government, and there was reason to
think his life would be sacrificed.   This was not told
to Henry ; but it made the Wilson's more anxious
to get him to leave the country.   When advised to go
off at once to his Uncle Patrick Henry in America,
he urged his desire to see his father and mother before going, and his inability to leave the country till
he got means from them to pay his passage.

Some weeks passed in this uncertain state ; but
matters were brought to a crisis by an unforeseen
incident, which caused him to see that it was absolutely necessary he should leave, as his remaining
might endanger the safety of his friends in Ballynacraig.   Mrs Rutherford having often expressed a wish
to see her sister-in-law and Mr Wilson, and her
health not being sufficiently strong to permit her to
visit them, it was arranged that they and Nannie
should go to Thornbrae, when Mr Wilson's farming
operations allowed him to leave for a couple of days.
It being necessary to remain over night, unless a pass
was got from the commanding-officer, permitting
them to return after night-fall, which it was thought
advisable not to ask for, lest it should be known that

Mary was left alone. On the evening of the day they left, as Mary and Henry were sitting at the fireside in the parlour, they were surprised at hearing the door opened, some one step in, and in a husky voice demand, " Who's here ?"

Mary at first did not recognise who it was, as the room was only dimly lighted by the fire ; she soon found that the intruder was one of the officers who had been previously billeted there. He had been returning from the mess, and seeing the hall door partially open, and one of the maids looking out, had rushed past her and walked in. Mary rose, and curtseying said, " Captain L——, you have mistaken the house ; it is a few doors farther on where you are quartered, and not here." She then perceived by his unsteady gait that he was intoxicated.

With a stammering voice he hiccupped forth, " Wrong house ! if I am in the wrong house, why are you not all in bed ? it is after beat of drum. Wrong house ! I tell you I am a British officer—a gentleman of family and fortune—I 'll not be shut out of any place, in your cursed country—I 'll prove to you, his Majesty's officers have a right to enter any of your houses at all hours." Then darting a look at Henry, he asked, " Who is this ?"

" A friend from the country," replied Mary.

" A friend," sneeringly replied he, " likely a rebel. Get a light at once, I 'll see if I know him—traitors must not be allowed escape."

" I am sure you do not know him," said Mary, glancing imploringly at Henry, to keep him from speaking, and placing herself so as to put him in the shade.

"A light—I say a light; if not I'll dragoon you." And he stamped and swore, still calling fiercely for a light.

This did not terrify Mary, who, coming close to him, said, "Captain L——, you know we are not permitted to have lights in the house, and therefore are not provided with candles at present. My father is absent from home; you are aware he is a loyal subject. To whom, then, should his daughter, if in any danger, apply for protection, but to a gentleman of family and fortune, and a British officer, instead of being threatened by him? I now tell you I am here a defenceless woman. I cast myself on your generosity, and call upon you, as a man of honour, to protect me from outrage and insult."

This nonchalant appeal quite cooled the Captain's valour, and he was flattered by Mary's words. Tottering to a chair, he seated himself, and vowed he would "stay and protect her with his life. But rebels," darting a glance at Henry, (who with difficulty kept silence,) "rebels must be taken. I think this is that rascal Gordon, son to that "——

Here he was interrupted by a sergeant coming in and delivering him an order from the colonel requiring his immediate presence.

It was some time before he was prevailed on to accompany the sergeant, often returning, and saying he would not go; "it was his duty to watch this rebel, and guard and defend this amiable young lady."

Mary thanked him, and said that now, as her mind was quite at ease, feeling assured of his protection, she would not trouble him to remain any longer. After repeatedly assuring him that in case of necessity she would not fail to apply to him, he left, greatly to the relief of all.

The active part Mr Gordon took in the approaching rebellion is already known to our readers; and Mary suspected that Captain L——'s unfinished sentence in connexion with the name of Gordon would have been, "son to that rank traitor, who deserves to meet a traitor's doom." She saw plainly that there was no time to be lost in getting Henry out of the way, as his presence, instead of being useful to his father, would only make his position worse, and might terminate in the lives of both being sacrificed. All this and much more passed rapidly through her mind.

Henry also became alive to the idea that his remaining there might endanger the safety of his kind friends and benefactors the Wilsons; but how could he bring himself to leave Mary, who every day was becoming more and more the idol of his heart? Mary first broke silence.

"Henry," said she, "you are now so much stronger, you can undertake a journey. You cannot with safety stay here any longer. Captain L——, in his inebriated state, might not have recognised you, or in the morning may have forgotten the interview; but from the significant look of the sergeant when leaving the room, I fear your being here cannot longer remain a secret. There is now no alternative but for you to go to America. You must not allow yourself again to be made prisoner. You know you can still be arrested on suspicion."

"Mary! O Mary! do you wish me to leave?" and Henry bowed his head, covered his face with his hands, and he who had borne to be flogged without betraying emotion now burst into a passionate flood of tears.

"Henry," said Mary, while she stepped up beside him, and put her hand on his shoulder, "this will not do. You must not give way now; for so far you have acted nobly. Do not now give up to useless inactivity, as there is not a moment to be lost."

"But Mary," passionately exclaimed he, "how can I part from you? Say, dearest, that you return my love, that you will be mine. The prospect of your becoming my wife, and of again meeting, only to be parted by death, will nerve me to tear myself from you for a time." Then in the warmest terms he poured forth words rendered eloquent by the impulses of his heart, vowing his resolution of living and working for her, if she would give him reason to hope that his love was reciprocated.

Mary had so long associated with him as a friend and companion, she could not bring herself to realise that she loved him; besides, her cousin John was still uppermost in her thoughts. True, he had not spoken plainly to her of his affection, and latterly he had not visited as frequently as formerly, and when he did his manner was constrained and cold, so that Mary felt rather piqued.

"Henry," said she, "we are both young. This is not a season to talk on these subjects. Your safety must first be attended to. If you love me, prove yourself a man by rousing yourself into action. Go to your worthy uncle. Like him, make your name honourable, and by so doing confer dignity on your wife."

"But how can I, almost penniless, proceed to America at once? I find I must leave this; but until I hear from my father I cannot go out of Ireland."

"Attend to me," replied Mary. "All this delay can be avoided. To-morrow's dawn must find you on your way to Londonderry. At the farm you can get a horse from Denny M'Durk to carry you to Dungiven. Mr M'Dougal, the landlord of the inn there, will, on my recommendation, keep you for the night, and supply you with a horse next morning to carry you to the Tirkeeran Arms, Londonderry."

"But "—— said Henry.

"No interruptions. I shall supply you with funds to pay your passage to America. Denny will follow you to Londonderry, to return the horse to Dungiven and bring ours back. You see all is arranged. Let us hope for better times. All may yet be well."

"How shall I ever repay you, dearest and best?" and clasping her in his arms, he kissed her repeatedly. "God will reward you for all your kindness to me and my father." Here again he broke down. "Won't you write to him, that it was not want of affection, but by your advice and stern necessity I was compelled to leave without going to ask the blessing of my parents, and bid them farewell. Oh, my father and my kind mother, I may never see you again! But oh, Mary, don't send me away without hope! May I not write to you?' and will not you reply to me?"

"Certainly," said Mary, "I will, and my heart and thoughts will often accompany you." And with convulsive sobs she rushed out of the apartment.

After spending some time (he knew not how long) absorbed in reverie, Henry roused himself, and went to his apartment to collect the few articles that he could carry with him. Morning was near at hand. After partaking of a cup of coffee a packet was handed to him. It contained a purse of guineas, a note to Denny and Mr M'Dougal, and a scrap of paper, on which was written, with a tremulous hand :—

"Farewell! Go without delay. May God protect you. Write on arrival. Your letter will be anxiously looked for by your friends—and   MARY."

Henry knew it was useless to ask Mary to see him again; so, with a sorrowful heart and agitated bosom, he left the house, and walked to the farm without meeting any one.

Delivering Mary's order to Denny, he was supplied with a horse, and proceeded immediately to Dungiven.

After Henry left, Mary's pent-up feelings and assumed composure gave way; and in the privacy of her chamber she relieved her bursting heart by shedding floods of tears. Often while performing, almost mechanically, the domestic duties of that day, did

Mary's thoughts revert to the poor wanderer in whose fate she was so deeply interested.

We need scarcely add that her image was seldom absent from Henry's mind and thoughts on his way to Londonderry ; and during his passage across the Atlantic he had ample time to think over and recall her every word and look. Many plans were laid by him for future happiness, of course always associated with Mary in " Love's young dream."

CHAPTER XXX.

WHEN Mr and Mrs Wilson returned, they were pleased to hear that Henry Gordon had left. They had heard that Government was taking more energetic measures, being determined to quash the rebellion by force of arms, and that strict inquiry was being made so as to seize all disaffected persons.

From Henry's father Mary had a letter, couched in the warmest terms, thanking her for inducing and assisting his son to leave Ireland, and in no sparing terms denouncing the government of the country, its laws, rulers, and institutions. Months passed over, and though unmarked by domestic events, the family at Ballynacraig were kept constantly on the *qui vive*, not knowing what a day might bring forth.

Francis and James Wilson were both on foreign service as surgeons in the navy. Nannie had formed an attachment to a young man in Ballynacraig, whom her parents did not think steady, and refused their consent to a correspondence being carried on. She took a sulky fit, and would not speak to her father, mother, or Mary, unless spoken to, but spent her time in dressing, altering, and making her clothes, and indemnifying herself for her silence to her family by scolding the servants whenever they came in her way. Between Mary and her sister there never had been a reciprocity of tastes or pursuits, so that her estrangement was not a cause of discomfort to either.

The looked-for letter from Henry came, announcing his safe arrival, and filled with ardent expressions of everlasting gratitude to his benefactors.

Mrs Rutherford's health was still very precarious; this, and the unsettled state of the country, prevented intercourse between the families, except on very rare occasions; and when Mary and John met, there seemed to be a tacit feeling of coldness or restraint between them. John evidently avoided being left alone with Mary, and never mentioned Henry Gordon's name, or alluded to his absence in her presence. Mary's worst fears about Mr Gordon were soon verified. His daring opposition to the Government being openly avowed, he was apprehended, confined in jail, brought to trial, convicted of high treason, and sentenced to death. Being popular with all classes, a strong memorial in his favour was numerously signed and forwarded to Lord Castlereagh, praying that his sentence might be commuted to banishment; but to this petition there was no reply.

Mrs Gordon, although a timid, shrinking woman, was nerved by strong conjugal love to force herself into Lord Castlereagh's presence; and attended by her five children, and an infant in her arms, she cast herself at his lordship's feet, and in agonising accents implored him to spare the father of her children and the husband of her love; but she was spurned from his presence. She was told mediation was now useless. Mr Gordon had been engaged in active rebellion, and by his advice and example many had been induced to become United Irishmen. He had been tried and convicted of high treason. It was necessary for the public peace that an example should be made; there was now no alternative but for the law to take its course; and as he had acted a traitor's part, he must therefore meet a traitor's doom. The next day Mr Gordon was taken out of prison, and, guarded by a strong body of soldiers, was led to the green attached to his own meeting-house. On one of the trees which surrounded it dangled a rope, and under it stood a cart, on which Mr Gordon was ordered to mount. He was then pinioned and blindfolded, the rope adjusted round his neck in a noose, the cart dragged away, and, after struggling for a short time, his life became extinct.

As a favour, his widow was permitted to have his body conveyed to the cottage, on the condition that the funeral must be strictly private, and to take place that evening.

Andrew was apprised of his father's death; but being unexcitable, and of an apathetic temperament, and his whole mind absorbed in his profession, to which he was devotedly attached, he did not suffer so acutely as Henry would have done. Mr Conway permitted him to go to his mother; and with the advice of her friends, Mrs Gordon sold off the farm implements, furniture, &c., and sailed to America, accompanied by Andrew and the rest of her family.

About the same time, a letter was received by Mr Wilson announcing that his son Francis had fallen a victim to yellow fever in the West Indies ; a high encomium was passed upon his services, and his books, apparel, and other articles forwarded to Ballynacraig. All the family mourned his death, as he was an affectionate son and brother ; but it was a solace to them to know that he had done his duty in his profession, and that his services were honourably mentioned. Shortly after this, the father of the young man who was anxious to be united to Nannie came to Mr Wilson to plead his son's cause, and offered to settle an annuity on her in proportion to the fortune given with her, if she became his son's wife. All was arranged to the satisfaction of both parties, and Nannie was married and settled down in Ballynacraig. Not having any children, she spent her life much as she had done previously, dawdling in her time. Years rolled over ; the country settled down into quietness. Politics, although still deeply engrossing the public mind, did not occasion disturbance, cause alarm, or prevent men from resuming their ordinary occupations, or women attending to their domestic duties, so that everything began to wear its former aspect. The streets were no longer silent and deserted at nightfall, but resounded with the voices and mirth of children ; and neighbours went from house to house to pass an hour in gossip at the fireside or tea-table, and retired to their beds without fear of being roused by the beat of drum, the clangour and discharge of arms, the tread of soldiers, or the crackling and smoke from the fire of the incendiary, or the yells of an infuriated mob.

The linen trade and agricultural pursuits were remunerative. Business was again resumed at the Royal Arms, and all was going on pleasantly and prosperously.

Mary had many offers of marriage, but rejected them, without assigning any reason for doing so.

Lord Southend's agent died, and his situation was offered to John Rutherford. By the advice and sanction of his mother and sisters he accepted it; and as it was more convenient to live in Slievedhu, he took a house there, and all the family removed, leaving Jamie M'Gwiggan's son Alick in charge, as his father had been before.

This was an agreeable change for all, as the cottage called forth too many reminiscences of former scenes to make it pleasant. Besides, Mrs Rutherford thought her daughters might be more likely to get established in life; and John had hopes that he might now bring his cousin Mary to Thornbrae. After their arrival in Slievedhu, the Rutherfords were called on by all the gentry of the neighbourhood; their health and spirits returned, and they were again happy.

John thought this was a good time to speak to his mother about his marriage. "My dear John," said she, "your cousin Mary is a good, clever girl, but do you not think she is engaged to some one?"

"Engaged!" exclaimed John. "Who to?"

"Oh, I never heard, but it is likely to be so; we have heard that she had many admirers."

"I have no doubt she has," said John, "but she has refused them all. I know, although I have not asked her, that her heart is mine."

"Well, my dear John, there is no hurry for you to be married. Mary will no doubt make a good wife, but your father and I had hoped you would have wedded into a higher sphere. Mr B—— has lately been paying marked attention to your sister Bessie, and as it would in every respect be a most desirable alliance for her, I will take it as a favour if you will not for a time speak to your cousin about matrimony, as your doing so might prevent your sister's settlement in life. Mr B., you are aware, is of a high family, and Bessie thinks he might object to being connected with an innkeeper's daughter."

John felt indignant at a slight being cast on Mary on account of her station in life; and replied, hastily, "Mother, I thought you all loved and respected Mary for her own merits, and that *you* were above being influenced by such paltry notions."

Mrs Rutherford was rather surprised at John manifesting such a spirit, and kept silence. Just then visitors were announced; and it was quite a relief to Mrs Rutherford not to have the conversation on the subject further prolonged.

The autumn weather proved very unfavourable for harvest work, and there was great difficulty in getting the crops saved. Mr Wilson took every opportunity of attending actively and promptly to have the grain stacked; he had nearly succeeded in saving all, but rain came on when he was finishing the thatching of a stack, and he was completely drenched. On his return home he changed his clothes, and did not think that the wetting would have any effect on him further than perhaps a slight cold. Being fatigued, he retired early to bed, having previously bathed his feet and taken some whey; but before morning he was so very ill Dr Conway had to be sent for, and at once he pronounced the case pleurisy of the worst kind. Every remedy was used, and all that skill could devise or love dictate was done to relieve the pain and reduce the fever, but without effect; within a week he died.

John Rutherford acted like a kind son and tender brother to his aunt and cousin during their affliction, assisting in all the last sad funeral rites.

James Wilson had a few weeks before written that he might soon be expected home; but as the time of his arrival was uncertain, the funeral was not delayed in expectation of his attendance. Nannie's husband and her cousin John were the only family mourners present.

The prospect of James's arrival roused the minds of the bereaved ones from brooding too much over their loss; but when weeks passed over, and he did not come, they began to feel great anxiety about his safety; and when it was reported that a man-of-war was missing, their suspense became torturing. After the delay of some months their fears were confirmed; the Admiralty had made every inquiry, and as the vessel had never been heard of after she left the Spanish main, they returned her as "lost at sea."

It was decided that as Mrs Wilson and Mary had sufficient means to keep them without business, they would dispose of the inn and farm, wind up their affairs, and retire into private life.

When cousin John heard this, he thought all was in a fair way to fall in with his wishes, hoping that when Bessie was married every obstacle would be removed, and all his hopes of being united to Mary realised.

Shortly after this, Mrs Rutherford was suddenly seized with paralysis, lost her speech and the use of her left arm.

When Mary Wilson heard of her aunt's illness, she at once hastened to render her assistance. She found Mrs Rutherford seemingly insensible to pain, but the remedies which Dr H—— had prescribed had not proved effectual.

With Mary's keen perceptions, she suggested the use of more active stimulants and blistering. The doctor said it might be a risk, as the patient was very weak; but Mary was so urgent, and so hopeful of the result, that more powerful means were resorted to, which, to the joy of all, proved in a degree beneficial, as feeling was restored to the arm; and although speech was still wanting, it was evident, from an incident which occurred, that consciousness had returned and her mind was still active.

During the time of applying lotions and blisters, Mrs Rutherford's rings had been removed; she had never worn any but on her ring finger, and on it were her two plain wedding-rings, which, contrary to the usual rule, she had worn as mementos of her two husbands. She was observed feeling over her left hand, and then looking imploringly at her daughters and niece. At first they thought it was pain which caused her to act so; but Margaret, who, from being so constantly her companion of late, could almost interpret her wishes from her looks, said, " I see what my mother misses; it is her rings." A gleam of intelligence and a slight smile showed that the supposition was correct. The rings were produced, and when put on her finger, she patted her hand with evident satisfaction, and looked as pleased and happy as a child on recovering a favourite toy which had been taken away for a time.

After a few weeks, speech returned to the invalid, but her health was ever afterwards very precarious.

Mary Wilson was obliged to return home, as the time was drawing near for the sale of the property. Previous to leaving, she began to notice that instead of being introduced as formerly to visitors as " cousin Mary," it was now merely " a friend," or Miss Wilson; nor was she appealed to or brought forward into conversation. Mary's high spirit could not brook being overlooked or slighted; it hurt and grieved her deeply, and rankled in her bosom, making her very indignant and unhappy on her journey homeward.

On arrival there, she found a letter from Henry Gordon, full of expressions of ardent love for her, painting in the most vivid colours the happiness he would enjoy if Mary would become his wife. His name and talents had placed him in a high position in America, and he could now offer her a comfortable home and a prospect of affluence. His mother and the younger members of the family were well provided for by his uncle. Andrew had gained a reputation for skill and experience, and was a physician, whose practice was large and daily increasing.

Mary had seen plainly that her cousins, Margaret and Bessy, thought her inferior to them in station; and, as John had never frankly avowed his love to her, began to accuse herself for loving when it was not returned ; so she at once wrote off to Henry Gordon that she consented to become his wife, and that after the disposal of the property, and when suitable arrangements should be made for her mother living with Nannie, she would go to America to Mrs Gordon's house, and there be married.

Mrs Rutherford still continued an invalid. Mr B—— did not propose for Bessie, and poor John felt that he had held out long enough ; and with more decision and energy than he had ever shown in his life, announced to his mother and sisters that he would no longer be deterred from declaring his love, and proposing to his cousin Mary to become his wife. The sisters pouted, and Mrs Rutherford looked grave, and remarked that there was no occasion for being "precipitate." But John, for once in his life, was resolute, and declared it was his determination to make his cousin his wife. Accordingly, a few days before the sale, he started off to Ballynacraig, buoyant with hope, little suspecting the blow he would receive.

Mary's announcement of her intentions fell on him

so unexpectedly that he could not utter a word, but rushed from the house a hopeless, crushed, prostrated creature. He did not return home till late; his mother had retired for the night, accompanied by Margaret; and in reply to Bessie's questions about his aunt and cousins, he merely answered, "Quite well," took his bed-candle, and proceeded to his room.

Next morning he left the house before breakfast, leaving a message that he was going to Thornbrae, and would not return till evening. His mother and sisters concluded that all had gone according to his wishes, and that he had hurried off to make arrangements to receive his bride as soon as possible; but when he returned, it was plainly to be seen from his moody, reserved manner that he had been refused.

In a few days a letter was received from Mary, saying she presumed that John had told them of her intention of going out to America to be married to Henry Gordon; but previous to her departure, she would go to see her aunt and cousins. John was present when the letter was read; he merely looked at his mother, heaved a deep sigh, left the apartment, and presently the hall-door closed on him, not to be entered by him again for many days.

He proceeded to Thornbrae, and wrote to his mother not to expect him back for a little. His sisters looked for his return on Sunday; and when he did not come, they went to him, and begged he would accompany them to Slievedhu. This he decidedly refused, but promised to go on the following

Sunday, escort them to church, and take dinner with them; but only on the terms that they were not to ask him any questions about his own affairs. This promise was given, and a taciturn hebdomadal visit was all the intercourse between John and his family for years.

Mary in the meantime had gone to America, had been most fondly and ardently received by Henry Gordon and his family. Mrs Gordon was all a kind, considerate mother could be to her daughter-in-law. Henry's anticipations were fully realised; he and Mary were blessed with affluence and health, enjoyed the respect and esteem of a large circle of acquaintance, loved each other dearly, and had a numerous family of sons and daughters.

Mary (or, as we should now call her, Mrs Patrick Henry Gordon) ever retained the greatest love for her native land—the name of Irishman or Irishwoman was a sufficient introduction to her, and called forth her strongest sympathies and kindest wishes on all occasions. By her the wants of the indigent, helpless, sick, and infirm were liberally relieved; the hopeless and down-spirited cheered; the struggling immigrant encouraged, and assisted to get into a way of earning a livelihood; the careless, improvident, and dissipated, warned, reproved, exhorted, and watched over. By her advice, hundreds of her countrymen and women had money remitted to them by their transatlantic friends to pay their passage to rejoin them in America, or to contribute to their comfort and well-being at home.

While she was pursuing an active and benevolent career, her sister Nannie and her husband went on "the even tenor of their ways." Mrs Wilson had died a few years after the emigration of her daughter. She had been an invalid for such a lengthened period that her death had often been expected; her mind, however, had been weaned off the world, and gentleness and resignation became so incorporated in her character that her "latter end was peace;" it was truly "putting off mortality to be clothed upon with immortality."

Mrs Rutherford made frequent attempts to win John round to his former sociability with his family, but found all means ineffectual. She did not long survive his estrangement from them. Her departure was so peaceful that her daughters Margaret and Bessie, who stood by her bedside, bending over her, anxiously and affectionately watching her every look, motion, and respiration, knew not when she ceased to breathe. Some minutes had elapsed before they could realise that she was really dead. The beams of the setting sun at that time illumined the chamber of death with its bright rays; and by the wonderful law of association, which excites the brain by a casual sight, sound, odour, or other trivial incident, caused the sunset at the Giant's Causeway to flash into Margaret's recollection. The glorious hues of the clouds, the radiance cast on all the scene around, the very expression of countenance of each member of the happy group who so deeply enjoyed it, rose up vividly to her imagination. Her mother's every word recurred to her memory—all passed before her in a few seconds in the words of the poet—

> " How quick is a glance of the mind
> Compared to the speed of its flight;
> The tempest itself lags behind,
> And the swift-wing'd arrows of light."

" Bessie," said she, " our beloved mother has passed over the troubled waters, which have evidently been smoothed to her; she has now entered through the bright portals to be united to our father, and her other friends who have gone before. May our end be peaceful and happy like hers ! "

After their mother's death John's sisters seldom saw him, as he lived constantly at Thornbrae, which he only left when his business required. He shunned society, sank into a morbid state, and became a moody, gloomy old bachelor.

Mr B—— had not proposed to Bessie, nor did she ever receive an offer of marriage; she and Margaret removed to London to be near Lucy and her children.

Hilary married in India. His wife died without having had any children, and having amassed a large fortune, he returned to England with the intention of purchasing an estate in his dearly loved native land ; but death called him off in Portsmouth, before he had reached his sisters in London.

Lucy also, since we last mentioned her, had bereavements and trials. She had lost several children. She and Edward had "beheld the fair bud and the beautiful blossom expand;" but while they looked, they saw it begin to droop, fade, and at last wither

and die ; still they sorrowed not without hope, knowing that their lovely flowers had only been trans-
planted to the garden of glory above, there to expand
fully, under the bright beams of the Sun of Righteousness ; and after time had assuaged the sorrow of
parting with their beloved children, they rejoiced at
the thought of being united soon to them, "where
parting is unknown." Lucy often sang to her husband in her sweetest tones—

> " Darlings we shall meet where the spoiler finds no prey ;
>   Where all lovely things and sweet pass not away.
>   Edward, this indeed is true ; speed, then speed the closing day !
>   How blest from earth's vain show to pass away ! "

After lives spent in usefulness and benevolence,
Edward and Lucy died within a short time of each
other, and were interred in Kensal Green Cemetery.
Several of their sons and grandsons are now honoured
members of professions, or merchants on 'Change.

Possessed not only with liberal means, but also
with a liberal spirit, the Messrs Talbot are munificent
donors to every charitable and benevolent institution
in London, and their purse is ever open to relieve the
wants of the indigent and suffering, irrespective of
creed or denomination.

Mary never left America. She survived her husband, Patrick Henry Gordon, whose death was sincerely regretted, and his memory universally respected. His three sons, members of the bar and
senate, followed his remains to the tomb, mourning
the loss of a kind, beloved father. Their mother

attained an old age, which to the last was occupied in works and labours of love for the comfort and happiness of her fellow-countrymen and women.

The morning of her funeral, the square in which she had dwelt was thronged with a weeping multitude of persons of both sexes, and all ages, bearing evidence by their appearance and speech that Erin had been their birthplace.

" Och, wasn't she cruel kind ? " " Didn't she do a power o' good ? " " An' so cliver, too ! " " Won't she be horridly miss't ? " " She was a sant on airth ! " These and similar Ulster expressions, uttered in the flat tone of voice peculiar to the greater part of the province by persons of staid looks and square impassive features, proved their northern origin.

" Wirasthrue ! Wirasthrue ! Heaven be her bed ! " and " God rest her sowl ! " was often fervently ejaculated in the rich flowing brogue of the midland counties, or in the plaintive, wailing accents of the southern part of Ireland ; and many a dark bright eye from Galway and Connemara was dimmed by floods of tears, while in touching accents the mourners poured forth their feelings in the expressive ancient language of their country, saying, in a wailing chant, " Beanacht Leat a ban usaila ! Beanacht Finbar, beanacht Brendan agus a companac seacht ! " (Blessings go with you, noble lady ! The blessing of Finbar, the blessings of Brendan and his seven companions go with you !)

The reader who has so far followed the events recorded in " Waves on the Ocean of Life " is even now

X

carried on by the never-ceasing billows of Time towards the boundless ocean of Eternity. The earnest wish of the writer is, that she and her friends and readers "may so pass through the waves of this troublesome world that finally they lose not the hope of eternal life, through Jesus Christ our Lord. Amen."

THE END.

Ballantyne and Company, Printers, Edinburgh.

www.ingramcontent.com/pod-product-compliance
Lightning Source LLC
Chambersburg PA
CBHW060513030726
47498CB00004B/928